DANNY COLMENARES

Faith of the Phoenix

FLAMESTRIKER
BOOKS

First published by Flamestriker Books 2026

Copyright © 2026 by Danny Colmenares

All rights reserved. No part of this publication may be reproduced, stored or transmitted in any form or by any means, electronic, mechanical, photocopying, recording, scanning, or otherwise without written permission from the publisher. It is illegal to copy this book, post it to a website, or distribute it by any other means without permission.

This novel is entirely a work of fiction. The names, characters and incidents portrayed in it are the work of the author's imagination. Any resemblance to actual persons, living or dead, events or localities is entirely coincidental.

Danny Colmenares asserts the moral right to be identified as the author of this work.

First edition

ISBN (paperback): 979-8-9905667-5-0
ISBN (hardcover): 979-8-9905667-6-7

This book was professionally typeset on Reedsy.
Find out more at reedsy.com

For my wonderful family, and everyone who has supported me while I wrote this book. This one's for you.

1

Ronan

Not again, Ronan thought.

It was the same dream he'd been having on and off for weeks.

A colossal stone door slammed shut behind him, the resonant boom echoing as it locked in place. From beyond the door came the clash of steel against steel, muted by the thick stone. A mournful weight settled around Ronan like a heavy cloak. Whatever battle raged beyond the door plagued him with a sorrow he knew wasn't his own, but felt too real for a simple dream.

Turning slowly, Ronan found a giant warhammer resting on the ground beside him. Its mythril shaft stood nearly six feet tall, and its head was as broad as the Great Anvil of Midral—well, before it had been destroyed. Ancient runes etched into the weapon flickered to life at his touch. A hammer like this would have been far too heavy for a human like him to pick up, much less wield in battle, yet his gauntleted hand plucked it off the ground and hoisted it onto his back without much effort.

Strange armor encased him. Its surface was a lattice of interwoven plates without a gap anywhere he could spot. The design was impossibly intricate, beyond even Brin's craftsmanship—and Brin was the best he knew. As he moved, Ronan could tell he was experiencing this dream from within someone else's body. He towered well over his normal height, and his steps carried an unnatural weight that he wasn't used to.

All around him, a dense violet mist curled like smoke, veiling the chamber in shadow and obscuring its boundaries. Two towering figures emerged from the mist—hulking shadows solidifying into forms of menace as they came closer. Their voices cut through the fog, but each word was distorted and unintelligible to Ronan's ears in this dream space. His pulse quickened as they approached. He didn't need to understand their speech to grasp the intent. Rage emanated from their very presence.

The shapes clarified as they drew nearer. Like Ronan, they were armored head-to-toe in the same seamless armor. One wielded a massive double-weighted staff, its ends capped in mythril-forged heads that glowed faintly with a pale violet energy. The other, shorter but no less imposing, gripped twin scimitars in her hands, simmering with the same dangerous energy as her partner's staff.

Embedded in the center of their chestplates was a metal orb, carved with dwarven runes. They swirled with turbulent energy—white and violet currents twisted around one another in dissonant chaos, matching the power in their weapons. The white energy, strangely, radiated the calm strength of Niradim, but the violet energy... it crackled with a chaotic hunger that turned Ronan's stomach. It was the same energy that Kyros had used to tear through his city not so long ago. He looked down and saw the same orb burning within his own armor, the white and violet cracks of light reflecting off his breastplate. If this had been his own body, a shiver would have run down his spine.

Energy surged from their orbs and powered their weapons to life. The unstable blend of opposing magics danced across the twin blades and staff as they advanced. But before Ronan could draw on his own power, they struck. The staff-wielder thrust forward, unleashing a shockwave that tore through the fog, while the scimitar-bearer darted in a blur of movement, her blades slicing in swift, ruthless arcs that left glowing trails of power in the air.

Ronan withstood the initial onslaught, his reflexes responding quickly despite the unfamiliar body he found himself in. As they advanced for a second assault, he looked down at the glowing orb in his chest and focused inward. He latched on to the white energy of Niradim within it and pulled. Niradim's power surged, wrapping tightly around the violet energy like a barrier, pushing the darkness inward and restraining it.

Immediately, warmth flooded his limbs, and the head of his warhammer ignited with Niradim's Flame. The oppressive mist around them recoiled, retreating to the edges of the room and revealing a large forge that glowed faintly with white fire from the inside. A massive anvil, etched with ancient dwarven runes, rested in front of it. It reminded him of the Soul Forge in Niradim's Cathedral, but older and different in subtle ways.

The sudden flare of Niradim's power stunned the scimitar-wielder mid-lunge, her movements faltering in awe or fear—Ronan didn't care which. He seized the opening, swinging his warhammer in a blazing arc, and struck her with a concussive force that cracked the stone floor. Her body crumpled. Another quick swing of the mighty hammer struck the orb in her chest, shattering it and leaving a lifeless body at his feet.

The staff-wielder roared in anger, and the power within his orb flared violently. Ronan raised his hammer, pointed to his own chest, then to the enemy's. Some unknown communication passed between the two that Ronan didn't understand in the dream. The armored man answered with action, leaping into a spinning assault. The staff spun like a cyclone, each strike landing with bone-jarring force. Ronan staggered back under the blows, the impacts vibrating through his armor like tremors from an earthquake.

But Ronan stood firm. He channeled Niradim's power, focusing Niradim's energy to strengthen his strikes and guide his limbs until the momentum of the duel shifted. He battered the staff-wielder back, step by step, until one crushing parry knocked the staff loose and sent it clanging across the floor.

Capitalizing on the opening, Ronan drove his hammer into his enemy's chest, hurling him into the far wall with a deafening crash. The armor cracked, and his body lay broken against the wall, but the orb in his chest still glowed. As Ronan approached, the fallen figure spoke. Words spilled from his mouth, but they bent in the air—distorted in the dream as before. Still, their meaning seeped into Ronan's mind. Whatever had been said, it filled him with fear.

Then, Ronan noticed something he'd missed before. Etched into the man's helmet was a face, and as he spoke, the metal mouth moved as if the armor itself were alive. This nightmare was twisting his senses—warping reality into something unnatural.

With a final distorted phrase, heavy with meaning Ronan couldn't decipher, the fallen warrior raised his gaze one last time and met Ronan's eyes. With deep sadness, Ronan lifted his warhammer and brought it down with a heavy swing, striking the glowing orb embedded in his enemy's chest with a loud crack. The orb shattered in a burst of white and violet flame, and silence reclaimed the forge.

This was the moment he always woke. Ronan braced himself for the jolt back to reality that would cause him to wake in a cold sweat—hopefully next to Brin if she was finished with her duties for the day.

But the jolt didn't come.

Instead, the dream continued. Reality within the dream sharpened rather than faded. Colors grew clearer, the weight of the hammer in his hand felt more tangible, and the air thickened with the scent of smoke and ash. Something had changed.

He rose slowly, raising his hammer to his shoulder with a grunt, and turned toward the stone doors—the ones he'd sealed at the beginning of his dream. Now they stood still and silent. The battle beyond them must have ended at some point during his fight. Ronan froze, unnerved. He'd never noticed the silence before.

Step by step, he approached the lever that would open the doors, each footfall echoing in the quiet forge like a countdown. His heart pounded in his chest, and the ever-present dread settled more deeply into his gut. Whatever lay beyond those doors, he feared it.

But in the end, his duty willed him to continue. If he did nothing, Niradim would die, and the guilt would be forever his to bear.

He pulled the lever, and heavy gears groaned—stone scraping against stone as the doors slowly parted. Beyond them stood a towering figure clad in armor nearly identical to Ronan's and the other two he'd just defeated. Across his back were two enormous greatswords. Each blade was six feet long and almost two feet wide, built for nothing but destruction.

Behind the armored titan stretched a battlefield of the dead. Bodies littered the area, some still smoldering with violet energy as they lay there. Renewed fear gripped Ronan's spine as he surveyed the scene.

The figure stepped forward, the ground trembling beneath his armored boots. He extended both arms outward and, with a metallic rasp, each arm split into two. Four hands reached up and gripped the twin greatswords hanging from his back as he glared at Ronan, eyes blazing with fury. He drew them free in a sweeping motion that screeched with power, a scream of steel against steel. At the center of his chest, a crystalline orb—not metal like the ones Ronan had only seen until now—glowed with pure, undiluted violet. Energy surged into his blades, wrapping them in streams of chaotic power.

Then, at last, he screamed. One word. Clear.

"CLASH!"

The violet mist rushed forward from the edges of Ronan's vision like a tidal wave, swallowing the world in deafening silence. Ronan barely had time to raise his hammer before darkness consumed him.

* * *

Ronan sucked in a ragged breath, eyes snapping open as though he'd surfaced from drowning. The sudden jolt disoriented him for a moment, until the familiar stone walls and simple furnishings of his room came into focus and anchored him back in reality. He exhaled slowly, then sat up and dragged a trembling hand through his fire-red hair, which was damp with sweat.

He turned with care, glancing over his shoulder. Relief loosened the tight coil in his chest—Brin was there, and, thankfully, still asleep. He hated when his nightmares woke her. She faced him, her long brunette hair a chaotic mess of half-undone braids with one limp strand plastered across her cheek. She hadn't even made it fully under the blanket before exhaustion claimed her. A soft snore escaped her slightly parted lips, and a thin line of drool glistened on her pillow. Ronan's heart softened. She was beautiful.

He slipped from the bed and silently wove his way through the many crumpled pieces of parchment littering the floor. Those were Brin's armor sketches, the fruits of stolen hours between shifts to help defend and rebuild the city of Midral after Kyros' attack. He even saw her working on some weapons and shields, though that wasn't her strong suit when it came to forging.

Ronan tiptoed into the kitchen, poured a glass of water, and downed it in a single, thirsty pull. The dream still clung to him. He wouldn't sleep again tonight, that was for sure. Maybe the cold air would help him clear his mind.

He set the empty glass on the counter, grabbed a spare shirt draped over a chair, and pulled it over sore muscles. The ache of yesterday's labor still gripped his shoulders. Skirting the clutter of gear strewn about the room, he cracked open the door. One last glance at Brin—still curled among the tangled sheets—and then he stepped out into the quiet veins of stone and shadow.

The Earth Sector was a rare hush of stillness at this hour, despite the influx of displaced souls now packed into its stone heart. Since Kyros' attack on Midral, refugees from the Sky Sector filled every spare chamber. The dwarves' age-old restriction on outsiders had been temporarily, though begrudgingly, lifted until the city recovered.

The broken husk of the Crucible Gate loomed ahead as he approached the division between the Earth and Sky sectors. This was one part of Midral that wouldn't rest until repairs were complete. Once thought to be impenetrable, the Crucible Gate now lay mostly in ruins. Ronan's fists tightened at the memory of the massive Starspawn that had destroyed their strongest defense. If only he'd been able to finish it faster... But dwelling on his failure wouldn't change the past. If anything, or anyone, dared to threaten Midral again, he'd be there to deal with it.

As he approached the checkpoint to pass from the Earth Sector to the Sky Sector, Ronan flashed his credentials and channeled a flicker of Niradim's light—just enough to confirm his identity. Satisfied he was who he said he was, the guards nodded him through. Couldn't be too careful these days.

Ronan stepped beyond the mountain's shelter into the Sky Sector—an open, sprawling city built at the mountain's base. This part of Midral was open to anyone. And until recently, it was considered the most secure stronghold in the north. Now, Ronan's city was more vulnerable than it had ever been.

Brisk mountain air surged into Ronan's lungs as he made his way toward the front gates of the city. His boots crunched over gravel and ash as he walked—lingering evidence of his failure to stop the madman that had attacked his home. The damage caused by the giants Kyros unleashed in Midral wouldn't quickly be repaired, but the residents were doing what they could to get back to a semblance of normal. Awnings were patched. Doors rehung. Even some of the rubble was cleared into neat piles.

The city's new front gates loomed ahead—thick timber lashed together to provide a temporary defense while they waited for the flow of supplies from the Earth Sector to catch up to the demand. In the meantime, the city guard had doubled its presence in the area in case another attack came while Midral recovered. However unlikely that seemed, the siege they'd just endured proved they needed to be prepared for anything. Midral would not be caught unaware again.

A flicker of green energy shimmered near the base of the gate, catching his eye. There, shaping vines and whispering to the wood, stood Ronan's closest friend—Astoro. As if sensing Ronan's approach, the florian turned and spotted him. Astoro lit up with a warm smile as he brushed leafy bangs from his brow and wiped sweat from his emerald-green face with some spare cloth that hung around his neck.

"Ronan!" Astoro called, waving both hands at him.

Ronan raised a hand in return and smiled back. "Hey Astoro, what are you doing out here this early?"

"Well, as they say, 'the flower that blooms first gets the best sun,'" Astoro replied with a mischievous wink. "But I could ask you the same question, my friend. The guards told me you finished your shift a few hours ago. Surely you're not back on duty already?"

"Nah," Ronan said, rubbing the back of his neck. "Couldn't sleep. Thought a walk might help clear my head." His gaze lifted to the wooden gates, where intricate plantwork wove itself like armor through and around the lumber. "What's all this?"

Astoro stepped back, admiring his handiwork. "Heard the guards grumbling about the lack of materials to repair the gates. So, I figured I'd lend a little help from Florana and strengthen the wood. Make it hold until enough mythril is ready to reinforce them properly. It'll take the rest of the day, but when I'm done, they'll hold like stone. Best I could do before I leave."

"Before you leave?" Ronan's voice caught on the words.

"Oh, thorns," Astoro cursed, sheepishly ruffling the leaves at the back of his head. "Yeah, sorry Ronan, I meant to find you yesterday. I got a letter. They want me back at Eldergrove—urgently. After hearing about the attack here in Midral, they want to hear a firsthand account. I guess they're worried. If Niradim was targeted..." His voice trailed off.

"Florana could be too," Ronan finished. Astoro nodded.

It made sense. After some digging, the Elders had pieced together the truth—Celestian, the imprisoned god, had orchestrated the attack through Kyros. If Niradim had been a target, Florana might be too. A thousand-year grudge still burned in the heart of the Fallen Star.

"Oh..." was all Ronan could manage to say.

"Yeah..." Astoro echoed quietly.

Silence stretched between them for a few heartbeats too long.

"I'd ask you to come with me," Astoro finally said, voice gentle. "But I know you can't. Not with all this."

Ronan nodded and cleared his throat, forcing the knot from his voice. "Sorry, I'm just... going to miss you. You gave me exactly what I needed right when I needed it. You defended Midral with your life, and then you stayed and helped this city breathe again. I couldn't ask for a better friend, Astoro."

Astoro's smile returned, bright and wistful. "Well, next time maybe we skip the thornin' death and resurrection nonsense and go straight to drinks and catching up?"

"Sounds like a good plan!" Ronan laughed, the sound easing some of the weight from his chest. "I promise, as soon as we've put this place back together, I'll come find you."

"Alright, *Mr. Phoenix*, I'm going to hold you to that," Astoro said with a wink.

"Oh, not you too!" Ronan groaned, rolling his eyes.

Astoro laughed. "You've gotta admit, it's a cool nickname."

"Yeah, yeah," Ronan said, returning Astoro's smile. "Alright, well I'll let you get back to it. I still have some walking to do. Niradim's blessings, my friend."

"Goodbye, Ronan," Astoro said. "May Florana's light guide you."

Astoro gave a small wave before turning back to his work, vines unfurling from his fingertips and weaving into the wooden gates.

Ronan turned and began the slow walk back toward the Earth Sector. There was one last place he wanted to visit before heading home.

* * *

Ronan retraced his steps through the winding paths of the Earth Sector, the stone corridors familiar beneath his boots. Before long, he stood once more in front of the towering doors of Niradim's Cathedral. It looked the same as ever—old, solemn, and slightly overdramatic with its looming spires. He let out a breath. It hadn't been that long since he'd stormed through those doors to renounce his faith. At the time, he'd thought that was the end of things between him and Niradim. But, as usual, Niradim had his own plans.

His faith hadn't exactly come galloping back—more like limped in, bruised and bandaged, when he needed it most. It wasn't what it had been before his death, not by a long shot, but he was trying to forge it back together, piece by jagged piece.

Still, questions lingered in the back of Ronan's mind like smoke after a fire. Why had Niradim let him die? And why did the magic feel stronger to him now, even though both his belief and the god's Flame were weaker? Maybe using the full power of the Flame during his duel with Kyros had changed him. Maybe he was still missing something important. That last bit seemed very likely.

Ronan shook the thoughts out of his head. Whatever the reasons were, they didn't matter right now. Aside from being plagued with strange dreams, there was too much work to be done in the city to be concerned with personal mysteries at the moment. He raised his hand to push through the large doors, but paused as he noticed they were already nudged open. Odd. Who else would be here at this hour? He pushed the door open the rest of the way and stepped inside.

"I left the door cracked for you," a familiar voice echoed gently from the front of the vast chamber. Brin knelt near the altar, haloed in the flickering glow of the Soul Forge. She turned and gave him a knowing wink. "Figured you'd find your way here sooner or later."

"And what are you doing here so early in the morning?" A light smile tugged at the corner of his mouth. "Didn't you just get to bed a couple hours ago?"

"Yeah, well..." Brin said, the twinkle in her eye dimming. "It's hard to sleep these days with so much going on."

Ronan nodded, the smile fading from his face. He moved beside her, the stone cold beneath his knees as he knelt before the Soul Forge. Together, they bowed their heads, the quiet between them filled only by the gentle pulse of the sacred fire—dimmer now than it once was, like a heartbeat fading.

"Do you feel it?" Brin's whisper broke the stillness in the cathedral.

"Yes," Ronan replied. Niradim's Flame was weaker than ever. At first, he hadn't believed the Elders when they told him that the Flame was dying—to him it had never felt stronger. In fact, even now he had a stronger connection with the Flame than he ever had before his death. But over time, the changes had become undeniable. Yes, the Flame was stronger to him than it used to be, but not as strong as it was when he'd fought Kyros.

"So," she asked, changing the subject. "Was it the dream again?"

Ronan nodded. "It went a little farther this time. I still battled the two armored figures, but then a new person showed up. Same type of armor, only his had extra limbs. He had four arms and drew two greatswords from his back before charging in. But when he spoke, I could actually understand what he said."

"You understood him?" Brin asked. "What did he say?"

"Just one word," Ronan said, gaze drifting toward the flickering forge. "Clash."

"Clash?" Brin asked.

Ronan gave a nod. "Then the dream ended with us sprinting toward each other to begin fighting. I can't make sense of it."

"Maybe it's just a dream?" Brin said. "You've been under a lot of pressure lately."

"Maybe," Ronan agreed hesitantly. "But it doesn't feel like it."

She went silent as they both turned their attention back to the Flame. The dream bothered him, but there was nothing he could really do about it at the moment. And anyway, it didn't matter. Midral came first. The city was holding on by a thread, and he wasn't about to disappear chasing down a nightmare in shining armor when they needed him here for protection.

"Ronan," Brin started. "I think you need to…"

The doors of the cathedral slammed open, cutting Brin off. A dwarven man staggered into the aisle and collapsed, hitting the stone floor hard. Ronan and Brin were already moving, instinct kicking in before they even knew what was happening. His robes were shredded, streaked with blood and dirt, and one of his eyes was swollen shut.

Brin reached him first, already channeling healing magic while Ronan eased the man upright against a pew, careful not to cause further injury. It took him a moment to recognize the face beneath the blood and grime.

Sorn. One of Vorkin's squad.

Ronan's stomach dropped. If Sorn was here, then where was Vorkin...

"Phoenix..." Sorn said, gritting his teeth against the pain, even as Brin healed him.

"Don't talk, Sorn," Ronan said. "Brin will have you feeling better in just a moment."

"No time," Sorn rasped, meeting Ronan's gaze. "Vorkin's in trouble. We were ambushed by draken after discovering some scrolls and got separated. I took out the few that were chasing me, but there were a lot more on him. He needs your help!"

Brin and Ronan locked eyes with each other for a moment, and they sprung into action. Sorn was stable, but wouldn't be able to lead them through the tunnels in his condition. Ronan would see what directions he could get from the bloodied man, but they'd need some backup. Brin could work on that.

"Go to the Forgehold and get word to the Elders," Ronan said to her as he gently lifted Sorn off the ground. He'd need to get Sorn to the medical quarters so he could recover. "Tell them to assemble a squad of Protectors and have them meet us at the sealed doors to the old Earth Sector, where Vorkin's team left."

Brin was already halfway turned when she answered. "I'll get them moving, then meet you back at your place to gear up."

She bolted through the open doors of the cathedral.

Ronan watched her go, tightening his grip on Sorn. He just hoped they weren't already too late.

2

Brin

Brin sprinted through the winding corridors toward the Forgehold, her mind a whirlwind of exhaustion mixed with anxiety. The ache in her legs from the day's labor faded beneath the raw surge of adrenaline sparked by Sorn's arrival.

Seven or eight would be ideal, she thought to herself, weaving through shadowy halls lit only by flickering torches on the walls. *But we could probably make do with just five, if we needed to.*

Her focus was so caught up on the mission at hand that she nearly slammed into a figure as she careened around a sharp corner.

"Whoa there!" cried a familiar voice as a dwarven woman with a sun-gold ponytail jumped out of Brin's way just in time, her boots skidding slightly on the smooth stone floor.

"Thalga!" Brin exclaimed, her face momentarily brightening with relief. "I'm so glad to see you!"

"See me? You nearly tackled me," Thalga teased with a smirk, brushing a stray wisp of hair behind her ear. "What's got you tearing through the halls at this hour? Rushing back to see your boyfriend, I'm assuming?"

Brin's smile faded, the weight of the current situation crashing back down. Right, this wasn't the time for a friendly chat. Every second Vorkin stayed out there alone was a second too long.

"Sorry, Thalga, I wish I could talk, but I've got to go," Brin said. "Vorkin is in trouble, and I need to let the Elders know."

Thalga's expression shifted to concern as Brin's words sank in.

"I'm actually heading that way," Thalga said. "I'll come with you."

Brin gave a quick nod and broke into a run once more, boots thudding against stone as Thalga kept pace with her.

"So how do you know Vorkin is in trouble, anyway?" Thalga called, breath quickening as they raced through the dim corridors of the Earth Sector.

"Sorn stumbled into the Cathedral," Brin said between breaths. "He was ripped to shreds—barely standing."

"Slag and ashes," Thalga muttered. "Did he say what happened?" They barreled around another corner, nearly colliding with two weary dwarves finishing their shifts. Almost everyone around here was putting in long hours to help with the rebuilding efforts.

"Ambush," Brin said between breaths. "The party ran into a group of draken and got split up."

"Draken?" Thalga said. "What in Niradim's name are draken doing in the old Earth Sector?"

"Add it to the growing list of problems, I guess," Brin muttered as their destination came into view.

The Forgehold was where the Elders lived and conducted their business within the Earth Sector. It was a grand building carved straight into the mountain's rock, its stone halls rich with gold filigree and veins of mythril, which glowed dimly in the torchlight. Statues of ancient heroes flanked the entrance, their faces weathered but proud, cloaked in flickering shadows cast by Niradim's sacred—though waning—flames. The current gloom gave the place a haunted feel, like even the mountain mourned its dying god.

Brin slid to a stop in front of the Forgehold and reached for the handle, but Thalga grabbed her arm. "Knock first," she reminded. What was she doing, almost barging in on the Elders like they were just common folk? Brin nodded to Thalga in thanks, then pounded on the heavy wooden door.

"C'mon, where are they?" Brin asked, bouncing on the balls of her feet as she anxiously waited for someone to answer.

"Brin, it's like two in the morning," Thalga said, folding her arms. "It might take them a minute to answer. It's not like they were expecting you."

"I know, but this is important," Brin complained, but she forced herself to stand still. Thalga was right, of course. It was unreasonable to expect anyone to answer the door right away at this hour. "Hopefully at least one of them is awake."

As if summoned by her words, the metal bolts locking the door slid back, and the door creaked open to reveal an aging, slim dwarf adorned in Elders' robes.

"Ah, Master Brillenia," Elder Oren said as he opened the door. Dark circles under his eyes told Brin she hadn't woken him. With the threat of Niradim's Flame weakening, the Elders might be working longer hours even than Ronan as they searched for a solution. He cleared his throat. "Niradim's Blessings upon you. How may I be of service?"

"Vorkin's in trouble," Brin burst out, the urgency spilling out from her. "We need a team of Protectors. Ronan and I are going, but I think we need-"

"Breathe, child," Oren said gently, lifting a hand. "Why don't the two of you come in? We can discuss the matter with the other Elders that are awake at the moment and see what can be done."

"Yes, of course, Flame Elder. Apologies," Brin said, pulling herself together. Even so, the urgency still simmered just under the surface. They really needed to get moving.

She stepped into the vaulted parlour, incense tickling her nose as she entered. Magical lamps glowed softly in alcoves, though many were flickering unnaturally or had completely gone out.

Thalga followed close on her heels as two other Elders appeared from a study room to the right—Leythia, the Shield Elder, and to Brin's dismay, Druden. The Armor Elder frowned in irritation as soon as he saw who was disturbing them so late in the night.

"What's all this racket about?" Druden grumbled, arms crossed over his chest. "As if we don't have enough chaos to contend with, now we have to deal with disturbances in the middle of the night?"

"Oh hush, Druden," Leythia said as she calmly poured water into a metal teapot for some fresh tea. "They wouldn't barge in like this unless it was important." She paused to look up over her half-moon spectacles at the two dwarven women who had disrupted their night. "Right, ladies?"

"Yes, well," Brin started before catching herself. She needed to be respectful here. No matter how much Druden grated on her, he was still an Elder, and therefore one of the top leaders of their faith. "Protector Sorn returned from his mission, barely alive. Vorkin is being hunted by a pack of draken in the old Earth Sector as we speak. Ronan sent me to tell you we need to ready a squad of Protectors immediately for a rescue mission."

Druden rolled his eyes and scoffed. "So, the Phoenix is giving orders to the Elders now, is he?"

"No, he-" Brin started.

"Well, no matter," Druden spoke over her. "We don't have the personnel to send on some random mission for the Phoenix. Now run along and let us get back to sleep."

"Honestly, Druden," Leythia snapped, glaring at him. Brin flinched—she'd never seen Leythia anything but calm and collected. If she was unraveling, it didn't bode well for Midral. "Vorkin's mission is vital.

Set aside your petty issues with the Phoenix and see the bigger picture. Besides, as the Shield Elder, the Protectors and their assignments are under my purview."

"And as the Armor Elder, in charge of the protection of Midral, your entire force is under my command until Midral is secure—correct?" Druden turned his head to Oren and raised his eyebrows, as if questioning.

"I'm afraid Elder Druden is correct in this matter," Elder Oren conceded. "The Protectors within the city are to be commanded by the Armor Elder when Midral is in a state of crisis. And Midral is unquestionably in a state of crisis."

"So, you see," Druden said with a self-satisfied smile. "I'm in command of the Protectors at the moment, and I say we don't have anyone to spare for Ronan's *supposed* rescue mission. I can't help but notice that instead of bringing Protector Sorn here for us to question and make a decision ourselves, you instead brought us orders. Well, you can report back to your Phoenix that while he may be blessed by Niradim, it doesn't grant him the right to do whatever he wishes!"

Brin stood frozen, stunned by how far Druden would go just to spite Ronan. Leythia hadn't been exaggerating. Vorkin's mission *was* vital. And yet Druden was willing to gamble the lives of the dwarves, and perhaps even Niradim himself, over politics. None of the Elders were particularly pleased with Ronan's new rank as Phoenix—there was no existing structure for what that meant. She knew that would create some friction between him and the Elders, but she never expected *this*. Her hands clenched into fists at her sides as she fought to steady her voice.

"Elder Druden," Brin said through gritted teeth, struggling to keep the frustration from her voice. She wasn't very successful. "Surely you would allow at least Ronan and me to go?"

"Elder Druden," Oren said gently. "Considering the circumstances, it may be prudent to allow the Phoenix and Brillenia here-"

"And me!" Thalga said, stepping forward. She turned and grinned at Brin, patting her on the shoulder. "I've finished my duties for the day, anyway. Let me go with them."

"Thanks, Thalga," Brin whispered, grateful her best friend was here for her.

Elder Oren nodded, continuing. "And miss Thalga here to go and investigate Protector Sorn's claims. Should there be any trouble, the three of them are capable enough to return safely with Lieutenant Vorkin."

It wasn't what she'd hoped for, but she'd settle for only three of them going rather than letting Vorkin die out there without any help.

Druden hesitated, then gave a curt nod. "Very well. The three of you may go. Find Lieutenant Vorkin and bring him back in one piece."

"Thank you, Elders," Brin said, bowing low to avoid meeting Druden's eyes. "Niradim's blessings."

Brin turned on her heel and sprinted out of the Forgehold, not waiting to hear another word.

It was time to save Vorkin.

* * *

Brin burst through the door to Ronan's home, barely catching herself on a wobbling table as her boot caught on a scatter of drafting tools littering the floor. The room was a chaos of casually discarded armor, weaponry, and design scraps—her own mess.

I should really keep Ronan's place cleaner, she thought, sighing as she began picking up and strapping on her armor, piece by piece.

Ronan stepped out of his bedroom, already clad in the Phoenix armor she'd forged for him during her Shaping Trial. Even now, the sight of it stirred pride in her chest—along with some butterflies because of the person wearing it. It was the finest armor anyone had ever created in the Soul Forge, of that she was sure. Crafting armor had always come easily to Brin, but that gift had been born from tragedy.

She shook the memory of her parents out of her head before it fully surfaced. This was no time to be thinking about them. Besides, her successful Trial meant future generations of Niradim's people wouldn't have to suffer the same fate as her family. Soon, all the Protectors would be wearing armor *worthy* of Niradim's most devoted Followers. Inwardly, she smiled at her personal victory.

"Did you speak to the Elders?" Ronan asked, snapping her out of her thoughts. He tightened the leather strap on his shield as he stepped toward her.

"Yes," she said, cinching her breastplate and reaching for a bracer. Her fingers fumbled, scanning the clutter. *Now where was that other one?* "But they only agreed to send you, me, and Thalga. And even that was a fight. You'd think by now they'd trust your judgment, after everything you've done."

She still couldn't believe how frustrating that meeting had been. Three of them to take on who knows how many draken? Ridiculous. Druden must have figured that trying to keep Ronan from this rescue mission was a losing battle. They all knew Ronan would have gone with or without the Elders' blessing. He probably only agreed to send them to save face in case they succeeded.

Ronan's resurrection had shifted him beyond the bounds of any existing rank in their faith. He was no longer a Disciple, but also not an Elder—he was something more. Something that had only existed once before, a long time ago. And that frightened them. A human granted the rank of Phoenix instead of one of the dwarven god's own people? That stung their pride and weakened their authority. Ronan's very existence was dangerous to them.

"Well, I turned down their mission," Ronan said, handing her the missing bracer. She quickly buckled it tight around her arm. "They're probably still sulking about it."

That tracked. The Elders had approached Ronan first when the Mythril Soul was discovered—an artifact that was still kept secret from the public. Its appearance coinciding with the Flame beginning to weaken seemed like no mere coincidence, so they'd asked him to investigate by delving deep into an older part of the Earth Sector that had been sealed off for centuries under the mountain.

But he had confided in her that the request had felt more like exile than assignment, so he refused, offering the Elders no explanation. She knew that his refusal, coupled with how many of Niradim's people now looked to Ronan for guidance, threatened the Elders more than the artifact ever could. But even though she understood why Ronan had made the decision to stay, she didn't agree with it.

"Well, I'm glad you're not the one being hunted by draken tonight," Brin said, tightening the last strap on her armor. "But I still think you should have accepted. You're the best chance we have to fix this."

He could do so much more to help save the Flame than simply tending to Midral's defense. Why couldn't he see what felt so obvious to her? But she knew what he'd say. She'd heard it before.

"Brin," Ronan sighed, rubbing a hand through his hair. "We've been over this. I can't leave Midral while it's so vulnerable. If something happens, I need to be here."

As expected—the same excuse he always gave. This topic was their only real unresolved argument. Everything else between them felt effortless. But here, their beliefs diverged so strongly. She believed Niradim wanted more for Ronan than being Midral's personal shield. The answers weren't here in Midral. They were *out there*, and Niradim's Phoenix was meant to find them. She was sure of it. She just wished she could convince him of the same.

"Ronan, the Flame is dying," Brin said, stopping what she was doing to face him fully. "You said it yourself—you can feel it. You're the strongest one of us, Ronan. It's *you* who should be the one out there searching for answers."

Ronan looked away, jaw tight. "Look, we don't have time for this right now. Vorkin's in danger—we need to get going."

Deflection. Again. When *would* they have time to talk about this?

She stepped in front of him. "You can't just ignore this conversation forever, Ronan. We *have* to talk about it at some point."

Ronan threw his arms wide, exasperated. "What do you want from me, Brin? We don't have time to hash this out right now! Vorkin is in real danger—real, *immediate* danger. I know you don't agree with me about staying in Midral, but now isn't the time for this."

She held his gaze, frustration giving way to resignation.

"Fine."

"Fine."

He grabbed her mace from where it leaned against the wall and held it out without a word. She snatched it from his hand, jaw clenched.

"Let's go," Ronan said, and strode out the door.

3

Ronan

Ronan raced through the rubble-choked corridors of the long-abandoned Earth Sector with Brin and Thalga following close behind. Dust hung thick in the air, stirred anew by their passage. This area had been sealed off for centuries—Vorkin and his squad should have been alone down here.

Just hang in there, Vorkin. I'm on my way, Ronan thought.

Dim torches flickered along the tunnel walls, giving them at least some light to navigate with. Without them, it would have been impossibly dark in the old Earth Sector, and they'd have had to use their own torches to give them light to see by. It was a miracle that any of Niradim's magic still worked this far into the old passageways. He idly wondered if they'd still be burning brightly if the Flame wasn't getting weaker.

He rounded a corner, and he finally heard something other than their boots thumping against the stone beneath their feet. The echo of clashing steel rang out from deeper within. The tunnel before him opened into a large room, now lit with flickers of combat. A jagged slab of stone that had fallen from the tunnel's ceiling blocked his path, but he vaulted it without breaking stride, making his way as quickly as possible toward the combat ahead of him.

Just ahead, three red-scaled draken surged past the far side of the chamber, their dragon-like features easy to pick out at a distance. A searing burst of white light flared from where they'd been headed, and one of them came hurtling backward, crashing to the ground with a bone-jarring thud.

Ronan reached across to the shield strapped to his left arm and drew the short sword from the embedded scabbard. As his fingers wrapped around the hilt, he whispered a prayer and summoned Niradim's power. The blade shimmered, then flared to life with crackling white energy. Before his death, it had taken everything in him to summon even a flicker of the Flame. Now, it answered his call as easily as taking a breath.

Sword glowing with Niradim's power, Ronan charged into the chamber. To his left, the draken who had been flung across the room was staggering upright, snarling and getting ready to rejoin the fight. Brin could handle that one. The scene to his right needed his immediate attention. The remaining two draken bore down on Vorkin in a brutal melee. Vorkin's tunic was slashed and bloodied, and his left arm hung limp and useless at his side. One of the draken swung his blade, and Vorkin barely managed to deflect what would have been a killing blow. Still, the force of the strike wrenched the sword from his grip and sent him crashing to a knee.

As the second draken raised his blade to finish Vorkin off, Ronan hurled his sword. A streak of burning light cut through the air and drove through the draken's chest, pinning him to the stone wall beside Vorkin. The sword in his hand clattered to the floor beside him. The first draken turned in surprise, just in time to see Ronan barreling toward him. In the moment he was distracted, Vorkin seized the fallen weapon and plunged it into his enemy's gut. The final draken collapsed, and so did Vorkin, sagging against the wall in exhaustion.

"Phoenix Ronan," Vorkin said, wincing in pain as he grabbed his left arm. "You always did know how to make an entrance."

"It gets easier with practice," Ronan replied with a light smile as he knelt next to Vorkin to assess the damage. "Where's the rest of your team?"

"We were ambushed… in the archives…" Vorkin said, wincing and grabbing his limp arm. "I'm the only one who made it out."

"Not the only one," Ronan said. "Sorn made it. He's the reason we knew you needed help."

"Well, thank Niradim he did," Vorkin said.

Ronan pressed one hand to Vorkin's injured arm, the other to the sword-and-anvil medallion resting against his chest—the symbol of his faith. He closed his eyes and channeled Niradim's healing flame. A flicker of white fire burned across Vorkin's body, sizzling as it both seared and soothed his wounds. He gasped as the magic surged through him, then sagged in relief when it was done, his head falling back against the wall with a shaky exhale.

With a quick glance across the chamber, Ronan could see that Brin and Thalga had indeed taken out the remaining draken. The immediate threat was gone for now, so Ronan took a moment to survey the large room around them.

This space had clearly once been a grand dining hall, wide and vaulted, but time had worn it down. Portions of the ceiling had crumbled, leaving pieces of rock and stone across the cracked floor. Most of the long stone tables had collapsed into rubble, though a few still stood near the walls. Scattered among the debris were more bodies—draken. It looked like Vorkin had downed at least five before they'd arrived. Impressive, considering Niradim's Flame was fading and he was on his own. That he had survived at all was a miracle.

Brin approached, but Ronan noticed the subtle distance she kept between them.

"Good work—both of you," Ronan said, nodding toward them.

"Thanks," Thalga said with a smile as she jogged up next to Brin. Brin only grunted a response, averting her eyes and crossing her arms, causing Thalga to shift awkwardly from the tension in the air. So, Brin was still angry with him. Ronan pushed the thought aside for now. There'd be time to patch things up when they made it back.

Ronan turned back to Vorkin and yanked his sword free from the wall, causing the impaled draken to slump lifelessly to the floor.

"How did these draken make their way into these halls?" Ronan asked as he wiped the dark blood off his sword using the draken's tunic. "These tunnels are supposed to be sealed."

"They were," Vorkin said, struggling to his feet. "But more than a few of the seals were magical. Now that the Flame is fading... there could be ways into the Earth Sector that we don't even know about."

Ronan slammed his blade back into the shield-scabbard in frustration. This changed everything. The front gates of Midral, the Crucible Gate—those were known vulnerabilities, and that was bad enough. But this? Entry points buried beneath centuries of stone, lost to history? How was he supposed to defend a city with so many holes in it? Especially when he didn't know where all the holes were?

Ronan took a deep breath to calm his growing anxiety. One thing at a time. Dwelling on it now wouldn't help. The priority was getting Vorkin back—alive and with the scrolls he'd found. If there were any answers left, hopefully the Elders would find them there.

Ronan offered a hand and helped Vorkin to his feet. "How are you feeling? Can you walk?"

Vorkin grunted, but nodded. "I'm exhausted, but now that you've healed the worst of it, I'll manage."

He turned to Brin and Thalga as Vorkin steadied himself.

"Let's move out. We—" Ronan stopped as his ears picked up a strange noise from the far end of the room.

A crossbow bolt punched into Ronan's shoulder with a loud thump, finding a small opening between his pauldron and breastplate. Pain exploded through his chest as the force spun him sideways. He stumbled, tripping over the fallen draken at his feet just as a second bolt hissed past—right where his head had been a heartbeat earlier. The impact of hitting the ground drove the air from his lungs and stunned him for a moment. Then came the sound. Footfalls, dozens of them, echoed from the stone corridors across the hall and were growing louder with each second.

"Ronan!" Brin's voice rang out, sharp with panic, as she dropped to his side. Vorkin and Thalga closed ranks, weapons raised, forming a wall between them and the enemy. Ronan groaned through gritted teeth as Brin hoisted him up. Across the chamber, more draken surged in with weapons drawn. The draken were advancing fast, but if the four of them moved now, they might be able to make it back through the corridor they came from and retreat back to the Earth Sector.

"I'm okay. Back to the entrance, let's go!" Ronan yelled to the group as he pointed toward their escape route. They broke into a sprint without hesitation. It was going to be close.

The two draken with crossbows had abandoned their ranged weapons, drawing curved blades instead now that there wasn't a clear line of fire through the draken horde. For now, it seemed they were safe from more bolts. But tightness gripped Ronan's chest as a cold realization set in. Even if their group reached the tunnel, they couldn't outrun the draken all the way back to the Earth Sector. Not with Vorkin staggering beside them, and the rest of them weary from travel and battle.

Ronan tried to raise his shield, but winced in pain as his arm refused to respond—dangling uselessly at his side as he ran. Gritting his teeth, Ronan reached across his body, seized the bolt, and tore it free. Hot blood gushed down his arm, and he stumbled from the pain before catching himself. He tossed the bloody bolt to the side and whispered a prayer to Niradim. The wound began to knit closed, white fire sealing the torn flesh with a sizzle of smoke. The pain dulled. His arm was still sore—but he could fight. That was all that mattered.

"Listen up," Ronan said, voice firm despite the pain. "Vorkin gets back to the Elders with that scroll, no matter what. You two make sure he makes it back in one piece. Understood?"

Thalga nodded at once, but Brin's expression twisted with worry. "What about you?" she asked.

"I'm going to keep them busy," Ronan answered. "Don't worry, I'll be right behind you." He locked eyes with Brin, holding her gaze just long enough to say what words couldn't. Then he turned and veered away from the group, charging headlong toward the draken horde.

As he ran, Ronan channeled Niradim's power into the ten knives strapped across his body. He raised his arms, ring and middle fingers of each hand forming an 'x' in front of his face. The blades slipped free from their sheaths with a metallic hum, gathering in the air behind him. A surge of Niradim's power pulsed through Ronan, and bladed wings flared and ignited with holy fire behind him. He was Niradim's Phoenix, and these draken were about to find out exactly what that meant.

He threw his hands forward, and the deadly blades shot into the oncoming draken, tearing through their front ranks with ease. Drawing his sword, he directed Niradim's power into the blade. As he did, he spared a glance back at Brin and the others. They were still far from the exit, so he'd need to keep the enemy's attention on him to allow their escape.

Ronan poured everything he had into his sword. The steel turned white-hot, then burst with Niradim's power. With a sweeping arc, he slashed the blade in front of him, and a wall of searing flames erupted from the earth itself, a blazing barrier that cut across the chamber. The first wave of draken slammed into it too fast to stop. Their screams pierced the air as their bodies burst into flames.

They were still screaming as Ronan leapt through the fire.

The front ranks of draken faltered, stunned as Ronan burst from the inferno as if he were born from the flames themselves. The Phoenix armor glowed with Niradim's strength, fire licking its plates without burning him. Niradim's Flame was his ally—but the draken felt every bit of its fury. Ronan tore into the stunned warriors, cutting down three before the others snapped out of their shock and began to counter with a roar.

He relied on constant movement, and the amazing power his armor provided him, to keep himself alive. The Phoenix Armor was a gift from Brin, born from Niradim's Soul Forge during her Shaping Trial, and it had no equal. As long as he channeled Niradim's magic, his power would protect all gaps in the armor as if it were seamless. But even Niradim's power had limits. Ronan sensed he would probably find that limit before the day was done.

Ronan carved a path through the tide of bodies, each swing of his blade leaving corpses at his feet. But they kept coming, pouring from the tunnels like a living flood. The Flame inside him flared, faltered, flared again. He could feel it thinning, unraveling under the sheer weight of the assault.

He dared a glance back and saw that the wall of flames behind him was dying down. Through the remaining glow, he saw Brin and Thalga reach the passage with Vorkin limping between them. She shoved him into Thalga's arms and turned—her eyes searching for Ronan.

That glance cost him. He took three blows in quick succession, and the Phoenix armor flickered. The fire finally died behind him, and some of the draken peeled off and charged after Brin and the others now that the path was clear.

Cursing under his breath, Ronan spun in a circle, cutting down a few of the draken around him with his blade, but more importantly, freeing up some space around himself.

Ronan drove his sword back into its sheath, inhaled once, and reached for the last of Niradim's power. It burned in his chest—pure, bright, final. He turned his gaze toward Brin.

Their eyes locked. Confusion crossed her face first. Then shock. Then horror.

She knew.

I'm sorry, Brin.

As the draken closed in, Ronan thrust both hands toward the ceiling above the tunnel's mouth and released everything. The chamber blazed white. Holy fire detonated, and the ceiling collapsed in a rain of rock and dust, sealing the passage completely.

His escape was gone. But they were safe.

He only hoped that Brin and the others would find the answers they needed.

Through the dust and flame, he saw Brin reaching for him, her mouth open in a silent cry. Thalga pulled her back, arm locked around her waist, just as the last stones fell and the world between them sealed shut.

He barely had time to turn before something struck the back of his skull. Light burst behind his eyes, then nothing.

The world vanished into black.

4

Brin

Brin stared in horror as stone and dust collapsed before her, sealing the tunnel back to Ronan. Her arm remained outstretched through the lingering haze, fingers trembling as if they could somehow pierce the wall of rubble and reach him.

He was gone.

"No!" She tore herself away from Thalga's grip, and dropped to her knees, clawing at the jagged stones with raw fingers. Dust hung in the air, and she could taste the grittiness in her mouth as dirt ground between her teeth, but she didn't care. She had to get through. She had to reach him.

"Master Brin!" Vorkin's voice cut through her panic like a blade. She froze, her hands buried in rubble, breath ragged. "These rocks will not hold the draken back forever, and we don't know if there are other paths they can take to reach us. Ronan gave us this chance. We can't waste it."

The cold truth of it twisted inside her. He was right. And she hated it.

Slowly, painfully, she lowered her hands, letting them fall to her sides. A shuddering breath escaped her lips. She nodded, tears slipping down her cheeks as Thalga gently took her arm and led her away.

Don't you dare die, Ronan, she thought, taking one last look over her shoulder at the tomb of stone. *I'm not finished with you. Not yet.*

Their return to the Earth Sector was mercifully uneventful, though the silence between them hung in the air for the entire return voyage. Vorkin moved with a visible limp, slowing their pace, but no draken pursued. After several hours, they reached the carved entrance that would take them back to relative safety.

Brin pressed her palm against the stone and channeled some of Niradim's power. Magic pulsed from her hand in a warm thrum, and the hidden door groaned open. Two armed guards stood just beyond, alert and poised.

"Phoenix Ronan, we wondered when—" one of them began until he noticed Ronan was missing. He looked to Brin. "Where is the Phoenix?"

Brin opened her mouth, but no words came. She shook her head slowly, the movement heavy with grief. The guards' eyes widened, but she didn't wait for them to speak again. Without a word, she brushed past them, guiding Vorkin forward. She had to get him to the Elders—then she'd return. She'd tear the tunnels apart stone by stone if that's what it took.

It only took a few minutes before they reached the Forgehold. Brin marched up the steps and pushed open the doors without knocking—the scent of burning oil and old parchment drifting out to meet her as she crossed the threshold. Inside, as she'd expected, all five Elders were assembled beneath the arched ceiling. Each wore the emblem of their sacred craft: pennant-shaped banners stitched in distinct patterns, either draped from their shoulders or tied at their waists.

The Hammer Elder stood for the artisans who forged the lifeblood of the city—its tools. This Elder oversaw the great forges, guiding what was crafted by the needs of the people. Though blacksmiths accepted commissions, the Hammer shaped the city's direction by choosing what the forges of Niradim would produce.

The Sword Elder represented Niradim's weapons. The Sword was in charge of outfitting the Niradim Protectors, Midral's main defense force, with weaponry and oversaw any missions sent beyond Midral's walls.

Then there was the Armor Elder. Elder Druden wore the title, so it fell to him to decide how the Protectors were outfitted for battle. But Brin had never trusted him. He guarded his own interests far more fiercely than the lives of those who followed Niradim. In addition to deciding what armor the Protectors would wear, his charge also included the security of the Earth Sector, a role once viewed as mostly ceremonial—until the world had come crashing in.

The Shield Elder represented those who specialized in the creation of shields, as shields could be both a weapon and armor. They were also in charge of assigning the Protectors to the other Elders as needed. The Sword and Armor Elders could request command of the Niradim Protectors for their own initiatives, but those requests had to go through the Shield Elder. Otherwise, they would assign their forces to patrol the Sky Sector. The Shield Elder had arguably the most responsibility of all the Elders. Leythia held the title at the moment and was the oldest among them. It was well known that she was training Master Ginmar to replace her when she retired. Brin couldn't think of a better candidate for that position.

And at the center of it all stood the Flame Elder, Elder Oren—the voice of the faith and the keeper of its sacred flame. His pennant bore the emblems of all the other crafts, circling the white Flame of Niradim in its center. When things required a vote, the Flame Elder would only vote if the other Elders were tied, and his vote would break the tie. Otherwise, he led from a place of wisdom and allowed the others to make their own decisions.

The Elders rose as she stepped into the chamber, Vorkin limping in just behind her. A strange realization crept in—this was the first time she'd stood before all five of them. Here, in this hushed sanctum of stone and fire, her voice felt small. She cleared her throat as her nerves betrayed her.

"Forgive the intrusion," she said, bowing at the waist. "We've returned with Lieutenant Vorkin."

"We expected the Phoenix to deliver the lieutenant himself," the Sword Elder said.

"He... didn't make it back," she replied, the words barely holding together.

"He sacrificed himself so we could make it back," Vorkin added, stepping forward. "He died so these records could reach your hands."

"We don't know he's dead!" She snapped at Vorkin before she could catch herself. Thalga placed a comforting hand on her shoulder, and she winced as she tried to regain her composure.

"He sealed the passage behind us so the draken chasing Lieutenant Vorkin couldn't follow," Thalga said calmly. "We... we didn't see him fall."

Elder Oren inclined his head. "The Phoenix has risen once before," he said softly. "Perhaps Niradim will see fit to return him again." The others murmured their agreement. "For now, the greatest honor we can grant him is to uncover the means to rekindle Niradim's Flame in the Soul Forge."

She could tell from the look in his eyes—he didn't believe Ronan had survived. None of them did. Despite all Ronan had done in his defense of Midral, there was still a rift between him and the Elders.

Vorkin stepped forward to hand a book and several tattered scrolls to the Flame Elder directly, snapping Brin from her thoughts. Oren took them gingerly and nodded his head to Lieutenant Vorkin in thanks. He then proceeded to give the Elders a detailed account of what happened in the tunnels and the deaths of the others. He'd grabbed the few records he could in his escape.

"You've done well, Lieutenant Vorkin. We will comb through these records to see if we can uncover the secret to restoring Niradim's Flame," the Flame Elder said. "Thank you all for your service to Niradim. We will call upon you if your services are required again. Niradim's Blessings to you."

With that dismissal, he turned to go, but Brin spoke up again, causing him to halt.

"What about Ronan?" she asked. "He could still be out there. We need to at least try to save him if we can."

Elder Oren turned back to address her. "I'm sorry, Brin, but we cannot spare the resources to recover the Phoenix or the bodies of the other Protectors who gave their lives to return these documents."

"But he could still be down there, wounded," she cried as she turned to Thalga, but her friend wouldn't meet her eyes. Ashes, she believed Ronan was dead too.

"Well, then I'll go!" Brin said, anger bubbling up inside her. "If nobody else will go with me, then I'll do it alone."

"Master Brin," Oren said, his usually gentle voice becoming firm. "We can't allow you to forgo your duties of rebuilding and patrolling while Midral is vulnerable. If the Phoenix is indeed alive, we will have to trust in Niradim to return him."

Those words hung in the air as he turned and followed the rest of the Elders into a room deeper in the Forgehold to pore over the ancient texts. That was it. They were going to leave him to die. Again. Her fists clenched at her sides.

Thalga squeezed her shoulder and slowly walked out of the room, head bowed. Vorkin turned and began limping towards the entrance, also placing a hand on her shoulder as he passed.

"What about you, Vorkin?" Her voice was barely above a whisper.

"He ran in there to save you. Are you just going to leave him?"

Vorkin sighed, his head hanging in defeat. "He's gone, Brin. I'm sorry."

He stepped past her and opened the door. "Thank you for coming for me. I am in your debt." He stepped out and left Brin alone in the foyer, tears falling once again.

They may have given up on him, but she wouldn't. The Flame Elder said she had to continue contributing to the rebuilding and patrols, but her free time was still hers. And she'd spend every moment she could spare to break through that rubble and prove Ronan was alive. Then, the Elders would have to agree to send a search party.

Vorkin knew the way back to the end of the tunnels where he'd first encountered the draken. Once she confirmed Ronan was alive, she could use his help to get her on the trail, and she wouldn't stop until she found Ronan.

Get better soon, Vorkin, she thought. *Because I'll be calling in that favor sooner than you know.*

* * *

Brin groaned as she rolled out of bed. Her limbs ached, and her joints were stiff from another restless night of sleep. Ronan had been missing for three days, and the Elders must be getting close to finishing their research into the documents Vorkin had recovered. Hopefully, they would find something to help restore Niradim's Flame soon. She didn't know how the city could recover without it.

She made her way to her favorite breakfast spot in the Earth Sector, Heart of the Forge, to pick up a couple of meat pies that would last her through the end of her shift at the city's front gates. The warmth of the food lifted her spirits a little as she walked.

Being on the front gates today also helped her mood. That was one of the easiest tasks in her rotation each week. All of Niradim's followers would rotate around the city to help rebuild, guard, or do whatever tasks were needed to help repair the damage that had been done as fast as possible. But certain things couldn't be repaired without a functioning Soul Forge.

The Crucible Gate, for one. If they couldn't forge the mythril required to reinforce the massive doors, they would have to make do with lesser materials for the time being. Same for the front gates to the city, though Astoro had graciously reinforced those with his nature magic.

She wished he had been able to stick around. He'd been called back to his home the same day that Ronan had gone missing. Though she'd already sent word of Ronan's capture to him, she doubted he'd get the news in time to help save Ronan. Astoro wouldn't be able to help her.

She'd also sent word to Master Ginmar, but he was on a diplomatic mission far from Midral to see if they could convince some of their allies to lend support while they rebuilt. There was no way he could return quickly enough to help Brin either.

And she hadn't spoken to Thalga since their meeting with the Elders. It was true that they were both busy with their duties as part of Niradim's Protectors, but in the past, they'd always made time to meet up and chat for a few moments each day. She still felt betrayed that Thalga hadn't backed her up.

Repeated petitioning of the Elders had gotten her nowhere. She'd made a request twice a day since she'd saved Vorkin, but if they were deep in research, she wasn't even sure they'd received the requests.

So, with limited other options, it looked like Brin would have to do this herself.

Aside from breaking up a minor scuffle close to the city's entrance, her shift at the front gates was relatively easy. Finally, after hours of trying to stay awake through her exhaustion, her replacement arrived to relieve her at the gates.

It was Thalga. Of course, it was Thalga. She really didn't need this right now.

"Oh, hey, Brin," Thalga said sheepishly.

"Hey," Brin simply replied. She wanted to get out of there before things got too awkward, so she quickly gathered her things and started to head out before Thalga grabbed her arm to stop her.

"Wait, Brin… I wanted to apologize for not supporting you the other day," Thalga said. "I was intimidated and didn't want to contradict the Elders. But that was wrong. If there's even a slight chance Ronan is still alive, we should be looking for him. He saved our city."

Brin took a deep breath, releasing some of the tension from her shoulders. "Thanks, Thalga, it's okay. I know being in front of the Elders can be a lot."

She squeezed Thalga's arm before hefting her bag over her shoulder and turning to go. "Well, I'd better be off. Have fun on your shift."

Now it was time for the real work of the day to begin. Despite her growing daily fatigue, the purpose behind her next task filled her with energy, and she all but jogged back through the Sky Sector and crossed the broken Crucible Gate back into the Earth Sector.

She made only two stops. The first was back to Heart of the Forge for a few more meat pies to give her the energy she would need, and the second was to drop off her latest petition at the Forgehold for the Elders to reconsider their decision to search for Ronan. Once that was complete, she made a beeline for the guarded door that led to the old Earth Sector.

She flashed her credentials to the guards at the sealed door, though that was mostly a formality at this point, and they let her through. For the last few days, she had been returning to the cave-in Ronan had made to seal their retreat, slowly clearing as much as her body would let her.

She grabbed the set of tools she'd left in a crate by the door—a mythril pickaxe, a small shovel, and a hammer—and began the two-hour journey back to where they'd found Lieutenant Vorkin. It was a grueling task, especially after a long day of work in the city, but she felt like she might be able to push through the last of the wreckage today. Her eagerness quickened her pace, and she hurried down the long, abandoned tunnels.

This portion of the old Earth Sector was relatively safe compared to how deep Vorkin's party had delved. Though she admitted to herself that the entire network could be compromised, as far as anybody knew. The thought sent shivers down her spine.

But that was a problem for another day. Today, her primary focus was breaking through. A small voice in the back of her head whispered that there was a chance she'd find Ronan's body among the others in the ruins, but she had faith, both in Niradim and in Ronan, that he wouldn't be there.

He'd better not be.

Finally, she reached her destination. The area around the cave-in was littered with pulverized rock—remnants of her work the past few days. She slid her pack to the ground, along with the shovel and hammer, and hefted the mythril pickaxe onto her shoulder while she pulled a wrapped meat pie out of her pocket.

She took a large bite, stuffed it back in her pocket, and wiped the crumbs from her mouth.

"Okay, Brin," she said through a mouthful of food. "Let's do this."

She lifted the pickaxe above her head and got to work.

* * *

Sweat poured from every pore on her body, and the mythril pickaxe felt like she was trying to carry the entire Midral mountain in her hands. Her dirt-streaked arms shook, but her grip tightened. She screamed with each swing of the pickaxe, letting her determination fuel her. She would break through tonight.

The only breaks Brin had taken were brief ones, either for a bite of food or a swig of water. She had run out of both hours ago. But nothing else mattered. Nothing else existed but her and the pickaxe. One swing at a time.

She paused, taking deep breaths to gather her strength. Over the last few days, she'd kept herself busy to keep her thoughts from wandering down dark paths. But every moment this barrier between her and the truth remained standing seeded anxiety in her mind. Now that her strength was waning, the one thought she'd been running and hiding from snuck through her defenses and found her.

What if she was wrong?

What if she broke through this wall only to discover Ronan's body on the other side? Was she ready to face that possibility? The unbidden thought froze her in place, and she dropped the pickaxe and slumped against the wall, lowering her head into her trembling hands.

Tension gripped her chest, and she could feel her heart pounding rapidly. Though she took deep breaths, it felt like she couldn't breathe deeply enough to get the oxygen her body needed. Her vision faded at the edges, and she thought she might pass out. She placed an arm on the ground to steady herself.

You're not dying, Brin, she thought to herself. *Get a grip!*

She forced her breathing into a cadence to calm herself down. In through her nose, and slowly out through her mouth until her vision returned to normal. As she did, she meditated and prayed to Niradim for strength and peace. Once she felt in control of herself again, she confronted the thought that had ignited her panic.

Okay, so what if she was wrong?

Could she do anything about it? No. When she broke through,

Ronan's body would either be there or it wouldn't. She had faith that it wouldn't, but letting thoughts of *what if* consume her wouldn't change anything. The only thing she *could* do was discover the truth and go from there. And the only way to do that was to keep hacking away at that wall.

She slowly got back to her feet and hefted the pickaxe back into her hands. With her food and water depleted, there was only one source of energy left she could tap into for some additional strength. She hadn't done so yet because it took more concentration than it used to, and once she'd expended that energy, she'd have nothing left. But she felt like now was the time.

She focused on the Flame of her faith and began to channel Niradim's magic. She felt the warmth flow through her, but where it used to feel like she was pulling energy from a raging campfire, now it felt like little more than a flickering candle was lending her strength. The head of the pickaxe flashed a few times as she directed Niradim's magic into it before finally glowing with an unsteady light.

Even as weak as the Flame was these days, her body felt stronger, and the pickaxe felt lighter. With renewed strength, she continued her efforts. Each swing now blasted chunks of rock away from the wall. She would only be able to keep this up for a few minutes. Then, she'd have to stop and rest, but she was determined to make as much progress as possible in that time.

After a few moments, the head of the pickaxe began to flicker again, but she felt like she was close. Grunting with effort, she flared as much of Niradim's power into the pickaxe as she could for one final strike. She screamed in frustration as she put her whole strength into this last blow.

As soon as she struck the wall, the pickaxe exploded in her hands. Chunks of rock flew in all directions, and Brin was thrown onto her back. She quickly covered her head as she was pelted with small stones ricocheting off the walls. Once the dust settled, she let her hands fall by her side and stared up at the tunnel ceiling. It didn't look like she would make it through tonight after all.

She rolled to her right and saw the head of the pickaxe lying next to her, still smoking from the explosion. She got up onto her hands and knees and slowly climbed back into a standing position. She was grateful for the breeze in the tunnel to help cool her off...

Brin's eyes widened as a thought struck her. There hadn't been a breeze before. She spun around and almost fell back to her knees. A small hole had opened at the top of the wall.

Sore muscles protested as she struggled to the wall and began to climb. Her spirit was strained, and her strength was sapped, but she would get to the other side, no matter what. The hole wasn't very big, but she scraped away the rubble as much as she could and pulled her body through to the other side. It only half-occurred to her that she should be more careful. There was no telling whether enemies could be on the other side of the wall.

She tumbled down the other side and scrambled to where she had seen Ronan last. Loose rocks and bodies caused her to stumble as she ran. The closer she got, the faster she pushed herself, still scanning the area for any signs of him, her hopes growing with each moment she didn't see him.

Finally, she reached the spot where she'd last seen him, and her heart skipped a beat. Among a pile of bodies, she saw a gleaming shield with the hilt of a sword extending from the top, as if the blade was sheathed directly into the shield. She'd recognize Ronan's unique design anywhere. Her mind fuzzed, and her heart rate increased as she forced her body forward.

She stumbled up to Ronan's weapon and slowly grabbed the edges of the shield. She was afraid of what she would find under it, but she reminded herself that she needed to know, so she moved the shield out of the way. It was on top of a pile of bodies. But none of them were Ronan.

Ronan was still alive.

5

Ronan

Ronan leaned his head against the back of his prison cell. Days had passed since he'd been captured, and the travel had been brutal. They dragged him through the tunnels of the old Earth Sector for the first day or so, before emerging somewhere on the northeast side of the Midral mountain. A few more days of travel through the snow and ice of dangerous mountain paths had deposited them at the base of a mountain in the northeastern portion of the Midral mountain range. Being so far from home while Midral was vulnerable made him uncomfortable.

They'd left his weapons behind, and stripped him of his armor—though he still felt the cool metal of his necklace against his chest. That left him little relief as they took dangerous, well-hidden paths through the icy cliffs of the Midral mountain range.

He'd been bound with some metal cuffs inscribed with what looked like novaborn runes, which somehow kept him from channeling any of Niradim's power to escape. He'd never heard of magic or technology that could do that, but the implications terrified him. Something that stripped away the power of Niradim's strongest warriors was a dangerous tool in anyone's hands.

He still didn't know why they bothered taking him hostage at all. He'd have to figure that out later. For now, simply being alive was a blessing he hadn't expected. As long as he drew breath, he'd try to figure a way out of this.

Though he had to admit, getting out of this situation seemed rather unlikely at the moment. Even if he managed to remove the cuffs, the enemy would overwhelm him without his weapons and armor. Of course, he couldn't fight any of them while he was bruised and battered from the initial fight and subsequent journey through the mountains. Sleeping in the cold weather had proved difficult without a fire to keep him warm at night, so he was exhausted. He would need to bide his time and recover while he looked for an opportunity to free himself.

Right, then I just need to retrace my steps through treacherous mountain paths, find the hidden entrance to the old Earth Sector, and make my way through ancient, uncharted tunnels back to Midral, Ronan thought, his head sinking into his hands. Easy as meat pie, as Brin would say.

Ronan sighed as he thought of her. He hoped Brin wouldn't blame herself for his capture. She couldn't have done anything to save him— he'd made his choice. But still, the look on her face as the debris sealed them apart haunted him. Worse, he hated how they'd left things between them.

After he'd agreed to take her on as an apprentice, they'd spent most of their time together. His feelings for her had snuck up on him. While he helped prepare her for the Shaping Trial, he was so distracted by his own struggles that he didn't notice the wonderful bond they'd formed day after day working in the forge together. He hadn't noticed the little signs that pointed to more than a simple relationship between master and apprentice. Late nights in the forge, easy conversation, laughing despite the hurt in his heart. The pieces had been right in front of him, and he'd completely missed them.

Then she'd saved his life for the second time and given him a precious gift. At that moment, everything finally fell into place for him. Everything was *right,* even in the middle of chaos.

Since that day, they'd been so busy rebuilding the city that they hadn't had much time to focus on their relationship. Still, he was committed to her, and she felt the same about him—or at least he thought she did. With their differences, they had some work ahead of them, assuming he got out of this mess and back to Midral. Back to her.

The group of draken had brought him to a large encampment within the base of a volcano. There were ruins inside that reminded him of a smaller version of the Earth Sector in Midral, almost as if Midral had been modeled after this little village. A current of lava flowed around the ruins, creating a moat that served as a natural defense, which also served to warm the air to a comfortable temperature. He suspected these ruins predated the draken that now lived here.

The far end of the ruins opened up to a large cavern, and that's where the majority of the draken had set up their camps. The contents of the cavern were beyond his sight, but the amount of activity in that area piqued Ronan's interest. Something important was going on here. He just didn't know what.

A hulking, green-scaled draken clanged a heavy mace across the iron bars of Ronan's cell, startling him out of his thoughts.

"You are the Phoenix, yes?" the draken asked. His lizard-like eyes didn't blink as he regarded Ronan in his cell.

"What gave you that idea?" Ronan said. The fact that they'd led off with that question after days of silence meant that his capture might not have been as random as he'd assumed. Maybe if he convinced them they had the wrong person, they'd let him go free.

The draken held up Ronan's breastplate, emblazoned with an ornate crimson phoenix on the front.

Well, there goes that idea, Ronan thought.

"Yeah, okay, that's me." Ronan admitted. "What do you want with me?"

"Come," the draken said. He unlocked Ronan's cell and began walking towards the cavern where Ronan had seen the increased activity.

They both knew Ronan had nowhere to run while the cuffs still blocked his power. So, wincing, he got to his feet and trudged after the draken. Gods, he was exhausted. And sore. But the draken was leading him towards the one place Ronan might be able to get some answers. And the more he knew, the better, so he willed his muscles forward.

Ronan studied his surroundings as he walked through the ruins. The draken tribe camped on the outskirts of the ramshackle settlement. Some were as tall as the draken leading him away, but others were on the shorter side, closer to the size of dwarves. And the colors of their scales varied as well—shades of green, blue, red, black, and white all intermingled throughout their camp. But after a few moments of walking, the draken population abruptly stopped. The draken had clearly been set apart from the rest of the camp.

Now that they'd crossed that invisible barrier, he saw a much more diverse crowd. Novaborn were the most prevalent among the people on this side of the camp, but he spotted several humans, elves, dwarves, and even the occasional florian. Some of them were carrying heavy barrels to a line of tents around the outside of the encampment. Ronan's stomach began to turn—something wasn't right here. What he'd originally assumed to be a group of scavengers or mercenaries hiding out in the mountains was beginning to feel distinctly more sinister.

They entered the cavern at the back of the camp, and the scene changed. Clean lines of deep purple tents lined the sides of the cavern, leaving a path straight down the middle towards a large stone door. A door that Ronan recognized.

The same door that appeared in his recurring dreams.

A few figures stood in front of the door, studying its design. Ronan saw the starlight freckles dotting their skin, marking them as Novaborn, but it was what they were wearing that made Ronan's blood run cold. Amethyst robes decorated with the symbol of a star falling from the sky on the back.

The Cult of the Fallen Star.

A novaborn woman with bright orange skin looked up as Ronan approached. She quickly dismissed the other cultists around her and glanced at Ronan with a self-satisfied smile.

"Well, well, well, the Phoenix has arrived," she said. "So gracious of you to honor us with your presence! Allow me to introduce myself. I am Treyla. Welcome to my humble city." She took a mock bow before straightening.

She reminded him of Kyros. Were all these cultists so pompous? He simply stared at her and waited for her to get to the point.

"That will be all, Dak'thor," she said, dismissing the green draken. "Back to the rest of the lizards with you."

He snarled, but turned and stalked back through the cavern. Ronan turned to watch him go. It looked like there was some tension between the draken tribe and the cult. He tucked that knowledge away for later.

"Now, you," Treyla said, giving Ronan her full attention. "We have a little project for you to work on."

"No, thank you," Ronan said. "Now if we're done here, you can call Dak'thor back to put me back in my cell. I was finally starting to get comfortable."

"Oh, I think you'll want to hear a little more before you say no," she said with a grin. "You see, it's about the Mythril Soul you recently discovered."

Ronan couldn't hide the surprise on his face, which only made Treyla's grin widen. The existence of the Mythril Soul was a tightly kept secret, even within Niradim's own followers. Only Disciples and Elders knew about the artifact that had been sealed within the Great Anvil.

"Oh yes, we know about it," she said. "And you *will* be helping us. Because if you don't, we'll go and take the Mythril Soul by force."

A knot in Ronan's chest tightened. Midral was weak right now, especially without him. This small group wouldn't be able to make a dent even in Midral's current defenses, but what if they had another like Kyros? He was able to bring Midral to its knees on his own—and that was when it was at its strongest. There's no telling what someone else could do to Midral in its current state if they had access to even half the power that Kyros wielded.

"I sealed the way back into the Earth Sector," Ronan said. "And even if you get past that, the entrance is well guarded."

"Oh my," she laughed. "It's adorable that you think there's just one way to get into the Earth Sector from the tunnels!" Her tone got serious. "Let me assure you—there are plenty of ways to get in now that the Flame is faltering."

Ronan's heart rate spiked. She'd just spoken his deepest fear. How many holes were there in Midral's defenses? And how was he supposed to defend his city when there were so many ways it was vulnerable?

Just then, another novaborn ran up to Treyla and whispered something in her ear.

"It's about time. Open it immediately," she said to the novaborn. He ran over to a group of cultists close to the door, and she turned back to address Ronan. "Now, I was about to explain the details of your little project, but I think it's better if you hear it from someone with a little more experience."

As she finished speaking, a massive sound of metal grinding against rock filled the chamber, and the stone door before them groaned as it began to open. Blinding light pierced through the opening, and the silhouette of a massive figure clad in armor strode through the opening. The figure was backlit by some light coming from the room behind him, so Ronan couldn't make out any details, but something about this man seemed familiar to him for some reason.

"Agent Steel," Treyla said, addressing the man with her hands clasped behind her back. "Glad you could join us. It is a pleasure to meet you and serve under your command."

Agent Steel? Ronan thought. *Didn't Kyros also go by the title 'Agent'?*

He wasn't sure what that meant, but those thoughts were immediately forgotten as the figure's details finally came into view. Ronan's blood ran cold as he realized just why the figure seemed so familiar. A looming man in armor covering his entire body strode toward him. Two massive greatswords, jagged and rusted from time, were crossed behind his back. Ronan had seen him many times before, usually just before waking up in a cold sweat.

This was the man who haunted his nightmares.

Agent Steel stopped next to Treyla and stared at her without saying anything. His neck twitched as he locked eyes with her, unblinking. Treyla's hands fell to her sides, and she shifted from one foot to the other uncomfortably.

Finally, she broke the silence and gestured towards Ronan. "Um, Agent Steel, this is—"

"Who was in charge of opening the door?" he interrupted.

His voice was the same warped, inhuman voice Ronan remembered, and somehow the metal mask he wore moved with his words...

No, Ronan thought with surprise. *That's no mask!*

And then something clicked into place in Ronan's mind, and he finally realized a major detail he'd never noticed in his dreams. Agent Steel wasn't wearing a full suit of armor—he *was* the suit of armor. Agent Steel was a man made of metal.

"Pardon?" Treyla asked. Her brow furrowed at the unexpected

question.

"Who," he said, bending down until his face was inches from hers. Barely contained rage laced his words. "Was the person in charge of releasing me?"

Treyla gulped, and Ronan noticed sweat beginning to bead on her temples. She gestured to the novaborn who had interrupted their conversation a few moments ago. "That would be Levon…"

Agent Steel was already on the move before she finished her sentence. He marched straight towards Levon, grabbed him by the neck, and threw him off the side of the cavern into a river of lava below. Levon barely had time to scream as he plunged to his fiery death.

Agent Steel then turned around and rejoined Treyla and Ronan as casually as if he'd been throwing away a piece of trash. Treyla's mouth hung open in disbelief as gasps from the surrounding bystanders faded back into silence.

"Why—"

"He took too long," Agent Steel said, cutting her off again. "You had direct translations from your source in Midral. The door should have been open hours ago. I will not suffer incompetence in this camp."

Treyla sputtered as she struggled with a response, but Agent Steel continued. He turned to Ronan, acknowledging him for the first time.

"You must be our new little Phoenix. I'm sure the details of your project have been explained."

Ronan stayed silent.

"Actually, Agent Steel," Treyla said, all the confidence she'd shown speaking to Ronan before vanished. "I thought you might want to give him the details…"

She cut off as a growl vibrated through Agent Steel's metal skin. He turned his head slowly and looked down at her with a rage that burned behind the lights of his eyes.

"Be glad you are a Nova Priest, Treyla, as your status in Celestian's church prevents me from sending you to swim with your inept doorman." The sweat on Treyla's forehead was easily visible now, and a small whimper escaped her lips. "Fortunately, I will be taking charge from here." He turned his focus back to Ronan, but the rage still burned behind those eyes. "You will be making us a new Mythril Soul, as only a Phoenix can forge one. You start immediately."

"No, I won't."

Ronan didn't even have time to flinch before one of those massive greatswords was at his throat, pulsing with a chaotic purple energy. Agent Steel's metal face was contorted in rage, and the blade trembled as if he could barely hold himself back from cleaving Ronan's head off his shoulders. He held the blade there—large, seething breaths puffing from his flared nostrils.

"Then I will raze Midral to the ground and pry the Mythril Soul from the burned corpses of those you love," he growled through clenched teeth. "Your choice."

Ronan shivered despite himself. It was clear that Agent Steel was unhinged, and powerful. A deadly combination. Ronan couldn't leave Midral to the whims of this madman. Perhaps he could buy some time to figure a way out of this by agreeing to this project, but he had no idea how to create a Mythril Soul.

"I couldn't even if I wanted to," Ronan admitted. "Until a few weeks ago, I'd never even heard of a Mythril Soul."

Steel hooked the greatsword onto his back and pointed to the room he'd emerged from. Ronan looked past him and saw a massive forge, even larger and more ornate than the Soul Forge in Midral. There were designs etched into the wall of the forge that vaguely resembled the Mythril Soul recovered from the Great Anvil in Midral. The etchings glowed with Niradim's white energy.

"You will use the Heart Forge for your Phoenix Trial," Agent Steel explained. "The orb inscribed on the forge will serve as the basis for your design, though each Phoenix always creates a unique Mythril Soul."

He didn't know what this Agent Steel was talking about, and he was a Disciple of Niradim. So why did Agent Steel sound so sure of himself?

"How do you know all this?" Ronan asked.

"Niradim was my god long before he was yours, little Phoenix."

Ronan scoffed. "That's impossible. Niradim is the god of the dwarves," he said. "I'm the first non-dwarf to be accepted into Niradim's ranks."

Agent Steel bellowed a laugh that lasted far longer than necessary—his warbled voice echoing off the walls of the surrounding caverns. Finally, the laughter cut off, and Agent Steel crossed his arms in front of him.

"Yes, Celestian has told me of Niradim's second attempt at creation—these dwarves you speak of," Agent Steel said. "I am the sole survivor of Niradim's *original* creation—a race of people forged directly from the veins of mythril that permeate these mountains."

Ronan's eyes widened in shock. It shouldn't be true—everything the Elders taught spoke of the dwarves being Niradim's only created people. Yet somehow, Ronan knew Agent Steel wasn't lying. Between the dreams he'd been having and seeing the proof standing in front of him, Ronan couldn't deny it.

Agent Steel met Ronan's eyes.

"I AM THE LAST MITHRALI. FORSAKEN BY MY CREATOR!" he proclaimed with a booming voice, arms wide as he addressed the crowded cavern around him. He leaned in until he was face to face with Ronan and lowered his voice to a growl of pure hatred.

"And Niradim *will* feel my wrath."

6

Brin

"He's alive!"

Brin burst through the ornate double doors of the Forgehold, stumbling with exhaustion and barely catching her balance. Hands on her knees, sweat dripping from every pore on her body, she repeated herself.

"He's *alive*."

"What is the meaning of this?" Elder Oren said, shutting the book he'd been studying and quickly getting to his feet.

Brin gasped for breath, barely able to talk as her body was running on pure adrenaline and nothing else at this point. She unslung Ronan's weapons from her back and dumped them on the ground in front of her, unable to hold them in her trembling hands.

"Ronan..." she said between wheezing breaths. "His weapons... were in the room where we found Vorkin... but his body... wasn't there."

She finally stopped to take a few deep breaths, banishing the spots of darkness that gathered at the edges of her vision, and composed herself as best she could. "They took him, Elder Oren. Ronan is still alive—this proves it. We have to go after him."

The Armor Elder stood with a huff.

"And how, might I ask, did you manage to get back into that area?" he asked. "You yourself confirmed the Phoenix sealed it upon your escape."

She leveled her gaze at him. "I broke through."

Druden's eyes narrowed at her, and a snarl pulled at the corner of his mouth. "You mean you specifically disobeyed direct orders and opened a hole for the enemy to use to sneak into the Earth Sector?" He said. "Am I hearing this correctly?"

"I was never ordered *not* to search for Ronan, I was told that I couldn't shirk my duties in order to do so, and I've attended every one of my shifts at the wall and on patrol," she lifted her chin in defiance. "My free time is my own to do as I wish."

"And yet you still–"

"Peace, Druden," Elder Oren said, cutting him off. "Master Brin is correct. Her free time is her own. One can hardly blame her for wanting to save the Phoenix."

Brin gave Elder Oren an appreciative glance, and some of the tension in her body uncoiled.

"Elder, I request we send a search party right away. Vorkin can show me back to where he was ambushed, and I–"

"No, Master Brin." Elder Oren held up a hand to stop her. "Our situation has not changed. We still need all our resources focused here on rebuilding our defenses."

Brin was speechless. She'd been so sure this evidence would convince them to search for Ronan. He had literally just saved the city from the worst assault in its history. How could they simply throw him away? Ronan was the reason the Flame was even still here in Midral.

"Furthermore, we have learned something from the texts Captain Vorkin reclaimed from the old archives."

Captain? Brin thought. *When did that happen?* Looks like they'd finally found Landren's replacement.

"What do you mean?" she asked.

"The key to restoring the Flame is to reforge the Great Anvil," Elder Druden said. "The texts confirm it."

"Well, I don't know that I would say they *confirm* it, Druden," Leythia cut in.

"Oh please, not this nonsense again, Leythia," Elder Druden waved his hand in the air, dismissing her comment. "It's obvious. The Flame was anchored to the Soul Forge when the Great Anvil was created. And as soon as it was destroyed, the Flame began to die. So the solution is simple—to save the Flame, we reforge the anchor."

"That's far from confirmation. We don't have the full context," Elder Leythia said. She reached up and pulled her spectacles off her face and pinched the bridge of her nose with her other hand in frustration. "But I'll concede that it's our best lead at the moment, so the matter is moot."

"Wait," Brin said. "You know how to reforge the Great Anvil? I thought it was here even before the dwarves?"

"That is correct, Master Brin," Elder Oren said. "And to answer your question, no, we do not know how to reforge it yet. Unfortunately, the texts do not reveal those details."

"Well then how…"

"The Disciples," Oren gestured to her. "Those of you who have completed the Shaping Trial are the best blacksmiths in Niradim's faith. We are confident that the Disciples will figure out the method of forging a new Great Anvil. We pray that will be enough to anchor the Flame back to the Soul Forge."

"Which means, *Disciple* Brin," Druden said. "You can't be running off on a suicide mission to find the Phoenix. Just because his body wasn't in the caverns doesn't prove he's alive. The draken may have taken his body as a trophy, or for food. Nobody knows what those beasts do with the bodies of those they kill."

Brin's fists clenched at her sides. Ever since the day she'd confronted him about her parents' death, her ability to control her temper around Druden had become more and more difficult with each interaction. She didn't know how someone like this could be a leader in Niradim's faith.

"I'm sorry, Brin, but Druden is correct, at least about needing you here," Elder Oren said. "There are only a few Disciples in Midral at the moment. We're recalling the others, such as Master Ginmar, but your skills are needed here in Midral. The Disciples are our only remaining hope to save Niradim."

Druden, Leythia, and the other Elders retreated to their quarters, but Elder Oren turned to address her one last time before he left.

"Get some rest, Master Brin. Reforging the Great Anvil begins tomorrow."

* * *

Once again, Brin found herself alone. She wandered back to Ronan's apartment, still in disbelief that the Elders had just discarded Ronan like a broken tool. She carefully leaned Ronan's sword and shield against the wall and made her way to the bathroom, discarding her clothes on the floor as she went. A full day of work—followed by a full night of digging—had left her absolutely filthy. Had she really appeared in front of the Elders like this?

One benefit of living in the Earth Sector was access to a hot bath at any time. Brin didn't know exactly how it worked, but living underground, they were able to siphon in water to some of the living quarters, and a little magic could heat it up to a nice temperature. She didn't know how she'd ever lived without it. She filled the tub, channeled some of Niradim's magic to heat it to basically scalding, and then slowly lowered herself in.

She didn't know what to do. It should be simple—she had direct orders from the religious leaders of the god she served to stay and help rebuild the Great Anvil, so that should be the end of it. Shouldn't she trust Niradim to take care of Ronan without her? But did she really believe Niradim really want her to abandon him? Or would he want her to disobey the Elders and go save his Phoenix?

That's why I sent you to him.

Those were Niradim's words to her in her Shaping Trial when she had insisted that she would protect Ronan with or without Niradim's help. Did those words still apply? Her mind kept wandering back to the last time they'd been together—before the mission to save Vorkin. They'd had a fight. Did she really want to leave things that way? Could she?

Her mind kept spiraling, and her heart rate increased. A wave of dizziness spread over her, and she quickly sat up in the tub, breathing hard. What was wrong with her? She needed to pull herself together. Taking a few deep breaths, she tried to steady herself, but a tightness lingered in her chest as she quickly washed herself and put on some new clothes. She was still exhausted, but she knew she wouldn't be able to sleep with this pressure and anxiety plaguing her.

So she grabbed some jerky and bread and left Ronan's apartment. She needed to pray, and Niradim's Cathedral was always open, even while it was being rebuilt. It was her safe place, and she needed some comfort right now. Maybe she'd even find some answers.

It was past midnight, so she didn't encounter anyone in the dark halls of the Earth Sector as she made her way to the Cathedral. Normally, she wouldn't expect to find anyone at the Cathedral at this hour, but with the recent attacks, two Protectors stood guard around the clock. She knew it wasn't just to keep people safe at night.

Only a handful of people knew the real reason for the ever-present guards—the Mythril Soul was still being kept inside. It was crucial that it remain guarded and safe in the Earth Sector, and the Elders hoped that keeping the Mythril Soul close to the Soul Forge would help preserve the Flame until they found a solution. She didn't know whether that would work, and she suspected the Elders didn't know either, but better safe than sorry. For now, it rested on what remained of the Great Anvil, covered by a ceremonial cloth to hide it from sight.

She stepped past the guards and into the Cathedral, choosing a pew close to the front to sit down. As near to the Flame as she could get. She bent her head in prayer and began telling Niradim what was on her mind—what she'd been through recently, her confusion about what the right thing to do was, and her feelings for Ronan. Above all, she prayed for his safety, and for a way to help him.

Eventually, her head bobbed, and she realized she could barely keep herself from falling asleep. She slowly sat up and stretched her neck, looking towards the ceiling. Just then, a strange movement in the shadows caught her eye. There was something up in the rafters. It moved silently as it climbed down the wall towards the back of the Cathedral. She quickly crouched down behind the pew in front of her and watched.

It looked like it was some kind of creature, but it only had three legs. When it reached the ground, it crept silently toward the front of the Soul Forge where the Great Anvil used to be—and where the Mythril Soul hid, tucked away. As the creature closed in, Brin finally got a better look at it. It surprised her to discover it was actually a small, red-scaled draken woman.

Most draken she'd encountered towered over her as a dwarf—they were normally the size of humans, or even taller, but this one looked like she was even shorter than Brin. She'd heard that there were groups of draken that were smaller, but she'd never seen one before. This draken was missing her left arm, though that didn't seem to slow her down much as she snuck towards the Mythril Soul.

A draken creeping around in Niradim's Cathedral was nothing but bad news. A horde of draken had taken Ronan, and now one was here attempting to steal the Mythril Soul. That couldn't be a coincidence. The passage she'd used the past few nights to search for Ronan was sealed and heavily guarded, so the draken's presence meant there was at least one more way into the Earth Sector that the dwarves didn't know about. That fact alone was a huge problem, but as she watched the draken draw even closer, she realized that this was a perfect opportunity to get some answers.

She pulled the warmth of Niradim's power into herself and ducked behind a nearby bench to wait for an opportunity. The draken reached out and grabbed the Mythril Soul, slipping it into a satchel slung over her shoulder. Brin focused on the artifact in the draken's bag and crossed her index and ring fingers of both of her hands in front of her. Just as the draken started climbing back up the wall, Brin reached her hand forward and then drew it sharply backward. The satchel around the draken pulled back—the Mythril Soul inside reacting to Brin's magic—and yanked her off the wall directly toward Brin.

She caught the draken in mid-air and slammed her face-first into the ground in front of the Soul Forge, pinning her arm behind her back.

"Guards!" Brin yelled.

"No, wait," the draken said. "You don't understand!"

One of the guards opened the cathedral door and poked his head in. "What's going on here?"

Brin waved him in and pulled the Mythril Soul from the draken's satchel. "I found her trying to steal this."

The draken struggled under Brin's grip, but Brin held tight while the guard turned and said something to his companion before running in to help Brin. They used some rope to tie the draken's arm to her side, and the guard started to lead her away.

"Please! I'm trying to help," the draken yelled, struggling against her bonds. "I can help you find the Phoenix!"

"Wait," Brin said to the guard, who paused. She walked up to the draken. "What do you know about the Phoenix?"

"They're going to make him create a new Soul," the draken said. "I heard them talking about it, and so I came straight here."

A new Soul? The Mythril Soul shouldn't even be public knowledge, and even the Elders didn't know its true purpose. What could someone want with a new one?

"So, Ron- the Phoenix is still alive?" Brin asked. "You're sure?"

"Yes," she said. "They need him alive."

A pit formed in Brin's stomach at the implication. "Who needs him alive?"

"I don't know what they call themselves," the draken responded. "But I heard several references to a falling star, and they said they were going to corrupt the Flame."

Slag and ashes. The cult of the Fallen Star had Ronan. This situation was getting worse every moment. The Fallen Star was behind the attack on Midral. If they were involved in Ronan's capture…

"Can you lead me to where they're keeping him?"

"Yes, I—"

"That's enough, Master Brin," a new voice said, entering the Cathedral. Brin looked over her shoulder to see Elder Druden walking toward her. What was he doing here?

"Elder Druden, this draken knows where Ronan is being held!"

"Lies, I'm sure. Clearly, your feelings for the Phoenix are getting in the way of rational thought—*again*." He ignored Brin's death glare and addressed the guards. "Now, take this vile little *wyrmling* away and lock her up."

The draken growled at the slur, and snapped her jaws at the Elder before the guard elbowed her in the stomach, causing her to double over. He yanked her back to her feet and started dragging her out of the cathedral.

"Please, it's the only way to save the Flame," she cried before she was out of earshot.

Druden turned back to Brin, who was still glaring at him. He held out his hand for the Mythril Soul, and she reluctantly handed it over to him.

"Thank you, Master Brin, for apprehending a thief. Now, as Elder Oren already told you once tonight, you should get some rest. Your work on the new anvil begins in about six hours." He turned and placed the Mythril Soul back on the pedestal. "Besides, we wouldn't want anyone to think you care more about your boyfriend than you do about saving your god," he said as he passed her and exited the Cathedral.

Brin let out a frustrated breath. Of all the people who could have interrupted her conversation with the draken, it just *had* to be him. She couldn't stand that man. Any other Elder would have allowed her to continue questioning the draken for any information about Ronan or the people responsible for his capture. Why did Druden seem so intent on preventing Ronan's rescue?

Things were getting so complicated. She plopped down on a pew and closed her eyes, letting her head hang over the back of the seat. What was she supposed to do? What would Niradim have her do?

Druden was an Elder. According to their faith, as the Armor, he represented a part of Niradim's will. Some people believed that even questioning his orders was like questioning Niradim himself. But she knew things weren't as simple as that. People were fallible, so even if they represented Niradim's will, it didn't mean they were always right. In fact, Niradim himself had never claimed to be infallible, though most followers either pretended or assumed he was. It was one of the reasons she worshipped him. She felt like her god put his faith in his people just as he asked them to put their faith in him.

What would Niradim do in her shoes if someone he loved was alive and in danger? As if in response to her unspoken question, the Flame flared for a moment from within the Soul Forge, and she realized she already knew what he'd do—he'd go save them.

She got to her feet and gently slapped her face with her hands to drive the exhaustion away. Her next move would put her even more in Druden's crosshairs than she already was. Well, slag him. Brin needed answers, and she knew exactly where to find them. She marched out the Cathedral doors and headed for the prison. She had a conversation to finish.

* * *

"Okay, explain it again to me."

Brin was standing across some iron bars from the small draken, whose name she'd learned was Gadjet.

"If I take the Mythril Soul back to the Heart Forge, I can activate its defenses and remove both the corruption and the Fallen Star simultaneously," Gadjet explained. "Thus, saving the Flame."

"How could you possibly know all this?" Brin asked. "Our Elders would have mentioned at least some of this if it were true."

"Well then, either they don't know, or they're keeping the knowledge secret for some reason. My tribe has guarded the Heart Forge and the Sword of Ashes for centuries, as directed by the Clash." Gadjet stood and paced in her cell, waving her only hand in the air as she told Brin her story. "For the last few centuries, a dragon of the north named Nivalthyr had taken residence there and enslaved my tribe to its service. We still guarded the Forge, but we did it under the oppressive claws of Nivalthyr. At least, we did until I killed her a few years ago."

"*You* killed the dragon that roamed the Midral mountains?" Brin raised an eyebrow at the small draken. "That dragon used to raid small northern villages, and we'd have to send Protectors to aid in the recovery efforts. I've seen firsthand the damage that dragon can do. I'm sorry, I don't mean any offense, but there's no way you killed it."

"And when was the last time you had to dispatch your Protectors to deal with Nivalthyr's raids?" Gadjet asked.

"I mean, it's been a few years, but—"

"You're welcome." Gadjet moved on. "Anyway, after I killed her, my tribe banished me."

"Wait, so after you *allegedly* killed the dragon that enslaved your tribe, they kicked you out?" Brin asked. "How does that make sense?"

Gadjet shrugged. "They were ruled by a dragon for so long, they'd grown comfortable with enslavement. People don't like change, even when it's good for them—even when they *know* it's good for them." Gadjet shook her head in frustration. "When I killed her and returned with her scales as proof, they branded me a traitor. A short time later, the cult moved in and filled the power gap left behind by Nivalthyr's death. My tribe traded one master for another. The cult has taken up residence outside of the Heart Forge, and they're attempting to corrupt Niradim's Flame at the source."

Ronan and Brin had done some research after Kyros' attack, and the Fallen Star served an old, banished god named Celestian. The cult had been around for a long time—centuries, probably—but they'd only recently come out of the shadows. Their aggressive actions in the last few months hinted at a greater plan.

"Okay, let's assume I believe you," Brin said. "What does any of this have to do with the Phoenix?"

"The Fallen Star wants a fresh Mythril Soul, and a Phoenix of Niradim is the only person with the ability to forge one."

"And why do they need a new Mythril Soul? Why not simply send a group or *individual*," Brin pointedly looked at Gadjet, "to steal ours and bring it to them?"

"Right, because a one-armed draken would be their best option," Gadjet said, rolling her eyes. "Look, I don't know why they want a new Mythril Soul, but do you really think it's a good idea to let them have one and find out?"

If Gadjet was telling the truth, it was a good point. If the Fallen Star wanted a Mythril Soul, then keeping them from obtaining one instantly became a top priority.

"Okay, and why do you care about any of this?" Brin asked. "Niradim isn't your god."

"My ancestors allied with Niradim long ago. It's why we were tasked with guarding the Heart Forge in the first place." Gadjet stopped pacing and let her arm fall to her side. Her shoulders dropped and her tone softened as she stared up, almost as if she was staring up through the rock of the mountain itself. "But to be honest, I just want the Fallen Star gone. My tribe kicked me out, but they're still my tribe." She looked at Brin, a small tear rolling down her cheek. "I still want to save them, even if it's from themselves. You have to get me out of here. We need to get the Mythril Soul to the Heart Forge before it's too late!"

This was… a lot to process all at once. She wanted to get to Ronan as quickly as possible, especially if Gadjet was telling the truth. But this was too big for her to deal with on her own.

"Look, I can't promise anything, but I'll at least go talk to the Elders," Brin said. "Get some rest. I'll be back in a bit."

Her body didn't want to do anything except collapse at the moment, but she forced herself to march back to the Forgehold. As she walked, she went over Gadjet's story.

She had to admit, the whole thing sounded crazy. She knew the Elders wouldn't alter their plans unless some of what Gadjet said matched up with what they were learning from the scrolls Vorkin recovered. If it did, maybe they would finally allow her to go save

Ronan. The alternative meant she'd be stuck in Midral working on an impossible project while her love was held prisoner by their fiercest enemy. She couldn't let that happen.

As she approached the Forgehold and prepared to wake the Elders, she saw some torches already burning inside. She knew Druden might still be awake, as he'd interrupted things at the Cathedral. Maybe he'd woken the others to discuss what had happened?

She reached for the door, but paused when she heard a familiar voice. What was Vorkin doing here so late? Instinct kicked in, and instead of making her presence known, she circled around to peer through a window and listen in on their conversation.

"I spoke with the draken, Armor Elder. And I read through some of those scrolls before I delivered them. The Heart Forge, the Sword of Ashes… These are both referenced—"

Druden slammed his hand on the desk in front of him, cutting Vorkin off. "Clearly, the draken read the scrolls and wove in truths with her lies," Druden said. "You can see why it's imperative we don't let her attempt to influence anyone else!"

Vorkin paused and visibly swallowed. "But can we really dismiss her claims without investigating further?"

It surprised Brin to hear Vorkin questioning an Elder. He was normally quick to obey any order. What was going on here?

"Vorkin, this is obviously a ploy to keep us distracted from the real solution." Druden leaned back in his chair. "She was attempting to steal the Mythril Soul—the one thing we *all* agree that we need to restore the Flame, correct?"

"Correct, but—"

"And the text says that the reason the Flame is here is because of the Great Anvil," Druden gestured down to the scroll that was splayed out across the top of the desk. "You said you read the texts, so you must know this is true."

"Yes, but it doesn't outline how the Great Anvil was forged," Vorkin protested. "Or how the Flame was anchored to it."

"Which is why we need every Disciple focusing on this," Druden said. "We cannot afford distractions. I need you to take care of the draken before she's able to poison anyone else's mind."

Take care of the draken? Surely, he couldn't mean what that implied, but a quick glance at Vorkin confirmed her fears.

"Elder, that seems extreme…" Vorkin said unsteadily.

An uncomfortable silence hung in the air, and the hairs on the back of Brin's neck stood on end. She held her breath, afraid to move a muscle as she waited for this conversation to play out. Finally, Druden spoke.

"Vorkin, do you know why I promoted you?" Druden stood and slowly circled his desk, arms casually held behind his back.

Well, that explained at least one thing. She'd been curious as to the circumstances of Vorkin's sudden promotion.

"No, sir."

"It's because you showed you were willing and brave enough to take on the most difficult missions, like the one the Phoenix stubbornly refused." Druden paused at Vorkin's side and placed a hand on his shoulder. His voice dropped to a low growl, and Brin could barely make out the next words. "And you proved you could follow orders. Now, did I make the wrong decision, *Captain* Vorkin?"

To his credit, Vorkin at least paused before giving his answer. But Brin's heart fell when she realized he was going to make the wrong decision.

"No, sir," Vorkin answered. "I'll take care of it myself."

Slag and ashes, Brin thought. Druden was even more crooked than she'd believed. And he had the captain of the Niradim Protectors in his pocket.

She had a decision to make. Their conversation confirmed at least part of Gadjet's story. It didn't mean everything Gadjet had said was true—in fact, some of the things the little draken claimed were flat-out ridiculous. Nobody in their right mind would believe this little one-armed draken had killed a fully grown dragon. But enough of Gadjet's story had checked out that Brin couldn't risk letting this opportunity slip away.

There was no way around it. Ronan was in trouble, and Gadjet was the only person who knew where to find him. Besides, Brin couldn't stand by and let Druden and Vorkin murder Gadjet in the night. She dashed back to Ronan's apartment to gather his sword and shield.

She had to help a draken break out of jail.

7

Ronan

Ronan woke up to the sound of Dak'thor unlocking the door to his cage. His prison was on the draken side of the ruined village, far away from the neat rows of tents where the Fallen Star camped.

"Phoenix, it is time." Dak'thor pulled the door open and waited for Ronan to rise and follow.

Ronan stood and stretched the soreness from his body. Sleeping on the hard ground in a camp full of enemies was not the most relaxing way to rest. At least the proximity to the magma meant he wasn't cold, so that was nice.

"Thank you, Dak'thor," Ronan stepped out of his cage and held up his hands. "Will we be taking off these lovely bracelets?"

"They tell me you keep them on until you enter the forge," Dak'thor replied in his deep voice. He had a strange accent, but then again, Ronan was sure he'd sound pretty strange to them if he tried speaking their language.

Well, at least he'd finally be getting these cuffs off. He could still feel his connection to Niradim, but it was impossible to channel magic with them on. It was like there was an invisible wall cutting him off from Niradim's power. If they were going to take them off of him, that meant he'd need to access Niradim's magic for the Phoenix Trial.

He wondered about that as they walked. The Shaping Trial was a three-day marathon, but the Phoenix Trial was different. Steel had explained some of the basics to Ronan before they'd thrown him back in his cell.

Where the Shaping Trial focused on faith, the Phoenix Trial was about learning a lesson through a series of visions. Instead of being in the forge for three days without rest, Ronan would exit the forge each night to reflect on the visions Niradim showed him.

The actual forging process happened in three stages as well. On the first day, he'd create the frame of the Mythril Soul, and then Niradim would show him a vision. Filling in the frame would happen on the second day, and then he'd receive his second vision. He'd finish the third day by inscribing the runes on the Mythril Soul and have one last vision.

The three visions served to teach him an important lesson from Niradim. If Niradim determined he'd learned the intended message, Ronan would pass, and the Flame in the Heart Forge would imbue the Mythril Soul with a new Soul Flame. If he failed, the Mythril Soul would remain empty. Or at least that's what Steel claimed.

They crossed the threshold into the Fallen Star camp and he could sense Dak'thor tense up beside him. There was an air of inherent distrust between the two groups that undercut all their interactions. The whole thing puzzled Ronan.

What did the draken gain out of this relationship except for unfair treatment and forced labor? Over the few days he'd been here, he noticed the number of draken and cultists in the camp were almost equal. He didn't know much about draconic magic, but he'd seen enough. With some organization, they should be able to stand up to the Fallen Star. Steel's presence complicated things, but he hadn't been here the whole time. So why didn't they fight back?

"Dak'thor," Ronan said. "There's something I've been wondering since I arrived. Why are you working with the Fallen Star? You don't seem to like them much, and they don't treat you well."

Dak'thor snorted. "They do not. But they are better than Nivalthyr."

"Nivalthyr?" Ronan asked.

"Yes, the dragon that ruled us before," Dak'thor said. "Nivalthyr. Dragon Empress of the North."

"Dragon Empress of the North?" Ronan imagined that was a self-imposed title. "Was she the large white dragon that used to terrorize this area? I didn't know she'd enslaved a tribe of draken. What happened to her?"

"She is dead," Dak'thor said. "The Dragon Empress ruled for generations. When she died, we were afraid of what that meant for us. She was a harsh ruler, but she provided for the clan and we'd grown reliant on her. Then, the Fallen Star came. Enslavement was familiar, so we did not resist. Well… most of us."

They walked in silence for a few moments, Ronan watching the slumped shoulders of the draken tribe around them. They looked so defeated, almost hopeless. He wished there was a way he could help them.

"What would it take to convince you to fight back?"

Dak'thor halted and turned so that he loomed over Ronan. "We do not wish to fight back. We used to have a purpose, but that purpose faded after the Dragon Empress took over. Our purpose didn't save us from her, so now we simply wish to survive."

Ronan nodded and Dak'thor proceeded with leading him to the Heart Forge. He understood better than Dak'thor realized. When Niradim resurrected him, he felt like he had no purpose. He'd wanted to fade back into his old life as a blacksmith so people would leave him alone. To simply… survive. But he eventually realized that was the wrong choice. Life needed purpose. It was easy to fall back on survival when it felt like you had nothing to live for.

"I'm sorry this has happened to you, Dak'thor," Ronan said.

Dak'thor studied Ronan's demeanor thoughtfully, perhaps expecting to sense sarcasm in Ronan's voice. Instead, he must have felt Ronan's sincerity.

"Thank you for your kind words, Phoenix. You are not what I expected. I hope they do not kill you."

"You and me both, my friend." They'd arrived at the massive doors to the Heart Forge. "Wish me luck."

* * *

Sweat poured down Ronan's face as he hammered the frame into place and then returned it to the fire. He wiped his brow as he lifted a wooden bucket to his mouth and swallowed several gulps of tepid water. Despite the circumstances, he enjoyed working in a forge again. He'd had no time since the fall of Midral to dedicate to his favorite craft, and he could almost forget that what he was doing here was exactly what his enemy wanted. The thought made him frown. He shouldn't be enjoying himself, he should be figuring out how to escape. The Elders needed to know about the Fallen Star's plans for the Heart Forge, and he needed to protect his city.

He only had three days left to come up with an escape plan, because as soon as he finished this project, they'd dispose of him. Agent Steel was already making a habit of tossing people who displeased him into the flowing lava below the ruins. Ronan would prefer to avoid that fate.

However, one additional benefit to being in the Heart Forge all day was that Agent Steel was absent. His captivity had left its mark on him, and he refused to cross through the doorway that once served as his prison. Crazed scratchings decorated the walls—workings of a man who'd lost his mind in solitude and imprisonment. He didn't know precisely how long Agent Steel had spent trapped in the Heart Forge, but he overheard some chatter in the camp that it was at least several centuries.

Ronan took one more swig of water, pulled the round frame back out of the fire, and hammered away. He was close to finishing his work, which meant he should receive the first vision soon. The Shaping Trial had strange hallucinations that tested him—he wondered if it would be something like that.

Three more strikes with the hammer finished the job. He quenched the metal in some nearby oil and then set it aside for the next day. As soon as he set the frame down, the fire in the Heart Forge blazed forward and out into the room, causing Ronan to lift his arm and cover his eyes.

When he lowered his arm, he was floating in a blank space, no longer in the Heart Forge. Before him, he stared at an enormous white flame that had taken the shape of a Phoenix. Wings of fire spread out to either side as far as Ronan could see, and two burning white eyes stared deep into his soul. This was Niradim.

Ronan could barely breathe, floating in the presence of Niradim like this. He'd never experienced the full breadth of Niradim's power, even when he'd taken the Flame back from Kyros in Midral. It was somehow even more than he'd imagined.

"Niradim?" Ronan managed to whisper.

The fiery bird shrank and morphed before him, taking on a dwarven-like appearance with a muscular build. White fire danced along the skin, and the eyes shone with a brilliant white light that Ronan knew intimately as the essence of Niradim's magic. An ever-shifting, lengthy beard of flames dangled from the form's chin, almost as if the fire was burning upside down.

"There we go." The timbre of his voice was like the deep, gentle roar of a steady fire, but his tone was as playful as a dancing flame. "Sometimes the phoenix-form can be a bit much." He beamed a smile at Ronan and walked closer. "Now let me have a look at you, my child."

He walked in the air with his arms behind his back, circling Ronan, inspecting him from head to foot. Ronan was too stunned to talk. It wasn't worth questioning whether this was his god. His connection with Niradim was stronger than it had ever been—there was no doubt that he was standing before Niradim himself.

Standing.

Anxiety froze him in place. Should he kneel? What was the protocol here?

"Don't worry, Ronan, you are my Phoenix," Niradim said as he sensed the uncertainty in Ronan's body language. "The first I've had in almost a thousand years, I might add, and I don't force my followers to prostrate themselves before me. Not like another god we know..."

The heaviness of the situation sunk in. He was speaking with Niradim in a way he'd always wished he could. This was an opportunity nobody else had ever had in his lifetime!

"Umm, I have about a million questions for you right now, but I don't even know where to start."

"Then don't!" Niradim said, chuckling again, though it faded quickly into a more serious tone. "But in all honesty, I can't answer the questions you have for me, Ronan. At least not the one that still plagues your heart and causes the rift between us."

"But why?" Ronan asked. "Why did you let me-"

Niradim held up a hand, cutting Ronan off, and shook his head. "You have to figure that out on your own, my Phoenix. I can't help you with that, or it defeats the purpose. That's as much as I can say on the matter. Do you trust me?"

"I do," Ronan said. And he meant it. He didn't know why Niradim had let him die, but he had decided to trust Niradim again in spite of it. It still hurt, especially after asking his god face to face without an answer. But he'd made his decision, and he was going to stick to it. Even if it hurt sometimes. "So then, why *are* you here?"

"Well, it's tradition for me to appear before the first lesson of the Phoenix Trial!" Niradim smiled and winked at Ronan. "Though this can't really be considered a proper Phoenix Trial, now can it? Seeing as you already passed."

"Wait, what?" Ronan asked. "That was it? I just needed to make the frame?"

"Oh, goodness no!" Niradim laughed. "No, Ronan, you passed it a while ago. But again, that's all I can say about that right now. The real reason I'm here is to give you some history lessons. You may already be a Phoenix, but by taking this outdated Trial, I can still give you knowledge that has been lost to time. I hope it will help you with what comes next."

"What comes next?" Ronan repeated. "And what *does* come next, Niradim? I'm trapped deep in an enemy camp that nobody knows about, with no means of escape, working for the enemy. I could really use some help here!"

"Don't worry, my child. It's already on its way," Niradim said. He sighed, and Ronan sensed the exhaustion of eternity in his god for a fleeting moment before it was gone. "It's time for you to see the past. I can't keep you in this space much longer."

Sure enough, the edges of this space began to burn with white flame that grew closer and closer.

"There's one more thing I wanted to tell you before you go." His eyes softened and his voice lowered. "You have a difficult decision ahead of you. One that has the potential to shape the future of our people, and the world itself." He stepped up to Ronan and placed a gentle hand on his shoulder. It was warm, but it did nothing to comfort Ronan against the profound sadness in Niradim's voice.

"It will be the hardest decision you've ever faced, and it will require a sacrifice that nobody should be asked to make. Just know that I have faith that you will make the right decision. Hopefully, these visions will help you when the moment comes."

"I don't want to die again, Niradim," Ronan said. "But I will, if it means keeping our people safe."

Niradim shook his head. The flames roared around them, closing in quickly.

"It's not *your* life that you will be asked to give, my Phoenix."

Before Ronan could respond, the flames swallowed him.

* * *

Over 1000 years ago

"Hey Ashe, what do you think the city looks like up close?" Clash hefted his heavy frame over another large boulder. It was a wonderful day for a hike. The cloudless sky allowed the sun to warm his metal body despite the cool mountain breeze as it reflected rays of sunlight on the surrounding path. The trek from Midralen had been a long one, and they were nearing the top of the tallest mountain he'd ever seen. Maybe the tallest in the world, for all he knew.

"I'm not sure, Clash," Ashe said, looking over her shoulder. "But it looked pretty impressive from far away."

She led the way forward on the path ahead of him. Ashe was small for a mythrali, at least a foot shorter than he was, but she carried herself in a way that made anyone she spoke to feel like they were looking up to her, rather than down.

"It better be, for all the trouble we're going through to get there," a voice said from behind.

"Oh, don't be so grumpy, Steel," Ashe said with a smirk. "We'll be there in no time, just you wait!"

Steel huffed in annoyance. He stepped up to the boulder Clash had climbed over and reached back to grab the two massive greatswords hanging across his back. In one swift movement, he smashed the swords down into the massive rock and reduced it to rubble before returning the blades to his back and continuing on. Clash rolled his eyes.

"At least we were allowed to bring Soul Flames for this trip," Clash said, tapping the glowing Mythril Soul embedded into his chest. "Imagine if we'd had to make the trip without Niradim's power."

"It's annoying we have to share these things in the first place," Steel replied. "Must be nice to have access to Niradim's power all the time, huh Ashe?"

Jealousy coated his words, but Ashe didn't seem to notice.

"It does have its perks," she said. "But don't worry, you're on the verge of being able to take the Phoenix Trial, and I'm sure Clash will follow shortly after, right Clash?"

"Right!" Clash cheerfully agreed.

Ashe was the first Phoenix of Niradim among the mythrali, but she said that the rank of Phoenix was open to anyone who could pass the Trials. As a result, she didn't have to use one of the limited number of Mythril Souls that were shared among the Disciples to channel Niradim's magic. Her old Mythril Soul had permanently embedded in her chest when she completed her Phoenix Trial, and the new one she created in the Trial had taken its place. So the total number of Mythril Souls had stayed the same, to everyone's relief.

Ashe's sword was slung across her back, always faintly glowing with Niradim's power. It was a long blade, etched with Niradim's runes. The hilt was forged into phoenix wings that folded shut when the sword was sheathed on her back. Clash thought it was beautiful.

"Want me to scout ahead and see just how close we are?" Ashe asked, a gleam in her eye.

"You know you just want to show off." Steel said, rolling his eyes.

"Guilty!" Ashe called out as she ran for the cliff's edge. Clash wasn't sure what that meant, but he assumed he was going to find out soon. Before Clash could react, Ashe threw herself off the edge of the cliff, disappearing from view.

"What-" Clash said in alarm. He ran after her until he saw her shoot back up into the sky. Massive wings of white fire flared out from her shoulders, propelling her gracefully through the air. She turned and hovered up in the sky, giggling to herself.

"When did you learn to do that?!" Clash yelled, a smile plastered on his face.

Steel grumbled as he passed Clash, not looking up to Ashe hovering above them. "You gonna scout, or just gloat?"

That finally caused Ashe to frown. "Oh, uh, yeah, sorry Steel. I'll be right back." She said before shooting off ahead of them.

"That was a little mean, don't you think?" Clash asked Steel as he jogged to catch up. "I'd be just as excited if I could fly like that."

"She needs to learn to control herself now that she represents all the mythrali," Steel said. "Acting like a child with a new toy makes us all look bad."

"I don't know…" He was about to say more before Ashe came flying back, landing in front of them.

"Oh yeah, we're close now." Ashe said. "I waved to a few of their scouts, so I'm sure they'll have people ready at the gates. Just a few more minutes around this curve and we'll be right there."

As Ashe said, only a few minutes later, they found themselves in front of some massive metallic and crystal gates. The work was extraordinary, unlike anything Clash had ever seen. Some well-adorned novaborn strode forward to greet them. The male had bright yellow skin and hair, with several earrings piercing his long, pointed ears. A female novaborn was at his side with deep orange skin and long black hair kept up with a pair of long, pointed crystals.

"Greetings, mythrali of Niradim," the male novaborn said. "I am Sola, and this is Galar. It is a pleasure to meet you three Disciples."

"Hello, Sola and Galar," Ashe said with a bow. "My name is Ashe, first Phoenix of Niradim, and these are two of the Disciples, Steel and Clash."

"Oh, my apologies. We didn't realize there was a rank of Phoenix," Sola said.

"Please! No apology necessary," Ashe leaned forward conspiratorially. "To be honest, we just discovered it ourselves," she said with a wink.

Sola smiled. "Well, either way, we are honored that you responded to our summons."

"Of course," Ashe replied. "We were happy to come. We believe that a strong alliance between our two peoples will be mutually beneficial. It has been difficult to forge strong connections with how remote our settlement is. We have reached out to the dragonkin tribes close by, but they are a segregated group, so it's been tough."

"Hopefully our friendship can serve as an example for others," Galar smiled at them.

"Well," Sola said, "Why don't we show you around first, and then we can celebrate the beginning of a wonderful partnership."

She stepped aside and gestured to the ornate gates, which began to open and reveal the sparkling city behind them.

"Welcome," she said. "To Celestian's grand capital—the beautiful city of Lumenova!"

* * *

Present

Ronan gasped as his vision returned to him in the Heart Forge. He stumbled backwards, barely catching himself on the Great Anvil before he hit the ground. A cold sweat slowly broke out across his skin despite the heat of the forge next to him.

Well, that was certainly different from the visions of the Shaping Trial. For one, he was a passive observer, rather than an active participant. That must have been an actual vision of the past, not some shaping of Niradim to test his faith.

There was so much to unpack from the vision, but seeing Agent Steel had surprised him. In the vision, he lacked the madness that consumed him now. Why had Niradim shown him this specific vision of traveling to a grand city at the top of a mountain? Lumenova... wasn't that the city that Kyros had re-discovered? But it was supposed to be in a valley, wasn't it? Something had changed in the centuries since that vision.

And Ashe, she'd been the very first Phoenix of Niradim. Until after the battle of Midral, he hadn't known 'Phoenix' was a rank. He thought it was just a nickname the people gave him. The Elders were the ones that eventually told him about the ancient rank. He wasn't sure why they'd never spoken of it before.

The doors to the Heart Forge opened, shaking him from his thoughts. A novaborn Ronan had never seen walked through the doors, trailed by Treyla. His skin was an orange-red, and he had short, black hair. But his most distinctive feature was his scars.

Long streaks of glass traced along the man's face and arms, as if some monster had torn him apart and glued him back together. The man dressed like a noble, and carried himself like someone who was used to people following his orders. As he came closer, Ronan realized those scars weren't glass—they were long veins of crystal, and they pulsed with the amethyst glow of Celestian's power. Ronan couldn't shake the feeling there was something familiar about this man, but he couldn't put his finger on it.

"Is this him?" The man stopped a few paces from Ronan. Agent Steel, predictably, hadn't crossed the door into the forge.

"Yes, my lord." So, someone else was here to supervise Ronan's Trial. Another agent, by the looks of him. Perhaps Celestian didn't trust the broken mind of Agent Steel to see their task through. "This is the Phoenix."

The Agent looked him over and sneered.

"So this is the man that gave my brother so much trouble?" He said. "Funny, he doesn't look like much."

Ronan sighed. He was tired—he didn't want to deal with some stuck-up novaborn right now. He just wanted to sleep.

"I'm sure I don't know what you're talking about," Ronan said, setting down his gloves and removing his apron. "I've finished today's work. Will you be escorting me back to my lovely accommodations?"

Anger flashed across the man's face, and the network of crystal scars lit with a vibrant purple as the man held out his hand. Ronan found himself yanked forward in the air toward the Agent before he slammed his fist into Ronan's stomach, causing Ronan to double over, trying to catch his breath.

The novaborn grabbed Ronan by the hair and pulled his face up to his own. "Looks like we could stand to learn some manners. I won't be as easy to deal with as my brother was."

He threw Ronan to the ground and walked away, but before he exited the Heart Forge, he addressed Ronan over his shoulder.

"You may call me Falrose. I'll give my brother Kyros your regards."

8

Brin

Brin knocked on Thalga's door, hoping she'd still be awake after her shift. To her relief, Thalga answered a moment later, surprised to see her friend standing there. Good, it looked like she hadn't woken her up. Brin would have felt bad about that.

"Brin, what in the world are you doing here at this hour? Shouldn't you be resting? You're supposed to start work on the Anvil in just a few hours!"

"I've… decided to focus my efforts on another way to save the Flame," Brin said, stealing a quick glance to either side to make sure nobody was around. Of course there wasn't. Everyone was sleeping. Still, it didn't hurt to be careful. "Can I come in real quick? I don't have a lot of time, but you're the only one I can trust with this information, and I'd rather we were behind closed doors."

"Of course, of course," Thalga opened the door wider to allow Brin to enter. "Come in. Want me to make some tea?"

"No, thanks." Brin entered Thalga's home and stood next to a chair Thalga had in the corner of her room. Brin didn't trust herself enough to stay awake if she sat, so she remained standing.

"Wow, no tea? Must be serious," Thalga smiled playfully before seeing the look in Brin's eyes. "Oh, it actually is serious. Is it about Ronan?"

"Well, yes," Brin admitted. "But not entirely. It's bigger than just him."

Over the next few minutes, Brin told Thalga everything that had happened since she'd seen Thalga earlier in the day. From her repeated efforts to dig through the rubble, all the way through her encounter with Gadjet in Niradim's Cathedral and the conversation she'd had with the draken afterwards in the jail.

By the time Brin finished her story, she was out of breath. The day's events spilled out of her like water from a broken dam. She stood there, waiting for Thalga's response as her anxiety threatened to send her into another panic attack.

"Brin, I can't believe you've been through all that." Thalga stepped forward to embrace her, and Brin squeezed her tight. "You poor thing!"

"Thanks, Thal," Brin said, breaking the embrace. "Listen, I need your help, but it's kind of a lot to ask…"

"Anything," Thalga said. "I owe you one."

"I need to free Gadjet from jail," Brin winced a little as she said it. "Druden is planning to have her killed, but I need to find out what she knows. Can you help me?"

Thalga paused. Brin knew this was a big ask, but she was hoping she could rely on her best friend to help her out, despite their recent squabble.

"Brin, I don't know," Thalga said tentatively. "Can't we just go to the other Elders and tell them what's going on?"

Brin shook her head. "Druden was the most vocal about abandoning Ronan, but the other Elders didn't fight him on it. Plus, it would be my word against Druden's. I need to question Gadjet myself and find out if she's telling the truth."

Thalga ran her hands through her hair and sighed. "Okay, Brin, I'll help. What do you need?"

"Meet me at the Cathedral," Brin said. "I can break Gadjet out of jail, but I'll need a safe place to question her. I just need you to keep a lookout to make sure nobody comes inside while we're there."

Brin thought about telling Thalga the rest of the plan, but she hesitated. If Thalga already had an issue with breaking Gadjet out of jail, she'd never agree to taking the Mythril Soul out of the Cathedral.

Because the fact of the matter was, Brin had already decided to trust the little draken, and that meant that the Mythril Soul couldn't stay in Midral.

She was going to steal it.

* * *

This is going to be tricky, Brin thought as she jogged through the silent halls of the Earth Sector. Her footsteps on the rocks echoed in the vacant corridors.

She was running on fumes. She hadn't rested since breaking through the rubble when she discovered Ronan wasn't dead. And that had been after a full day of work. It was well past midnight now, and the Earth Sector was quiet around her. She stuffed a bite of meat pie into her mouth as she ran. Thank Niradim she'd remembered to swipe some food at Ronan's place when she retrieved his sword and shield.

As she approached the building where they were holding Gadjet, she nodded to the guard out front and told him she was under direct orders from the Elders to bring Gadjet in for questioning. Her standing as a Disciple gave her some authority among the Protectors, and he didn't have any reason to question her, so he let her right in.

She grabbed the key to Gadjet's cell from a hook on the wall and unlocked Gadjet's prison, opening the door for the little draken. "Gather your things. We're leaving."

Gadjet jumped to her feet. "What do you mean, leaving?"

"Midral. We're leaving Midral," Brin said as she found Gadjet's bag and tossed it to her. "One of the Elders is planning on having you killed. So I'm getting you out, and you're taking me to where they're keeping Ronan."

She caught the bag and strapped it over her shoulder. "I'm not leaving without the Mythril Soul." She said it as if it were a challenge.

Brin still couldn't believe she was doing this.

"We're picking it up on the way." She stepped up to the little draken and pointed a finger in her face. "You'd better not be lying about all this."

Gadjet brushed Brin's hand aside and snarled. "I swear to you, we need the Mythril Soul if we're going to save the Flame."

Brin studied Gadjet's eyes one last time, searching for any hint that she was lying. But there was nothing. She had to take this risk. For Ronan, and for Niradim. So she nodded. "Then let's go."

Brin led Gadjet out of the building and through the Earth Sector without incident, but she knew it was only a matter of time before Vorkin discovered Gadjet's disappearance. Hopefully, they would just assume that Brin and Gadjet had fled the city and give up the chase.

They crept up to the Cathedral and Brin signaled to Gadjet to hang back. Where was Thalga? She should have had enough time to get ready and meet Brin here.

Brin sighed to herself. Thalga had probably decided this was too risky and stayed home. It disappointed Brin, but it made sense. Their friendship hadn't been strong these last few days, so she couldn't blame her friend too much for not wanting to go against the Elders' orders. When Thalga still didn't show after a few moments, Brin decided she couldn't wait any longer. She'd have to do this herself.

She approached the guard at the door and let him know she'd be relieving him of his watch and taking over. The guard relaxed and left without asking any questions. They'd all been working long shifts, and any chance to go home early was welcome. Once they made sure he was gone, Brin signaled Gadjet to follow her inside.

"Now listen," Brin whispered to Gadjet. "Understand that I am taking a huge leap of faith here breaking you out, so my one condition is that the Mythril Soul stays in my possession the entire time. Got it?"

Gadjet nodded. "That's fine with me. We just need to bring it to the Heart Forge. I don't care who carries it." She paused and held up a hand to Brin. "I could use a weapon, though."

"Yeah, I don't think so," Brin responded, brushing past Gadjet. Brin would trust the draken to lead her to Ronan, but she wasn't stupid.

They moved through the silent aisles of the Cathedral, quickly but carefully. Brin didn't want to be here any longer than she needed to be. However, she did pause as she passed the Soul Forge, with Niradim's Flame still flickering inside. It seemed so much weaker than before.

Niradim, please let this be the right decision, Brin prayed as she glanced at the Flame. It may have been her imagination—confirmation bias playing tricks on her—but it almost seemed as if the Flame grew brighter and warmer, almost encouraging, as she prayed for guidance.

Either way, she knew Niradim cared for his people, and he wouldn't want them to murder a person in secret. She knew it wasn't right, and that gave her the confidence she needed to keep moving forward. That would have to be enough until she learned more from Gadjet.

She crept up to the pedestal with the Mythril Soul, but as she reached out for it, she heard a sharp hiss from Gadjet. Acting purely on instinct, she ducked, raising Ronan's shield just in time to deflect a magical bolt of energy that would have knocked her out cold. She peered over the shield to see where the attack had come from.

Vorkin lowered his hand back to his side—a bit of smoke still wafting from his palm where the attack had originated. That wasn't too much of a surprise, but she took a sharp breath and her eyes widened when she saw Thalga step out from behind him with a sad look on her face. Druden was closing the doors behind them, shutting their way out.

Brin blinked back the tears threatening to run down her face as she looked at the woman she once thought of as a friend. "Thalga, I trusted you."

Druden latched the door shut behind him and then turned, clasping his hands behind his back as he addressed them. "Brin, I'm disappointed in you. I wonder how long you've been working with our enemy."

Brin ignored him and looked around, trying to come up with ideas for an escape as Gadjet moved closer to Brin. Hadn't Ronan said there was a secret back entrance to the Cathedral? He and Ginmar used it to trap Kyros, but she had no idea where it was, and there wasn't exactly time to search for it.

"Any chance you've changed your mind about giving me a weapon?" Gadjet asked under her breath.

Yeah, she'd have to revise that policy if they were going to get out of this. But she didn't want to give Gadjet anything too deadly. "Grab something off that workbench you can use to defend yourself. We don't want to kill them."

Gadjet stepped over to the bench with a huff. "I don't think they're going to show the same restraint."

She grabbed an iron rod of some kind off the workbench and held it out in front of her to defend herself. Brin was initially surprised she hadn't grabbed a hammer, but then realized the draken was playing to her own strengths. A blacksmith hammer wasn't meant for battle, and Gadjet was small enough that she'd have trouble swinging it around effectively, especially with only one arm.

Brin finally acknowledged Druden. "Mind explaining why you ordered Vorkin to come assassinate a prisoner in secret without a trial or formal questioning? As far as I remember from our sermons,

Niradim doesn't condone murder."

Vorkin shifted on his feet. Looks like he still wasn't sure that killing Gadjet was the right thing to do. Good, maybe she could use that. To her surprise, it was Thalga that jumped to Druden's defense.

"The Elders have every right to defend Niradim's Flame by whatever means necessary!" Thalga stepped forward and pointed at Brin. "But it's clear you care more about your boyfriend than you do about your own god. You've disobeyed the Elders at every turn, and now you're trading Niradim for someone who renounced Niradim until a few weeks ago when it was convenient. Take a good look at yourself, Brin. This is way out of line!"

Brin fumed. How *dare* she? Ronan had essentially given his life to Niradim twice in a matter of months. Thalga could criticize Brin all she wanted, but Ronan had proved himself in a way that was unquestionable. Even though Brin sometimes disagreed with the way he wanted to protect Midral, his heart was in the right place. She knew Niradim was proud of that.

Brin took a deep breath to settle her temper as best she could. "It's sad how quickly everyone seems to forget what Ronan went through to protect them." She reached over and slipped the Mythril Soul into her pouch and tucked it away. "I don't expect you to understand, Thalga. I can see how much you value your relationships."

"Enough of this nonsense," Druden cut in. "Brin, we are taking you and that little wyrmling into custody. You are both under arrest as traitors to Niradim. If you resist, lethal force will be permitted in your apprehension, as the safety of Niradim's Flame takes precedence above all else. Now, place the Mythril Soul back on the pedestal and drop your weapons."

Gadjet looked over her shoulder at Brin with a determined look in her eye. No, Gadjet would not go quietly no matter what Brin said. And that's when Brin knew Gadjet was telling the truth. Nobody would lay their life down for something they didn't truly believe in. It was vitally important to Gadjet to get the Mythril Soul back to the Heart Forge, and Brin could tell it wasn't because she was working for the Fallen Star. There was something about Gadjet that reminded her of Ronan. She fiercely wanted to protect her people, and would die trying if that's what it took.

Brin raised her hand to the side of her head where she'd woven a symbol of Niradim into her braid and began to channel Niradim's Flame. It was so weak compared to what she was used to, but she felt like it was giving her as much strength as it could. Ronan's shield flared with power, and Brin grabbed the hilt of Ronan's short sword and drew it from the shield. The sword rang in the silent air of the cathedral.

"If you want the Mythril Soul back, Druden." Brin shifted into a defensive stance. "Come and take it."

"Very well, Brin." Druden's mouth curled into a smirk. Brin suspected he'd be happy to rid himself of her, once and for all. "Captain Vorkin, Lieutenant Thalga, please dispose of these traitors and return the Mythril Soul to its rightful place. This is no longer the Brin you remember. Her actions prove she is working with the Fallen Star to destroy Niradim. Show no mercy. Protect your god!"

Thalga unclipped her mace from her belt and held it with one hand out to her side as Vorkin drew his sword. He held up his shield in one hand, and they began to advance.

"Gadjet, you take Thalga," Brin whispered over her shoulder. "She's the less experienced fighter, so you'll have an easier time with her."

Gadjet scoffed. "I believe I told you already that I've killed a dragon. I can handle an angry little girl just fine."

"Fine, then try not to hurt her too badly," Brin said, rolling her eyes. Gadjet sighed in response, but nodded and began circling to the side to get closer to the wall and create some separation between her and

Brin.

Thankfully, Thalga followed, despite her pride. She knew Brin was beyond her ability. Brin still doubted this little draken had slain a fully grown dragon, but hopefully she'd at least been in some fights. Thalga wasn't the best fighter, but she'd been training. Fortunately, she didn't have much field experience, and she hadn't learned to channel Niradim's magic in battle yet.

Vorkin, on the other hand, was a completely different story. He had a lot of experience. He may have achieved the rank of Captain because of Druden's meddling, but he would have gotten there himself before long. As Thalga broke off to deal with Gadjet, Vorkin advanced straight down the aisle toward her.

"Brin, we can still settle this without bloodshed," Vorkin pleaded. "I don't want to hurt you."

"Then back down, Vorkin," Brin responded. "I've made my choice. What about you?"

"Mine is the same as always." Vorkin's eyes simmered with white energy. "I serve Niradim."

He rushed forward in a flurry of attacks, and Brin instantly went on the defensive. She didn't want to hurt him, and from the way he was attacking, she could sense he didn't want to hurt her either. Unfortunately, he was a better fighter than she was in normal situations, and she was already at her limit. She needed to end this quickly.

Channeling as much of Niradim's power as she could, she pushed out a wave of energy as Vorkin slammed his weapon into her shield. The move made Vorkin stumble backward, and Brin pressed her advantage. She drove Vorkin to the side and onto the unstable footing of the wooden benches, but he recovered before she could disengage and make a break for the exit.

The obstacles made the fight more even for Brin, but it took all her skill to keep Vorkin contained. If they were going to get away, both

Gadjet and Brin would need to find an opening to break away from their opponents. A small flash of energy caught her eye, and she saw a small red draken flying through the air and slamming into the far wall. *Ashes*, it looked like Thalga actually *did* know how to channel Niradim's power in battle. She must have been practicing.

The brief distraction allowed Vorkin to knock her sword to the side and get inside her guard. He used his own shield to knock hers away and then kicked her straight in the chest, sending her tumbling backward. Using the momentum from Vorkin's kick, she rolled and regained her footing. A quick glance to the side confirmed Gadjet was slumped against the wall, unmoving.

Slag and ashes, she thought. *I need to-*

A powerful force of energy slammed into her side and sent her crashing across the cathedral floor. Her weapons went tumbling from her grasp, and her hold on Niradim's power faltered, causing her exhaustion to hit her like a hammer. She lay there, gasping for breath and holding her side. Her ribs were definitely broken.

Where had that... Druden. She'd focused so much on Vorkin that she'd forgotten to keep an eye on the Elder.

Vorkin ran up to her side and held his sword pointed down at her neck. "Stay down, Brin."

"Vorkin..." Brin said, wincing at the pain in her side. It hurt to breathe. "Why? After everything Ronan's done... You were there... You saw him battle the Starspawn... You saw him defeat Kyros..."

"That's enough, traitor," Druden said, walking up to Vorkin's side. "Captain, finish her off and replace the Mythril Soul. We will need to remove her body and clean up this mess before the other Disciples arrive to begin work on the Great Anvil."

"Sir..." Vorkin paused with the tip of his blade still keeping Brin in check. "Can't we just... imprison her or something? This doesn't feel right."

Brin saw the struggle in Vorkin's eyes. His grip on his sword tightened, fingers grinding into the leather wrap of the handle as he hesitated.

"I gave you an order, Captain."

Vorkin raised his sword over his head, the sharpened tip pointing down at Brin.

"Vorkin, please…" Brin pleaded.

His muscles tightened as he readied the finishing blow.

"Now," Druden said.

Vorkin took a deep breath and closed his eyes for a moment before opening them to meet Brin's. With one quick movement, Vorkin slammed a gauntleted hand into the back of Druden's head, knocking him out. He then reached down and pressed his hand against Brin's armor, and a burst of healing magic surged through her. She gasped as her ribs popped back into place and her cuts sizzled and knit themselves back together. Her body still protested at how long she'd been pushing it, but the pain had vanished.

"Ronan has saved my life at least twice now, and the enemy has him because of me," Vorkin said, helping Brin to her feet. "I don't know why the Elders refuse to help him, but I can't pretend that what Druden asked me to do here was right."

"Vorkin, what are you doing!" Thalga yelled from the other side of the Cathedral.

Gadjet's eyes snapped open while Thalga was distracted and she slammed her iron bar through Thalga's thigh, causing her to scream in pain. As she was doubled over, Gadjet took a deep breath and huffed out a concussive blast of draconic magic directly into Thalga's chest, sending her flying back the way Gadjet had come a moment ago.

"That should keep her down for a while," Gadjet said, casually brushing off some dust from her clothes. She leveled her gaze at Vorkin. "Have you decided to let us go then?"

Vorkin frowned. "Yes, against my better judgment." He looked down at the unconscious Elder at his feet. "And to my enormous detriment."

"Come with us," Brin said. "You can help us locate Ronan."

He turned back to her. "No, Brin, this mission is yours. I don't know that I completely agree with it, and I intend to stay and help rebuild the Great Anvil… if they'll let me. Besides, I'm not just going to leave an Elder here on the ground. Once you've left, I will heal him and Thalga and then accept my punishment."

Life was about to get much more difficult for all of them now. She only hoped that he wouldn't suffer too much because of his actions here. Maybe some day she could come back and save him from whatever fate Druden would cook up for him. Until then, she'd have to make sure to repay his gift by finding and saving Ronan. His sacrifice wouldn't be in vain.

"Thank you, Vorkin," Brin threw her arms around him. "You're a good man, and I'm sorry you're caught up in the middle of this. I promise I'll bring Ronan back."

Vorkin gently pushed her back and held on to her shoulders, shaking his head. "I wish you luck, Brin, I really do. But… you can't come back." He gestured down to the unconscious Elder. "Druden will spread the word about you being a traitor. If you step foot in Midral again, there's nothing I'll be able to do to protect you. He will have you executed."

He was right—she had already crossed the point of no return. So she simply nodded and tried to hold back the tears that were threatening to blur her vision. Returning home would never be an option for her. "I understand."

He saluted her and turned his back. "Now go, before I come to my senses and change my mind."

Gadjet walked up to Brin and handed her Ronan's sword and shield. She smiled and strapped the items to her back. She then unstrapped a knife from her belt and handed it to Gadjet, who took it with a raised brow.

"You earned it," Brin said with a wink, and Gadjet smiled back.

They turned and walked toward the door, cautiously opening it and checking the surrounding area. There wasn't anyone in sight. Gadjet crept out the door first, and Brin paused to turn back one last time.

"Goodbye, Vorkin."

"Goodbye, Brin."

9

Ronan

Ronan was up and ready before Dak'thor came to gather him. Despite the stakes at hand, Ronan was looking forward to getting back in the forge. If nothing else, it would give him time to think about how to get out of this predicament.

"Thank you, Dak'thor," Ronan said as he stepped out of his cell.

Dak'thor closed the door behind him. "You are a curious one, Phoenix of Niradim. Most people despise their captors."

"Sounds like you speak from experience," Ronan said, raising his eyebrow at the powerful draken. Dak'thor didn't answer, so Ronan shrugged. "You haven't given me any reason to hate you. You haven't been unnecessarily cruel to me, you're just following orders from people who are oppressing you. I've seen how they function—they don't tolerate people who question their orders."

Dak'thor led them through the camps, back to the Heart Forge. He didn't see Agent Steel anywhere, but Falrose was waiting for him on the other side of the doors. Based on his previous interaction with Falrose, he suspected that the novaborn stayed on that side of the door often, simply to remind Agent Steel of his weakness.

Falrose saw them approaching and stepped toward them. "Ah, the mighty Phoenix has arrived." He directed a nearby cultist to insert a key into Ronan's cuffs to release him. "As a reminder, any sign that you're not holding up your end of the bargain, and I will send this tribe of reptiles to finish the job my brother started in your city."

Dak'thor bristled at Falrose's insult to his tribe. "That seems unnecessary-"

Falrose backhanded the large draken with a magically enhanced blow, cutting him off and causing him to stumble backwards. "Did I ask for your opinion, wyrm?"

Dak'thor snarled and took a threatening step towards Falrose, but Ronan put his hands up to Dak'thor's chest and held him back. Dak'thor met Ronan's eyes, and Ronan subtly shook his head.

"Don't." Ronan said under his breath. "He's not worth it."

Dak'thor held Ronan's eyes for just a moment longer as he let out a low growl. After a tense moment, he took one quick glance at Falrose, and then snorted and stomped away. Falrose chuckled.

"Shame, it would have been fun to play with him a little longer." Falrose turned his attention back to Ronan. "Remember what I said, Phoenix. Any funny business at all, and Midral is done."

With that, he left Ronan to get to work. It didn't take long to fill in the frame to create the spherical shape of the Mythril Soul, but he was frustrated that he didn't have longer to think of a plan to get out of this mess. He kept wishing there was a way for him to convince the draken to take up arms, but nothing would come to him. Before he knew it, the next vision was upon him.

* * *

Over 1000 years ago

"Settle down, everyone. Let's get started."

Ashe struggled to get the council in order. Clash didn't blame her—

the news of their trip had already spread. All four of the elder Disciples, plus Ashe as the only Phoenix, gathered in a circle around the Great Anvil. As was the custom, each of the elders removed their Mythril Souls and placed them in their designated slots on top of the anvil. Since Ashe, as a Phoenix, no longer had a Mythril Soul, a slot had been created in the center of the Great Anvil. She pushed her sword point-first into the anvil until the phoenix wings on the hilt rested on its surface.

"So, Ashe," Cinder asked as soon as the room quieted down. "Tell us exactly what happened."

Ashe took a deep breath to compose herself and then explained the events of their diplomatic trip to Lumenova.

"The novaborn have been gifted magical items called Star Crystals from their god, Celestian. They claim that integrating them with their bodies grants them magical abilities, similar to how Niradim's Mythril Souls grant us our magic." Ashe crossed her arms as she addressed the rest of them. "The difference is that the crystals are integrated permanently, they cannot be swapped out as our Mythril Souls can." She paused here, bracing herself for the reaction to what she was about to tell them.

"The novaborn told us that Celestian has blessed them with an abundance of Star Crystals, and they are offering some to us in trade. They believe we would receive the same magical benefits as they do by integrating them into our bodies."

"So, if I'm understanding you correctly," Cinder leaned forward with his elbows on his knees. "Anyone who accepted a Star Crystal would be able to use magic? They wouldn't have to share the limited Mythril Souls we have available?"

"That's exactly what she's saying," Steel said. "We could finally have permanent abilities!"

"Sharing these four Mythril Souls between all the mythrali achieving the rank of Disciple *is* becoming a bit of a burden," Saber said from her seat on the other side of the anvil. "It would be nice if we could start granting abilities that were more permanent to the Disciples."

Ashe held up her hand and placed it on her chest, which no longer had the same circular cavity theirs had for the Mythril Souls. "If I might remind you all, there is already a path to us having permanent abilities. Perhaps it would be better if we put our efforts into having more people attempt the Phoenix Trial."

"Of the few who have, you are the only one who has passed, Ashe," Saber leaned back in her chair as she gestured at Steel. "Steel's most recent attempt proves it's not a guarantee, even with multiple tries."

Steel visibly simmered in his seat at the mention of his failed attempts at the Phoenix Trial, but the point was helping his cause, so he stayed silent for the moment.

"If Steel feels that he's learned the lesson Niradim was trying to teach him-" Ashe started.

"It doesn't matter." Steel stood and gestured to Saber. "Her point still stands. It's not a guarantee, and sharing the Mythril Souls is not a viable option if we want to stay strong in this world. There are several dragonkin tribes in the surrounding area, and the trip to Lumenova proved that the novaborn are far more technologically advanced than us. How are we supposed to protect ourselves if only five of us can wield magic at a time?"

Cinder gestured for Steel to sit back down. "Peace, Steel. The dragonkin are allies. We're in no danger from them. And it sounds like the trip to Lumenova went well, so forging an alliance with the novaborn seems likely." Steel sat back down in his seat so Cinder continued. "There are no elven or human settlements anywhere near Midralen, and they wouldn't have any reason to venture so far north. We aren't in any danger."

"The humans will push north eventually," Saber said, the disgust plain on her face. "Showing them the power of our mythril was a mistake that will come back to haunt us—mark my words. They are too greedy for their own good."

"That's not up for debate at the moment," Ashe countered. "Both sides have made their points. We need to hold a vote." She held up her hand. "I don't think we should accept these gifts from the novaborn. We don't know enough about the Star Crystals, and Niradim has already laid out a path that leads to the same result, but using his power instead of a foreign one."

Steel immediately raised his hand and shot a glance at Saber. "I vote we accept."

Saber nodded and raised her hand as well. "I side with Steel. The benefits are too great, and I don't see much of a risk, if any."

Cinder cleared his throat. "Well, I'm with Ashe on this one. Niradim has a path for us. We should stick to it. He is our god after all."

"It's up to you, Clash," Ashe said, as the four mythrali turned to him at the same time. "You've been silent throughout all this. What are your thoughts?"

It would be down to his vote. Why did it fall to him to make such an important decision for his people? He could see Ashe and Steel leaning forward, each hoping that he'd cast the deciding vote in their favor, when an idea struck him. Maybe there was a compromise that could be found here.

Clash stood to address the group. "I don't think we have enough information to make a final decision yet, but the offer sounds like a good one. Maybe it would be a good idea for one of the Disciples to take the novaborn up on their offer and try this method. After seeing if and how it works, we can make a more informed decision."

Steel flashed his teeth in a grin, standing up to support Clash's idea. "I can agree to this, and I'll happily volunteer to test this method."

Saber nodded her consent, and after a brief pause, Cinder did as well.

Ashe let out a disappointed sigh. "Very well. Steel will travel with Clash back to Lumenova to test how the Star Crystal interacts with a mythrali." They nodded to her, and Steel's smile widened. "Only take one Mythril Soul with you to share on your way to the city. If everything goes well, Steel won't need one for the way back. We are dismissed. Go with Niradim's blessing."

Each of the Disciples took their Mythril Soul from the Great Anvil and walked out. Clash was the last to grab his before he turned to go. After Ashe retrieved her sword, which flared back to its normal pristine form at her touch, she caught Clash's arm.

"Keep an eye on him, Clash. And keep him out of trouble. I don't completely trust the novaborns' sudden altruism. There may be something more at work here."

Clash nodded. "Don't worry, it'll all work out."

Clash turned and left Ashe standing there staring at her own reflection in her sword, deep in thought.

* * *

Clash and Steel sat in the Grand Observatory of Lumenova as the novaborn prepared the crystals needed for Steel's transformation. The normal way the novaborn integrated crystals into their bodies wouldn't work for the mythrali, but they theorized they could modify a large crystal to fit within the chest cavity that normally housed a Mythril Soul. They also confirmed that it was a permanent integration—it couldn't be removed and replaced like a Mythril Soul could. The thought of it made the surface of Clash's metal vibrate with anxiety. To him, it felt like a betrayal of Niradim.

Clash tapped his foot on the ornate marble floor as they waited, each tap echoing in the large room around them. "Are you sure about this,

Steel? What if something goes wrong?"

"Well, then we'll know it's not a viable option." Clash could tell he was eager to get the process started. "And I'll go back to begging Niradim to give me the power I deserve by now."

Clash didn't like the entitlement in Steel's voice, but he couldn't help commiserating a little. Steel had attempted the Phoenix Trial on three separate occasions and had come out angrier each time. He didn't know the lesson Niradim was trying to teach him, and Ashe said there was nothing she could do to help. It was a personal thing each of them had to learn on their own. Clash knew Steel was beginning to think Ashe was just hoarding the power for herself.

"Will you…" Clash wasn't sure how to broach this subject, so he figured it was best to just come out and say it. "Will you still serve Niradim after the transformation is complete?"

Steel waved his hand in the air as if it was a silly question. "Of course. In fact, I'll be serving him better than before. I'll become an ambassador to the novaborn, and I'll be bringing power to Niradim's people. *Permanent* power."

"Do you think their price is fair? The amount of Mythril they're asking for is higher than we thought."

"Well, it will depend on the results—" Sola and Galar walked in, and Steel cut his comment short. Galar was holding something in his hands covered by an ornate cloth. Steel's mouth curled into a hungry grin as his eyes stayed locked on the cloth. "Finally, they're here."

Sola gave a slight bow when she reached the two large mythrali. "Apologies for the delay, but we believe we have a Star Crystal that will work."

"It took more crystal material than we expected to create a Star Crystal that would work with your unique bodies." Galar stepped forward with the bundle in his arms. "If this is to become a trade between us, it would require more mythril than we previously discussed."

Clash's eyes went wide. "More—"

Steel held up a hand to cut him off. "Let us see if this even works first before we discuss costs. You said we could try it first before finalizing the deal, correct?"

Sola's lips pursed. "That is correct." She also held up a hand to prevent Galar's incoming protests. "Now, shall we begin?"

"Yes, let's." Steel stepped forward eagerly. He removed his Mythril Soul and tossed it over his shoulder to Clash without looking, not caring about the sacred artifact any longer now that what he ultimately wanted was within reach. Clash caught the Mythril Soul and inserted it into his chest, feeling the warm embrace of Niradim's power flow through him. He always loved that feeling. Would the Star Crystal's power have a similar effect?

"As you know, this is still untested," Galar said, as he removed the cloth to reveal a polished crystal orb with a glowing core in the center. "But if you insert this—hey!"

Steel had reached forward in one quick motion and snatched the Star Crystal as soon as it was visible. He shoved it into the slot in his chest, and immediately, the star crystal pulsed with a bright violet light.

Power seemed to seep out from the crystal and through Steel, who hunched over and screamed as the energy flooded him. Clash took a step forward to help, but Steel held out his hand to stop him as his scream slowly transformed into laughter. The light dimmed, and Steel stood up straight, taking a deep breath. Clash could see his eyes now glowed with a faint purple light.

"YES!" Steel laughed as he held up his hand in front of himself and flexed his fingers. "This is what we've been missing!"

Clash stepped forward and tentatively put a hand on the larger mythrali's shoulder. "Steel, do you feel ok?"

Steel looked up as if he'd forgotten Clash was there. He laughed again. "Better than ever, Clash! This will change everything." He looked to Sola and Galar. "Name your price. We'll pay it. I'll be back with more mythrali who wish to have the power Niradim has been holding back from us."

Sola nodded, and a sly grin spread across her face. "Very well, Steel. We'll have formal documents drawn up."

Steel walked out with Sola and Galar, completely forgetting about Clash, who stood there, too stunned to speak and trying to process what had just happened.

* * *

Present

Ronan opened his eyes back in the Heart Forge. So, Agent Steel had been the first of these mythrali to accept a Star Crystal, but it sounded like there were more to come. Clash had been confused and concerned at the outcome, but Ronan didn't know what that meant for Clash's future. He also didn't know why he was watching these visions through Clash's senses. Was it simply because he was present for each of these events, or was there more to it?

Falrose approached, seeing that Ronan had come out of his meditation. He picked up the solid sphere that would become the Mythril Soul and held it up to inspect it.

"This is all you've accomplished? It seems like you could have done this and more on the first day." Falrose closed the distance between them, staring daggers at Ronan from just inches away. "One would almost be inclined to think you were stalling."

Ronan didn't back down, meeting Falrose's stare with his own. "I don't make the rules, Falrose. If you have a problem with it, talk to Steel. He's the one who gave me the instructions."

Falrose's crystal scars flashed violet, and Ronan found himself hurled through the air. He hit the ground with a grunt, and the room spun for a moment before he got his bearings back. He slowly got back to his feet, and Falrose continued as if nothing had happened.

"Yes, I'm sure the words of that madman are completely trustworthy," Falrose slammed the unfinished Mythril Soul back on its resting place. "Fine, you will have the three days that were promised, but not a moment more. If we don't have a Mythril Soul we can use for our purposes by the end of tomorrow, I will make you watch by my side as we destroy your city before I kill you myself."

10

Brin

Brin and Gadjet only got a few steps into the abandoned tunnels before Brin collapsed from exhaustion.

Gadjet turned to Brin, who was struggling to catch her breath on the floor. "You should rest before we make the rest of the trip. It'll take a day to get out of the abandoned part of the Earth Sector, and then it's a two-day hike in the cold to get to where we're going."

"Just... give me a few minutes," Brin said between breaths. "I can keep going."

Gadjet shook her head. "If you push yourself, it will only make the trip longer. Take some time to recover before we're out in the cold. Your people don't know about this exit, so we'll be safe here."

Brin nodded. She knew Gadjet was right. Brin had pushed herself to her absolute limit since she'd been awake. It was hard to even keep her vision from blurring. "Okay, but promise me one thing—"

"I will not leave you, Brin," Gadjet interrupted. "I give you my word."

She supposed she had no choice but to believe her new companion, so she nodded once more and gave in. The ground was uncomfortable, but she barely had time to notice before sleep took her.

She dreamt of death.

She watched as two small groups, clad in armor from head to toe, clashed together on a bridge surrounded by lava. One group advanced towards an open room with an ornate forge behind it—the other fought to defend it. The defenders' armor was warped by crystals that glowed with an angry violet, but gave them magical abilities that the advancing group didn't seem to have.

A large man wielding a massive hammer advanced through the corrupted ranks and broke through to the large room before sealing it behind him. Stone doors slammed shut, and a cascading flow of lava fell from above to block the entrance.

The group without magic continued to push forward, and slowly they defeated the corrupted ranks, but not without heavy losses. Five of them remained, breathing heavily and standing in front of the lava and closed doors.

A scream of rage erupted behind them, and the group turned to see a large figure with two greatswords strapped across its back. In the dream, the monster was a dark shadow, outlined in violet energy that radiated power from its form. It drew its weapons and leapt toward them, cutting them down with ease. Brin watched through the eyes of the last survivor as the monster stepped over her and raised its colossal blades above its head.

The last thing she heard was its roar as the blades descended, leaving the beast surrounded by nothing but corpses.

***

Some time later, she woke to a gentle nudge, which caused her to jump awake with adrenaline.

"Apologies, Brin, you looked like you were having a nightmare." Gadjet stood and shouldered her pack. "Besides, we have to get moving."

However long she'd been out wasn't enough to satisfy the rest her body craved, but Ronan was in trouble. So she forced herself up into a sitting position and rummaged around in her pockets.

There should be one more around here somewhere...

There it was. She pulled out a half-eaten meat pie and took a bite. A little stale, but better than nothing.

"Do you just... keep those on you at all times?" Gadjet asked.

"Oh, sorry," Brin said, wiping some dirt off the remaining chunk of meat pie in her hand and holding it out to Gadjet. "Did you want some?"

"No, thank you," Gadjet said. She pulled out some kind of dried meat from a pouch at her waist and chewed on it.

Brin shrugged and stuffed the rest in her mouth. "Gotta eat something, might as well be something delicious." It dawned on her that this might be the last time she'd be able to enjoy her favorite Midral pastries, and her shoulders slumped. "I wish I'd grabbed more while I could."

She patted down the rest of her pockets, discreetly checking to make sure the Mythril Soul was still in her pouch, and then looked to Gadjet. "Okay, let's go."

Gadjet led them through winding tunnels for hours. Brin had no idea how the draken was able to guide their way, but Brin was glad she could. The old Earth Sector seemed vacant, and what remained of it wasn't organized in a way that Brin could recognize. There had also been cave-ins over the years, which only added to the confusing layout. They finally reached what seemed to be a dead end, where Gadjet stopped and studied the wall.

"What's wrong?" Brin asked.

"I've never used this exit before," Gadjet said. "I just need to figure out how to open it. It'll take a few minutes, so you should get some rest. We'll be hiking through snow from here on out. We might be able to stop and rest for a few hours at night, but we should try to get to the Heart Forge as quickly as possible."

"If you've never used this exit before, how did you know how to get here?" Brin asked.

Gadjet gestured to some markings hidden in one of the corners of the wall. "I followed the glyphs. My tribe has come through these tunnels plenty of times, and they left markers to follow. The exits all require draconic magic to open, but each one is slightly different."

Brin studied the random scratches on the wall, running her fingers over the rough grooves as a thought struck her. If this were the old Earth Sector, why did the draken have so much access? She turned to look at Gadjet. "Only draconic magic will open the doors? That seems odd. Why wouldn't they be keyed to Niradim's magic?"

"Well…" Gadjet said hesitantly. "I don't know the details, but our ancestors had several ways to get inside the mountain that the dwarves didn't know about."

Brin let her hand fall from the markings as she considered Gadjet's words. "Interesting…"

"Now, just give me a moment and I'll have it open," Gadjet said, turning back to the wall.

Brin couldn't decipher what Gadjet was doing, but after a few minutes, the small draken made some gestures with her hand and then exhaled a small flame against the stone. Glowing arcane lines flashed blue across the wall, and then it ground against the surrounding rock as it slid aside and cold arctic air blasted them.

"Are you ready?" Gadjet asked.

Brin wrapped her cloak tighter around her. "Ready."

The icy wind cut straight through Brin's cloak as they stepped out into the mountain air, but Gadjet seemed strangely unfazed by the cold weather, despite her meager clothing. Brin pulled her cloak closer around her and focused on putting one foot in front of the other as she followed the small red draken through narrow mountain paths.

Initially, Brin was worried that they might run into some dangerous wildlife along the way, but after a few hours of hiking, she didn't see any signs of life. She couldn't imagine many creatures would want to brave these elements. The valley ahead of them descended several hundred feet before leveling out and extending northeast, deeper into the Midral mountain range.

Once they got down to the base of the valley, the wind died down quite a bit. It hadn't snowed much in the last several days, and Brin caught faint traces of a path carved in the snow along their same trajectory. She guessed it belonged to the draken that had captured Ronan.

She desperately hoped he was still ok. Gadjet assured her he was, but she'd been gone for a while, so Brin didn't know if she could trust Gadjet's assessment of the situation. They needed him alive for an important project, but what would they do to him if he refused? She tried not to think about that.

So instead, her mind drifted to their last interaction. They'd gotten in a fight over the same argument they'd had for weeks. Midral was important to both of them, but they had drastically different opinions on the best method of serving their city. She knew Ronan at least partially blamed himself for Midral's current state. He'd expressed to her that if he had just joined Ginmar earlier in apprehending Kyros, they might have been able to avoid the entire disaster. As a result, he thought the only way to protect Midral was to remain within its broken walls. Brin knew he still had some lingering trauma to work through from his death and subsequent resurrection, but she didn't know how to help him realize that he couldn't stay in Midral forever.

Ronan had given her details about the circumstances of his death that she didn't think he'd told anyone else. He'd been in the middle of a fight against a large Starspawn. Not nearly as big as the one he'd ultimately defeated in Midral, but this one had still towered over him. When he'd tried to use his signature spell, Niradim denied Ronan access to his power, pulling it away right as the beast descended on him.

That meant Niradim had deliberately let Ronan die in that fight. Brin knew it still bothered Ronan that he didn't know Niradim's reasoning, but, in the end, he'd decided to put his faith in Niradim again anyway. Ronan later told her that he might not know the reason for his death, but he finally believed that there was one.

And Brin believed it too. Just as it was no accident that Niradim had let Ronan die, it was also no accident that Niradim resurrected him. Maybe it was the only way to get Ronan back to the city before it was under attack. Or maybe it was so he'd be able to stop what was happening right now with the corruption of the Heart Forge. It was possible that they would never know the reason.

Either way, whether it was for something he had done or was yet to do, they believed. That was what faith was—putting your trust in something without knowing the answers up front, and knowing that the answers may never come.

But whatever the reason, the resurrection had granted Ronan something that even the Elders of their faith didn't believe was possible—the rank of Phoenix. When Ronan found out that his new nickname was also a long-forgotten rank of Niradim that the Elders had been keeping a secret, he demanded answers. He hadn't learned much, but there were records of the first Phoenix of Niradim and her weapon, the Sword of Ashes.

Unfortunately, the records did not paint the best picture.

According to the histories the Elders presented, the appearance of the first Phoenix had almost wiped out Niradim's people and Niradim himself. The first Phoenix turned her sword against her own people, almost completely wiping them out.

Now that she thought about it, it made sense why the Elders had pushed back so much at her attempts to save Ronan. Maybe they believed that the appearance of another Phoenix was a sign of impending doom. Well, if there was one thing she knew about Ronan, and the Elders would know too if they had their heads on straight, it was that Ronan would never turn against the people of Midral. That was one thing she and Ronan had in common—their dedication to protecting Niradim's people.

Even if they had different philosophies on *how* to protect them.

* * *

After a long day of hiking, Gadjet led them to a small cave hidden off the path so they could rest for the night. The brief nap she'd had before they started this journey had been far from recuperative, not after she'd pushed herself so hard in the days before their escape. Her muscles groaned in protest as she heaved herself up a short incline to the mouth of the cave. As soon as she crossed the threshold, she collapsed against the wall to catch her breath.

Gadjet didn't even have the decency to pretend to look winded from the long day of hiking as she went to work bundling some sticks together to build a fire.

"Sorry," Brin said. "Do you want me to light the-"

She cut off as Gadjet gave her an exasperated look, lowered her head without breaking eye contact with Brin, and breathed fire onto the sticks.

"Oh, right," Brin chuckled, "Sorry."

Gadjet smiled back at her and took out some jerky. She handed some to Brin and began to chew on some herself.

"Eat and warm yourself," Gadjet instructed between bites. "Use the fire to dry anything that's too wet from the snow and then get as much rest as you can. It's too dangerous to travel at night. The temperature drops so much that even I get cold."

"Yeah, I was going to ask about that," Brin said, taking a bite of the dried meat. Wow, that was some really good jerky. "You're barely wearing anything. How are you not freezing right now?"

Gadjet looked down at her simple clothing—a long-sleeved tunic with the left arm tied off at the shoulder paired with some dark brown trousers that had been ripped at the bottom of the legs to make them short enough for Gadjet's small stature. She didn't have boots on her feet, a glove on her hand, or anything to cover her head.

"Oh, we can use our magic to keep ourselves warm enough for most weather," Gadjet explained. "It's kind of like how we breathe fire, but we keep the warmth inside of us instead. It doesn't drain us very much unless we have to do it for really long periods of time. This two-day hike is nothing."

Brin swallowed the piece that was in her mouth. "And how about the fact that you don't seem to be tired at all? Does that also have to do with your magic?"

Gadjet nodded. "That's correct. Though that kind of magic is a little more complex and taxing than simply keeping warm. Not every draken can increase their strength, and most can only do it for short bursts. I'm a little more advanced, but even I would get tired keeping a pace like this for more than a few days."

"Wow, I had no idea," Brin said. "That seems pretty useful for living in remote places like this."

"It is." Gadjet turned to look out into the cold night beyond the border of their little cave. The wind had picked up, and snow began to fall—sparkling in the darkness from the light of their fire. "Draconic magic helps us survive even the harshest climates when we need to."

They finished the rest of their meal in silence, but Brin had one last thing she needed to ask Gadjet before they got some much-needed rest.

"Gadjet, can you tell me a little more about what we're walking into? You told me the Fallen Star is involved, but not much more than that."

"You're right. You need to know what's waiting for us at the end of this trip." Gadjet sat down across the fire from Brin, with her one hand resting in her lap. "The Fallen Star brought in about a hundred people, who are all camping in the ruins just outside the Heart Forge. They've created a clear separation from my tribe, so to get to the Heart Forge, we'll have to go through my people first, and then through the Fallen Star camp."

"Is there a way to get around them into the Heart Forge?" Brin asked.

Gadjet shook her head. "There's only one way in, and it's been sealed off for centuries by a falling flow of lava and big stone doors that are locked shut. The Fallen Star were getting close to figuring out how to open it before I left, and I heard they were communicating with someone on the inside."

Brin furrowed her brow. "Inside? How could someone be inside if it's been sealed for centuries?"

"That's just what I heard," Gadjet said with a shrug. "But what's important is what they're planning to do when they get the door open. Since the tether that kept the Flame anchored in Midral shattered, the Flame is slowly returning to the Heart Forge. As it gathers, they're going to have Priests working to corrupt the Flame at the source. If they succeed, it might take away the dwarves' ability to channel Niradim's magic."

"That would leave Midral even weaker than it already is," Brin said. "And it would prevent us from rebuilding the defenses we had in place. Most of the forges were already operating at limited capacity. If the Flame completely returns to the Heart Forge, it means we won't be able to forge mythril or any of the other magical weapons and armor we use to defend ourselves."

Brin's heart sank. So, they didn't have much time to figure out a solution.

"So, what does any of this have to do with Ronan?" Brin asked.

Gadjet took a deep breath and let it out slowly. "They want him to forge a new Mythril Soul. I don't know why they need one, but until an opportunity presented itself to capture the Phoenix, they were planning on attacking Midral for the one we're carrying."

Brin's hands moved protectively over the Mythril Soul tucked away in her pack. "So we're bringing them exactly what they want? We should have left it back in Midral!"

"The Phoenix is creating a new one for them anyway," Gadjet countered. "We need this one to stop the Priests from corrupting the Heart Forge. We had to bring it!"

"But what if Ronan refuses?" Brin said. "What if he—"

She cut herself off as the truth dawned on her. No, Ronan wouldn't refuse—not if they threatened to attack Midral. Ronan would do anything to protect Niradim's people. Slag and ashes, this was *bad*.

"It looks like you came to the same conclusion I did," Gadjet said.

Brin took a deep breath. "Yes, you're right. Ronan would work with them if it had a chance of keeping Midral safe. They will have what they need, regardless of whether we bring this one to them."

"Thank you," Gadjet said, tension visibly releasing from her body. "You're more level-headed than the Elders would have been, had I been allowed to explain this to them."

"Yeah, you're probably right," Brin said. "Okay, so then what's the plan? How are we supposed to get through a camp full of draken and cultists to save the Flame? Because even if we make it to the Heart Forge, there's too many of them to guard it ourselves. We can't just shut the door again if they've figured out how to open it."

"I have a plan to get my tribe to fight for our side," Gadjet said.

Brin waited for the rest of her response, but that seemed to be it, so she prodded. "And that plan is?"

Gadjet looked away from Brin. "I'd... rather not say. I have to ask you to trust me on this."

Brin sighed. That was not ideal. She didn't want to go into such a dangerous situation without knowing Gadjet's plan, but she'd gone too far to turn back now.

"Ok Gadjet," Brin said. "I'll trust you. Let's get some rest. It sounds like we're going to need it."

11

Ronan

"It is time," Dak'thor said as he unlocked Ronan's cage.

Ronan was already up and ready to go. He didn't know what was in store for him today, but it was hard to sleep when he knew this was the final day of the Phoenix Trial.

Ronan stepped out of his prison and nodded to the draken. "Thanks, Dak'thor."

Dak'thor shook his head. "You should not be thanking me for this, Phoenix."

Ronan shrugged. "It's just the way I am, I guess." He smiled up at the large draken, who returned the smile. They walked in silence for a few moments before Dak'thor spoke up.

"I did not thank you for what you did yesterday," Dak'thor said.

Ronan furrowed his brow. "What do you mean?"

"I have given it much thought, and I believe you have saved my life," Dak'thor said as they walked. "If you had not stopped me, I would have lashed out at the novaborn. And he would have killed me with ease. So you have saved my life. I am in your debt, though I do not know how I will repay you in our current circumstances. For that, I am sorry, Phoenix."

"It's okay, Dak'thor," Ronan said. "I understand the position you're in. You're trying to protect your tribe. It's the same reason I'm working with them—to protect my people."

Dak'thor nodded in agreement. "This is true. But I still wish it were not so. If there is an opportunity for me to repay your kindness, I will look for it."

Agent Steel met them at the border between the two camps and took Ronan from there. Dak'thor lingered long enough for Ronan to notice the battle of emotions the draken was dealing with before he turned to head back into the draken camp.

Steel began to lead them towards the Heart Forge, where he'd inevitably hand him off to Falrose. He still wouldn't go near his old prison. "I hope you're ready for the end of your trial, little Phoenix. Today, you determine the fate of your people. I have to admit, it would entertain me greatly to see you fail. It has been ages since I've been able to let loose."

Ronan could tell Steel was trying to get under his skin. Frustratingly, it was working, but two could play at that game.

"Well, if I fail, I'll be in good company. Wouldn't you say, Steel?" Ronan asked with a smirk. "How many times did you fail before betraying your people? Twice? Or was it three times? I forget."

Agent Steel spun, eyes blind with fury, and backhanded Ronan to the ground. His right arm split into two, and they both grabbed one of his greatswords from his back as he loomed over Ronan.

He pointed the enormous blade at Ronan. "You should shut your mouth before it gets you into trouble, little Phoenix. You speak of things you know nothing about."

Ronan spat some blood out of his mouth and rose to a knee, looking up at Steel towering over him. "I don't know why Ashe ever thought you could pass the Trial. It's clear you only ever cared about the power, and nothing else."

Steel raised the greatsword over his head and slammed it down toward Ronan. Ronan rolled backwards and raised his cuffed hands in the air above him. The greatsword slammed into the cuffs, shattering them—and Ronan's wrists—in the process. But as soon as the cuffs came off, Ronan felt his connection to Niradim flood his senses, and he healed his wrists as he got to his feet.

Warm power coursed through him, and he somehow felt even stronger this close to Niradim's original forge. Of course, he was still unarmed and facing down an irate man made entirely of mythril. And that's not even considering Steel was wielding a greatsword so large that Ronan probably couldn't even lift it, so he was at a distinct disadvantage.

As Steel stalked closer, a voice sounded from the Heart Forge. "That will be enough, Steel. I'll take it from here." A sinister grin spread across Falrose's face. "Unless you'd like to accompany Ronan into the forge itself?"

Agent Steel growled and looked back at Falrose over his shoulder. "You should show more respect for your elders, Agent Falrose. You may be Celestian's *newest* toy, but I was one of the first."

"Yes, yes," Falrose said, waving a hand dismissively. "Regardless, at least wait one more day before you bisect our dear Phoenix here. We still need him."

Ronan considered his options. Part of him wanted to fight it out right here, but his death would only cause them to revert to their plan of invading Midral, and he couldn't let that happen. If he thought fighting his way out of this was an option, he'd gladly take it if it gave him a chance to return to Midral to prepare them for an attack. But there was no way he'd be able to fight off two Agents, much less the droves of minions they'd brought with them, in his condition. So he stood up and stopped channeling Niradim's power in a show of surrender.

Falrose noticed and inclined his head toward Ronan. "It was unwise of you to antagonize our dear senior citizen, but at least you have enough brains to know when you can't win. Try any other stunts and I will allow Agent Steel to punish you as he sees fit, even if it forces us to procure a Mythril Soul the hard way."

Ronan sighed and walked past Agent Steel, who stared daggers at him. He fell into step with Falrose heading toward the Heart Forge. It was time to finish the Trial.

* * *

Over 1000 years ago

"What do you mean you left one of our Mythril Souls with them?!" Ashe yelled.

Clash and Steel had just returned from Lumenova with the most recent batch of volunteers to accept the Star Crystals. Cinder and Saber were out on missions, so it was only the three of them in the council chamber today. Clash wished he was anywhere else.

"They are simply borrowing it so they can refine the process," Steel said cooly. "A dozen of us have already benefited from the Star Crystals, but what if there were a way for us to use both Niradim's power *and* Celestian's power? Think of how strong we'd be!"

"Steel—those are precious!" Ashe said. "We can't afford to just loan them out! Who did you even get to agree to give up their Mythril Soul?"

Clash raised his hand. "I volunteered mine." Hopefully, he could soothe things before this conversation got too out of hand. "I'm sorry Ashe, perhaps I should have notified you first, but we've been trading so much mythril with them for access to the Star Crystals, and they said they'd renegotiate for more favorable terms if we allowed them access to a Mythril Soul for testing until we return."

Ashe's head snapped to Clash, and the force of her glare almost made him take a step back. "Clash, what were you thinking?!"

"Well, we don't need them as desperately as we used to, right?" He gestured to the other Mythril Souls lying atop the Great Anvil. "I mean, we still have the other three to use, but with twelve mythrali now wielding power that rivals one of our Disciples, we're stronger than ever. I figured we could afford to lend one out for a short time to get a better deal in the long run. They were crippling our mythril supplies, Ashe!"

Ashe buried her head in her hands. "We could have just stopped trading with them. We didn't have to agree to *this*."

"What, and deny the other mythrali access to magic?" Steel cut in. "Why do you seek to limit our power at every turn, Ashe? Is it because you no longer have to share yours?"

Ashe's head snapped in his direction. "Oh, that's ridiculous, Steel, and you know it. I willingly shared my Mythril Soul with any Disciple who had need of it before I was a Phoenix. And to remind you *again*, I have already proven that there is a path to getting power that is permanent without having to seek it out elsewhere. Besides, I don't think it's right that people should be able to obtain such power without having to earn it and prove they deserve it."

"Deserve it according to who? You?" Steel asked.

"Of course not!" Ashe threw her arms up in exasperation. "Niradim has always made the decision."

Steel sneered at her. "Yes, and you are the one who keeps the secret of passing the Trial to yourself!"

"There is no secret, Steel!" Ashe yelled back at him. "You're either ready, or you're not! I'm sorry you failed your Trial multiple times, but let me make it *perfectly* clear to you—that was nobody's fault but your own!"

"And yet, here I am, stronger than ever, and I've done nothing but make our people's lives better!" Steel pointed a finger in her face. "What have you done, Ashe? Fly around with your fancy sword and kill some monsters that barely threaten us? Well now I've made your job obsolete because the people can defend themselves, and I think you're jealous that they don't need you as much as they used to."

Ashe was visibly seething at this point, her eyes wide with anger. Clash sensed that Steel had hit a nerve with that last statement. It was time to step in.

"Peace, you two," Clash said. "Ashe, they are only borrowing the Mythril Soul for as long as it took us to bring back the latest mythrali that had accepted the Star Crystals, and return with the next batch and *much smaller* payment of mythril ore. We can pack that up and take the next group of volunteers today if we need to, and I'll collect the Mythril Soul as soon as we arrive."

Ashe and Steel locked eyes with an intensity that seemed to electrify the air between them. Clash thought they were on the verge of attacking each other before Ashe finally broke the deadlock. "Fine. But don't you *ever* do this again without consulting the council." With that, she picked her sword up from the anvil, restoring it to pristine condition, and stormed out of the room.

"Well, that went better than expected, I'd say!" Steel clapped Clash on the back. "Thanks for the support back there."

"I still don't feel great about it, Steel," Clash said. "But I do agree that our people deserve the power to defend themselves. Besides, there's no way I was going to let us keep paying those prices for the Star Crystals."

"Indeed, I think what you've done may be the greatest thing to ever happen to the mythrali," Steel said.

Clash wished he felt the same.

* * *

Within a few short days, Clash stood next to Steel back in the Grand Observatory of Lumenova speaking with Sola and Galar.

Galar welcomed them with open arms as they arrived. "And how are the most recent volunteers faring with their newfound powers?"

"Wonderful, as always!" Steel said as he clasped hands with the novaborn. "We've brought a full six this time!"

"Fantastic!" Sola said. "We weren't expecting so many. It will take a few more days to get things ready for them."

Steel waved his hand in the air. "Not a problem, my friends, we can wait."

"Umm," Clash said, cutting in. "I wanted to ask about the Mythril Soul we left in your care. You said we could collect it upon our return."

"Oh yes, of course!" Galar said. "I'll go fetch it right now while Sola explains what we've been able to accomplish. It's very exciting!" Galar practically ran out of the room to collect it.

Clash turned to Sola as Galar left. "What does he mean?"

Sola's eyes lit up with excitement. "Oh, we were able to conduct some very interesting research! As we suspected, we believe we've found a way to grant an individual both Niradim's magic and Celestian's magic *simultaneously!*"

"Is that so?" Steel asked, perking up. "I would love to try out this new method. Is it ready to be tested?"

"Well, yes, but it won't work on anyone who has already integrated a Star Crystal." Sola pointed to the latticework of crystals on Steel's chest. They'd grown deeper into his body, expanding from the center of his chest as he grew in power over time. "The Star Crystals are embedded in your body in a way that's permanent. We can't remove them to integrate this new creation."

Steel instantly deflated. "But don't worry, my friend," Sola reassured him. "We are working on other ways to enhance your already impressive powers. In time, your power may grow beyond what a

Starsoul can do, because you won't have to rely on the delicate balance between the two powers."

Steel looked down at his hands and grinned. "Well, I like the sound of that."

"Is it dangerous?" Clash asked.

"We don't believe so-" Sola started before Galar rushed back into the room.

"Here it is!" Galar came to a halt in front of them, breathing heavily. "Behold—the Starsoul!"

He removed the cloth covering the bundle in his arms and revealed Clash's Mythril Soul, or at least what it had become. The Starsoul crackled with violet energy, and with an almost-white light that had the slightest purple tinge to it.

"Wait, you modified the Mythril Soul *itself*?" Clash asked in surprise. Ashe really wasn't going to like this. "I thought you were only using this for research! Can this be undone?"

"Undone?" Sola asked. "Why would you want to do that? We've enhanced it!"

This was a nightmare. Why did he agree to this? This left them with only three pure Mythril Souls back in Midralen. What would that mean for the mythrali who weren't comfortable with this new power and only wanted to use Niradim's? They'd only be able to share three now.

Clash's head fell and his shoulders slumped. "Ashe was right. We never should have left it here."

"Calm down, Clash," Steel said, putting a hand on his shoulder. "You heard them. They enhanced it! It still contains a Soul Flame, which will grant Niradim's magic, but they've added Celestian's magic to it as well. It's marvelous!"

Clash pushed Steel's hand off his shoulder and turned to look at his companion. "Steel, we didn't agree to this. There were only a few

Mythril Souls to begin with, and now this one may not even work anymore for all we know!"

"Pardon," Galar cut in. "But if you're willing, we can test it right now."

"That's a good idea," Steel said. "They have already integrated Star Crystals into plenty of mythrali, so there's no reason to believe this won't work. At least try it before you criticize, Clash. You said you were holding out on accepting a Star Crystal so you could attempt your Phoenix Trial. Well, this won't prevent you from being able to take the Trial. If this doesn't work, or you don't like it, just take it out."

Clash looked at the crackling energy of the Starsoul. Ashe was going to have his metal for this, he just knew it. But Steel might be right. If it worked, and he could channel both Niradim's power *and* Celestian's, then this was a net-gain for the mythrali. It was already done, and it wouldn't be right to ask someone else to test the Starsoul. They had used *his* Mythril Soul for the experiment, and so it should be *his* responsibility to test what they had created. So, reluctantly, he agreed.

Clash sighed. "Okay, let's test it. But to be clear, I am not happy that you made these modifications without our prior consent. I'm going to take this into consideration when we renegotiate our contract."

"Apologies." Sola bowed her head. "It won't happen again, I assure you." She straightened and held out the Starsoul for Clash. "Now, you can place the Starsoul into your chest just like you would with a Mythril Soul, but you should have access to both sets of power instead of one."

Clash carefully picked up the Starsoul and inspected it. Taking a deep breath to steady himself, he placed the glowing orb into his chest, and it locked into place. Immediately, a hot bolt of new power shot through him. It wasn't the normal warmth of Niradim's power, but the heat of a star that surged within his body, almost painfully. Purple lightning sparked around him for a few moments until the energy stabilized and settled within his body.

He stood up straighter and looked at the rest of them. Raw energy vibrated through him, discordant from the two opposing sources, but powerful indeed. This technology would change things. The mythrali would reach new heights with this, he knew it instantly.

"How do you feel, Clash?" Steel asked.

Why hello, Clash. I've been looking forward to meeting you, something said in his mind. *Let's change the world.*

"Amazing," was all Clash said out loud. "I feel... amazing."

* * *

One year later

"This is wonderful, Steel," Clash said as they strode through Midralen. "Nearly half of the mythrali have been outfitted with a Crystal Star, and there is only one Mythril Soul left to enhance."

Steel huffed. "Ashe may pose a problem. You know she still doesn't believe we should have enhanced the other three."

"Cinder, Saber, and I have all successfully converted our Mythril Souls into Starsouls, and we've all voted—this is the new way forward for the mythrali." Clash pushed open the doors to the Council chamber. "If Ashe still respects the Council as she claims, she'll have to give us the last Mythril Soul. Besides, she's out on assignment, so if she has any complaints, it'll already be too late."

They walked into what they thought would be an empty chamber, only to find Ashe standing behind the Great Anvil, waiting for them. The final Mythril Soul rested in a slot on top of the anvil in front of her, with her sword resting behind it, crusted in ash as it always was when it wasn't on her person.

Ashe nodded to the two of them. "Clash. Steel. A pleasure to see you both."

"Ashe," Clash said, abruptly coming to a halt. "I thought you were dealing with the giant incursion to the east."

"Yes, I was. Fortunately, that took less time than I thought, and Midralen was only a quick flight back." She flared her fiery wings behind her to make her point and then let them dissipate. "What, may I ask, brings you here if you suspected I was away?"

So it came to this. Clash had hoped they'd be able to avoid this conversation, but it looked like Ashe was being stubborn as always. He crossed his arms. "We held a vote."

"A vote?" Ashe raised one eyebrow. "Without me?"

"You weren't necessary for the vote, because the vote was unanimous," Clash said.

"That's not how we've always done it," Ashe said.

Steel grinned. "Well, times are changing, Ashe. Despite your best efforts."

She glared back at him. "You can't have the last Mythril Soul."

So, she *did* know what they had planned. This would make things even more difficult.

"I knew you would try to hoard it for yourself," Steel said, pointing at her.

Clash took a step forward. "That's not your decision to make, Ashe."

She regarded him for a long moment without speaking. The pause gave Clash time to notice the state she was in. She was tired. What had started as simple debates a year ago about how to proceed after the discovery of the Starsoul had evolved to the brink of a civil war—separating the mythrali into two groups with contrasting ideologies.

Her stance had always been to cease trading with the novaborn and return their focus to Niradim, but too many of the mythrali had grown frustrated with Niradim's leadership and craved the power Celestian freely gave when they saw the results of the Star Crystals and Starsouls. The feud had taken its toll on her, especially after Cinder and Saber had taken and failed the Phoenix Trial and decided to enhance their Mythril Souls. She was still the only mythrali who'd ever passed the Trial.

"What happened to you, Clash?" Ashe asked. "You never used to be like this. Ever since you took the Starsoul, you've changed. You've pushed others to take Star Crystals, you convinced the other Disciples to give up their Mythril Souls, and you've completely abandoned any notion of taking the Phoenix Trial."

It was true. Shortly after returning with the Starsoul, he'd attempted the Phoenix Trial and failed like all the others. Since then, he'd left the Star embedded in his chest longer and longer, until he'd stopped taking it out altogether.

"I finally saw that Niradim put too many pointless obstacles in our way," Clash said. "This way is much better. Celestian talks to his followers, giving us guidance on how to live our lives. Why can't Niradim just give us the answers to our questions? That would make things so much easier. But he doesn't. He claims to love us, but instead of giving us his blessings, he's a silent god, leaving us to fend for ourselves in a harsh world. And we're tired of it."

"Do you even hear yourself? Niradim has always blessed us through our *faith*," Ashe said. "It's not faith if we're just given all the answers. He's laid out a path for us, Clash. There is a reason he doesn't just give away his power to anyone who wants it."

He was not going to get dragged into a lengthy debate with her on this. "Ashe, we're taking the Mythril Soul. The Disciples all agree, so it's four against one." He reached out his hand to take the Mythril Soul, but Ashe snatched it from the Anvil before he could.

"If you want it, you'll have to take it from me."

Clash unclipped his Anvil Hammer from his back. "Ashe, don't do this."

Ashe scoffed as she studied her old disciple and shook her head. "You think I'm going to fight you? I thought I taught you better than that, Clash." She picked up her sword, which flared to life at her touch, and slammed it point-first down into the center of the Great Anvil. The sword sank deep into the anvil, almost to the hilt.

When she let go, the sword immediately crusted over with ash. "I forged this blade to protect our people. It will never be used against a mythrali."

"Come on, Ashe, just give us-"

"This is taking too long," Steel said. His Star Crystal flashed with violet light and with one swift motion, he plunged one of his greatswords into Ashe's chest. Her eyes went wide with surprise at the sudden betrayal.

"You have no idea how long I've been wanting to do that," he whispered in her ear before yanking the blade free. She clutched her chest and stumbled before falling to the ground. The Mythril Soul rolled out of her limp hand.

"Steel!" Clash yelled. "What have you done?"

"Oh, come on, Clash. You were the first to draw your weapon," Steel replied, pointing to the glowing weapon Clash was holding. "How did you think this was going to end?"

Clash looked down at the massive hammer in his hands, already pulsing with power as if ready for a fight. He didn't even realize he'd called upon his power.

"Not like this..." Clash said.

"Well, what's done is done." Steel picked up the Mythril Soul and tucked it away. "Now, I'm going to take this to Lumenova to get it converted into a Starsoul. Cinder and Saber are working on a special project at the Heart Forge that they'll need your help with. When I get back, we can celebrate ushering in a new era of power for the mythrali!"

He turned and put his hand on Ashe's sword and tugged on it, trying to pull it from the anvil, but it wouldn't budge. He gave Ashe one last look and snarled before turning and leaving.

"Clash..." Ashe said. He didn't know how she was still alive. He walked over to her and knelt by her side.

"Ashe, I didn't mean for this to happen," Clash said, tears forming in his eyes.

"Clash, I need you to remember who you were..." Ashe said. "Who you were before Celestian's power poisoned your mind... Protect Niradim's people, Clash... *our* people... That's what matters most..."

How had it come to this? She was right. He had succumbed to Celestian's influence. At times, he could hear Celestian in his mind, and he even saw him in the occasional dream. His opinions and morals had changed—slowly at first—but then quicker the longer he held the Starsoul in his chest. He'd strayed so far from his path. Maybe there was still time to make it right.

"I'll try," Clash said. "If they won't follow me, maybe they'll follow your sword." He reached up to take her sword, but it wouldn't budge for him either.

Ashe coughed. "Only a Phoenix can wield that blade, Clash... It won't work for you.

Clash dropped to his knees next to her. "Then how am I supposed to fix this? I need the sword to be worthy enough to save our people."

Ashe looked up at him and reached up to gently touch his face. A gentle smile curled at the edges of her mouth.

"A sword is just a sword, Clash," Ashe whispered. "Until... someone..."

Her hand dropped to the ground before she could finish. The light slowly faded from her eyes, and she went still.

Clash held her body and wept.

* * *

Present

Ronan was knocked out of the vision by a violent kick in the face. He looked up to see Falrose standing over him, gloating while holding the Mythril Soul Ronan had created.

"Wakey wakey, Mr. Phoenix," Falrose said. "Consider your Trial over."

"What?" Ronan said, wiping fresh blood from his face. "The Trial wasn't done! What are you doing?"

Falrose held up the empty Mythril Soul. "We have what we need. There's no reason for you to continue. Steel's instructions say that if you successfully completed your Trial, it would fill the Mythril Soul with a Soul Flame. Well, that would just create extra work for us, and nobody wants that. This empty vessel is perfect for us to fill with a power that will create something a little different from your typical Mythril Soul."

Ronan didn't like where this was going.

"We call it a Starsoul."

12

Brin

Seven years ago.
"Good morning, my little sweet bun," Brin's mother, Bellina, whispered as she gently nudged her daughter awake. "I need some help at the market today. Would you keep me company?"

Brin rolled onto her back with a groan, squinting her tired eyes to look up at her mother. She was kneeling next to the lumpy mattress, if you could even call it that, lying on the ground where Brin slept. There wasn't even a hint of light outside.

Brin pulled the thin sheet over her head and yawned. "Can I sleep just a little longer?"

"Not if we want to get the best groceries!" Bellina exclaimed.

"I'm too tired." Brin rolled over and adjusted one of the lumps under her hip. "Just go without me."

Bellina got to her feet and dusted off her skirt. "Well, if you're sure." She turned and began walking away. "What a shame. I heard Dorna has a new breakfast meat pie stuffed with eggs, potatoes, and sausage that sounded really tasty…"

Brin had already thrown off the covers and was stumbling into a pair of boots before her mother finished her sentence. She was not about to miss a new meat pie from her favorite place, especially a breakfast one! "Can I get two?"

"Yes, my little sweet bun, you can get two," Bellina chuckled. "Let me comb and braid that mess of hair on your head. We can spare a few minutes before we head out."

"No, I don't like the braids, Mom," Brin said, tying her hair up in a quick ponytail. She hated how young the braids made her look. She was growing up—it was time to change. Besides, she didn't want to get picked on again by the other girls at school.

"Oh, but I love it when you and your mother have the same hairstyle," Brin's father said as he entered her room.

"None of the other girls do their hair like their mothers," Brin said, matter-of-factly.

"Yes, well, none of them have mothers as amazing as yours," he replied, giving her mother a quick kiss as she and Brin exited her room. Bellina blushed at the compliment.

"Oh, stop, Delvin!" she said before planting a bigger kiss on him.

"Eww, you two are gross!" Brin tugged on her mother's arm. "Come on, Mom, we have to go get those meat pies!"

Both of her parents laughed. Her mother gathered a few coins—they didn't have much—and a basket to carry any purchases they made.

"Take care, you two," her father said. "How long will you be out?"

"Well, the Festival of Fire is happening today, and it's been a while since we've had a girls day…" Bellina turned to her daughter and raised an eyebrow. "Maybe we'll stay out late and have fun at the festival, what do you think, Brillenia?"

"Yes!" Brin squealed. Festivals meant food, and lots of it.

"Well then, we will see you tonight, my love," Bellina said with one last quick kiss.

Delvin waved as they left. "Have fun!"

BRIN

* * *

The festival was amazing as always, even though the Acolyte who had attempted the Shaping Trial failed. It just meant they'd continue to train and study in Niradim's faith and come back to try again. Most people didn't pass on their first try.

The vendors had outdone themselves on the food this year, too. More and more people were coming from further away to take part in the festivities, and it meant that Brin got to try all kinds of food from other cultures.

She'd tried some fantastic fried balls on a stick that were an ancient draken delicacy, or so the vendor claimed. Some florians were selling these little rolls, stuffed with fried vegetables—she must have had 5 of them before her mother cut her off. She loved every minute of their day, but eventually the vendors began to close up their shops, and they had to go.

"Did you have fun on our little mother-daughter day?" Bellina asked her as they shuffled through the crowds on their way out.

"So much fun, Mom," Brin said, beaming. "The food was delicious!"

Bellina chuckled and patted Brin on the head. "You do always love the food. Now, let's head home before it gets too late. You know how your father worries."

"Why didn't Daddy come with us today?" Brin asked.

Bellina held out her hand, and Brin took it. "He was on assignment, patrolling one of the other parts of the city. Most of the Protectors had to work today because of the festival."

Brin looked up at her mother. "But you didn't have to work?"

"No, I was lucky this year," Bellina said. "I got to spend the day with my wonderful daughter!"

Brin smiled. She could give her parents a hard time sometimes, but she loved them so much. Both of them served as Protectors, so

Brin rarely got to spend time with both of them at the same time. Sometimes she wished they did something else so they could spend more time as a family, like her friends did with theirs. She didn't know what she wanted to do when she grew older, but she thought she might pick something different from the path her parents took. Maybe she'd be a chef or a baker, something that involved food and wouldn't make her travel too much.

The crowds thinned as they left the Court of Fire. The Dawnstars lived pretty far away from the Earth Sector, very close to the outer walls where the homes weren't as nice. Brin knew it was all they could afford, but she didn't mind too much.

"Mom," Brin asked. "Are you ever going to do the Shaping Trial to become a Disciple?"

"Actually, I did try it once, when I was younger," Bellina said. "I didn't pass, and decided I didn't want to try it again."

Brin's eyes widened in surprise. "You didn't pass? But Daddy always says you're so strong!"

"I *am* strong!" Her mother laughed and poked her in the side. "But that's not all there is to it, my little sweet bun. I think Niradim knew I wanted something different for my life. I've always wanted a family, and being a Disciple is a lot of responsibility that would make that a lot harder. Shortly after I failed, I met your father, and the rest is history."

"So you're not upset you failed?" Brin asked.

"No." Bellina smiled and looked up at the night sky as they walked. "In fact, it's probably the best thing that's ever happened to me. If I'd passed, I'd probably be far from home, with no husband or daughter to fill every day with joy like I have now."

Brin gave her mother a hug. Yes, her parents weren't too bad at all.

After several more minutes of walking, Brin noticed the streets were mostly empty. The moon wasn't out, so they only had light from some of the magical torches that were spread throughout the city.

Unfortunately, the further they got from the Earth Sector, the less light there was. Their part of town didn't always get repairs as quickly as some of the more frequently visited areas.

Suddenly, Brin noticed her mother become more alert, and her grip on Brin tightened ever so slightly as they walked.

"Brin." Her mother's voice was calm, but serious. "Do you know the quickest way home from here?"

"Yes, if I turn down the alley here, it's just a couple more blocks, but shouldn't we stay on the road?" Brin was starting to suspect that something bad was happening. "What's wrong, Mom?"

"Nothing, sweetie," Brin's mother said reassuringly. "Everything's going to be okay. There are some people following us I don't recognize. It's probably fine, but I'd rather be safe than sorry. Let's turn down that alley and then we'll hurry along to get home, okay?"

"Okay." Brin's heart began to race as they approached the alley. As soon as they'd turned out of sight of the people behind them, Brin's mother picked up the pace. She wasn't running, but Brin still had a hard time keeping up with her.

They were about to emerge from the other side of the alley when a shadowed figure stepped out to block their path. Bellina was already holding on to Brin's arm, so she turned them both around and started back the way they came, but the two that had been following them turned the corner and blocked their way back.

Brin's breathing quickened as fear took her. Her mother squeezed her hand and turned to her. "It's okay, sweet bun, just breathe. It's going to be okay. I'll take care of you." She knelt down and took Brin's head in her hands. "I'm going to distract them. As soon as I do, I want you to run home as fast as you can, okay? Go get your father. Do you understand, Brin?" Brin nodded, but she was trembling as the figures closed in on them.

"Looks like you ladies have gotten a little lost," one of them said. He had a deep black beard with gaudy jewelry woven throughout. Bellina moved Brin behind her and backed them up against the wall as the three men closed in around them. "Perhaps we can lend the two of you a hand." The other two laughed in response.

"Thank you for the kind offer, but my husband just finished his shift with the Protectors, and he's waiting for us. In fact, there he is now." She pointed to one side of the alley, and the thugs turned their heads to look.

As soon as they did, Brin's mother tackled two of them to the ground and screamed, "Run, Brin!"

Brin did as she was told and started running to the end of the alley that would take her to safety. But her fear and adrenaline got the better of her, and she stumbled and crashed to the ground. She recovered quickly and got her feet under her. The sound of her mother wrestling with the thugs echoed off the alley walls behind her, but she didn't dare look back. She had to get to her father as fast as possible.

Just before she could turn onto the street, a powerful arm grabbed her and hauled her back into the alley. The man with the beard pinned her against the wall, easily overpowering her as she struggled in his grasp. Her ribbon fell out of her hair and across her face as her cheek pressed into the cold, hard stone.

"Now where do you think you're going, little one?" She could smell the alcohol on his breath as he whispered into her ear. "We're not done with the two of you yet."

Her heartbeat hammered in her ears, and her vision was going dark around the edges as fear paralyzed her. She struggled to get enough air into her lungs. What were they going to do to her? To her mother? The world around her fuzzed, and she couldn't focus on anything as she fought to stay conscious.

The sound of the others struggling stopped, and Brin vaguely heard footsteps approaching through the haze she was in. She whimpered—

tears streaming down her face. This was it. The footsteps got louder and faster as they neared. She felt the man pinning her turn his head in confusion. "What-"

Something powerful slammed into him from the side, and Brin was released from his grip. Her mother caught her before she hit the ground.

"Don't you *dare* ever lay a finger on my daughter again," she growled at the bearded man sprawled out on the ground in front of her, clutching his head and groaning in pain.

Brin looked back into the alley and saw the other two thugs lying on the ground, unconscious but breathing. She gazed in awe at her mother. Bellina was a little dirty from the scuffle, and blood trickled from the corner of her mouth from a split lip, but she was otherwise unharmed. It was like the fight was barely an inconvenience.

Daddy was right—her mother was *very* strong.

Bellina brushed some dirt from her dress and wiped the blood from her mouth. "Now come along, Brin," she said, gently taking Brin's hand and leading her out of the alley. As soon as they were back on the road and found some light, she stopped and studied Brin's face. "Are you okay, honey? Are you hurt?"

"No, Mom, I'm okay." Brin jumped into her mother's arms and sobbed. They stayed like that for a moment until Brin got herself together. Her mother wiped the tears from Brin's face and took a new ribbon out of one of her pockets.

"Here you go, honey," her mother said as she gathered Brin's hair. "There we are—a ponytail just like you like it."

Brin sniffled and wiped her nose. "Hey, Mom?"

"Yes, my sweet bun?"

"Can you do my hair in braids before school tomorrow?" Brin asked. "You know, like yours?"

Bellina smiled.

"I would love to."

* * *

Present day.

The next day of travel was as uneventful as the first, with one major exception. Brin noticed a significant change in her access to Niradim's magic. Something was impeding her connection, almost as if it was being slowly choked off. She did not like the implications of that, and she forced herself forward at the fastest pace she could manage behind Gadjet.

Gadjet still didn't have any issues with the travel, and Brin couldn't help but be impressed with the small draken. As a dwarf, Brin was used to most people of other races being taller than her, especially draken—they averaged taller than most races, but they also had the largest difference of sizes as exemplified by Gadjet.

Gadjet was so different from the other draken Brin had met in so many ways. She was shorter even than Brin, but carried herself with the full poise, self-confidence, and authority of any draken she'd known. Maybe more so. Gadjet had a strength to her that Brin was coming to envy, and though she still didn't believe that Gadjet could possibly have felled a full grown dragon, she was coming to see that Gadjet was a lot more capable than Brin initially gave her credit for.

"We're getting close!" Gadjet yelled over her shoulder. "A couple more hours and we'll be there. You can see the volcano from here." She pointed to a smoking peak in the distance.

"Will they spot us at the entrance?" Brin called back.

"There are more than a dozen ways into the ruins," Gadjet replied. "We've never needed to guard any of them because of how remote this location is. We'll pick one at random, and I'm confident we'll get in without being spotted."

She had a point. This settlement was so far removed from the rest of the world, nobody would ever just accidentally stumble upon it. She hoped the Fallen Star would be similarly lax in their defenses. Now knowing about the entrances to the old Earth Sector that the draken tribe had kept secret, she figured they would probably keep many of the entrances into their own settlement secret from the Fallen Star as well.

Gadjet gracefully pulled herself over a large boulder, barely slowing as Brin struggled over the top of the same obstacle. It was remarkable how well the small draken traversed the difficult terrain.

"Gadjet, I hope you don't mind me saying," Brin said, catching up to Gadjet and falling into step with her. "It's really impressive how well you manage with only one arm. Is this how you were born?"

"No, I normally have two," Gadjet said, chuckling to herself. "But thank you for the compliment. My left arm was taken from me by Nivalthyr a long time ago, so I learned how to manage without it. At least until I made a replacement."

"You... made a replacement?" Brin asked. "How did you manage that?"

Gadjet shrugged. "I'm good at putting things together. Always have been. I found a lot of mythril ore around our settlement, and there was an arm I used as a blueprint. So, I took the mythril I found and forged a new arm for myself. It wasn't easy, but the result was amazing, if I do say so myself."

Brin placed her hand on Gadjet's shoulder, and they both stopped. "Okay, listen, I like you, Gadjet, and I don't know how you come up with some of these stories, but anyone with a basic knowledge of forging mythril will know you're lying. Forging mythril requires access to a forge powered by Niradim's Flame, and those are only found in the Earth Sector of Midral."

Gadjet smirked. "Well... let's just say that two days ago wasn't my first time in the Earth Sector."

"You expect me to believe that you snuck into the Earth Sector with enough mythril to forge an arm, and somehow secretly used somebody's forge without them knowing?" Brin asked. "You're crazy, Gadjet. Between this and your story about killing a dragon, I don't know which one I believe less. You have a wild imagination."

"How about we make a little bet then," Gadjet said with a glint of amusement in her eye. "When we get into the city, I will prove that both stories are true. And if I don't, I will supply you with as many of those little meat pies as your heart desires."

Brin's mouth began to salivate at the mere mention of meat pies, and she licked her lips. "Oh, you're on! Assuming we survive this mess, I can't wait for the feast you're going to bring me."

Gadjet held up a finger. "But *when* I prove both of those things, I want you to use Niradim's power to enhance my mythril arm, a set of armor, and my spear."

"Not that it's going to make a difference, since I'm definitely winning this bet," Brin said, "but I can only promise the arm and the armor. I'm not great with weapons."

"Then have the Phoenix do the weapon. You two are dating, right? I'm sure you can find some way to persuade him." She winked at Brin, who blushed at the comment.

"Okay fine, Gadjet," Brin said, laughing. "You have a deal. If you can prove that you killed a full-grown dragon, *and* that you forged a mythril arm, I will use Niradim's magic to enhance your arm and set of armor, and I'll have Ronan enhance the weapon."

Gadjet held out her hand, and Brin shook it.

They continued walking, and Brin placed a hand on her stomach. "Good thing I'm working up an appetite with this hike. I'm going to be nice and hungry by the time this is all done."

Gadjet only smiled as they continued on.

***

Sure enough, they didn't see any signs of life as they made their way into the volcano. The path was quick, and the temperature steadily increased as they delved deeper, much to Brin's relief.

The ruins themselves weren't as large as the Earth Sector of Midral, but they reminded her of her home. It was as if the Earth Sector had taken inspiration from this place when it was built. If this was where Niradim's Flame originated, then it made sense that the dwarves built the Earth Sector in a similar way when they migrated south to establish the city of Midral.

Something occurred to her that seemed strange now that they were here—why was Niradim's Flame moved to begin with? If Gadjet's story was correct, this is where the dwarves would have come from if the Heart Forge was here. So what caused them to pack up and move south? Maybe it was some kind of external attack? Gadjet had mentioned the draken were tasked with guarding the Heart Forge and that there was someone inside. Who was this person, and were they the reason the dwarves had moved? And why wouldn't the dwarves just guard it themselves?

If they were there under any other circumstances, she would have loved to research and discover as much about the history of this place as she could. But Ronan was here and needed her help. Nothing else mattered right now. Maybe someday they could find out what happened, and why the Flame had been relocated.

They found some high ground, and Brin finally got a good look at the situation. Gadjet pointed out the Heart Forge at the back of the settlement, and Brin's heart sank at the number of Fallen Star tents and cultists she saw walking around. There were definitely too many of them for Gadjet and Brin to take on themselves.

A little further out, she saw a lot of draken hanging about, looking bored. She didn't see any tents on their side, but the draken probably lived inside the ruins, as this was where they'd always lived. The only strange thing that stood out was a rectangular cage out in the open on the draken's side of the settlement. Brin couldn't guess what that was for, but the draken seemed to keep away from it.

On the far side of the settlement were more ruins, but the side where they'd entered was flattened in a large circle. Brin noticed there were actually scorch marks along some walls and nearby ruins, and she even saw the glint of what seemed to be broken dragon scales scattered around. Well, at least Gadjet hadn't been lying about a dragon living here.

They watched for a few minutes, and Brin gasped as she picked out a massive figure among the camps of the Fallen Star. It was hard to miss him, glittering in a full suit of armor with two enormous greatswords hanging across his back. That whole setup must have weighed a ton—how did he even move in that? She watched as he approached a group of cultists, exchanged a few words, and then picked one up by the neck and threw him over the edge of the ruins. Brin could hear the man's scream even at this distance as he plunged into the slow current of lava below. The rest of the group around the armored man scattered as the cries of agony slowly subsided.

"Gadjet," Brin whispered, almost as if she was afraid the man would hear them from across the settlement. "Who is that man?"

Gadjet shook her head. "I've never seen him before. He wasn't with the Fallen Star when I left. Maybe he's the one they freed from the Heart Forge? He is... frighteningly large. I think it would be best if we avoided him."

Brin nodded. He also matched the description of the armored man that had been plaguing Ronan's dreams. That couldn't be a good sign. But before she could follow that line of thought, the door to the Heart Forge opened, and out came the man she was here to save—Ronan

Flamestriker, the Phoenix of Niradim.

A smug-looking novaborn with orange-red skin and short black hair yelled something she couldn't hear to the armored man. Brin spotted something round in his hands before he retreated back to the Heart Forge. The armored man marched up to Ronan and picked him up by his collar, and Brin stiffened. Gadjet reached out her hand and placed it on Brin's shoulder. She wasn't sure if it was to steady her or hold her back.

As the man held Ronan up in the air, he walked toward the edge where he'd thrown the cultist off moments ago, and Brin's heart rate spiked.

Brin pushed Gadjet's hand off her shoulder and got to her feet. "I have to go!"

Gadjet grabbed her arm before she could rush off and pulled her back. "Hold on, Brin, wait." She pointed at Ronan. "Look, something's happening."

Brin shook Gadjet's hand off, but she looked up and saw that the novaborn had reemerged and was yelling at the armored man again. They argued for a moment, and then the man holding Ronan screamed in frustration and threw Ronan forty feet in the air towards the draken side of the settlement.

He walked over to Ronan, still lying on the ground, and kicked him in the ribs hard enough that Ronan slid five more feet before he slid to a stop, clutching his stomach. The man grabbed Ronan by the hair and dragged him across the ground before tossing him into the rectangular cage Brin had noticed earlier. Ronan slammed against the bars and fell still inside the cage.

Brin's hand went up to her mouth to stifle a scream that was threatening to escape. He had to be okay—he just had to be. They wouldn't have thrown him back in the cage if they were going to kill him. This was clearly just a man with anger issues taking them out on

Ronan.

The armored man stalked off, punching a draken on his way out. Brin heard a deep growl from behind her. Apparently, Gadjet had not liked that. Brin continued to watch Ronan for any signs of life, and to her relief, he finally rolled over onto his back—clearly in pain, but also definitely alive. Brin turned back to Gadjet, who was still staring daggers at the armored man. Smoke curled out from between her teeth, and her eyes flickered with draconic power as the growl deepened.

"Gadjet," Brin said. "Gadjet, snap out of it."

Gadjet looked at Brin and then back at the armored man. After a moment, Gadjet shook her head, and that murderous aura faded.

"I am going to make him pay for that," she snarled.

Suddenly, Brin saw a different side of Gadjet. A feral, protective predator who had just identified her prey. Her gaze was more intense, her focus—sharper. If there were a version of Gadjet that could kill a dragon, Brin had just caught a glimpse of it.

"We need to get Ronan out. Tonight," Brin said. "I don't know what they're doing to the Flame, but I can feel my connection to Niradim's power waning. If I'm going to heal him, it has to be before they finish whatever it is they're doing."

Gadjet took a deep breath. "I can get him out, but we need to wait for nightfall when there's less activity."

Brin didn't want to wait another moment, but Gadjet was right. They needed to wait for the cover of night if they had any chance of freeing him.

"Okay," Brin said. "But as soon as things have died down, we get him. Is there a place closer to him where we can take cover?"

Gadjet nodded. "I have a place we can wait. It's a place the rest of the tribe avoids, now that the Fallen Star has taken over."

"Why?" Brin asked.

"Because it reminds them of the promise they broke," Gadjet said. "It's too close to the Clash."

* * *

Gadjet led Brin carefully around the outside of the settlement. Far enough from the center that they didn't risk running into any wandering members of Gadjet's tribe. As they did, Brin began to get anxious. All she wanted to do was run to Ronan right now and break him out. But she held back, trusting Gadjet could accomplish what she said she'd be able to.

Gadjet led them to an abandoned building along the outskirts of the ruins. It was close enough that Ronan wouldn't have to go far to get to her, but far enough that the draken wouldn't stumble upon them by accident.

"Wait here," Gadjet said.

"Please hurry," Brin said. "I can feel the Flame dying. I don't know how much longer it will last."

"I'll do my best," Gadjet said, before she ducked out of the building toward Ronan's prison. Brin only hoped Ronan would be here in time for her to help.

It was excruciating waiting for Gadjet to rescue him. What if someone saw her? The cage was right in the middle of the settlement, so they wouldn't be able to hide. Her heart began to thud in her ears, and she struggled to get enough air into her lungs. She stood up and started pacing, but that only made it worse, and she started to get lightheaded.

She loosened the collar of her shirt and sat down, closing her eyes so she could focus on her breathing. It was a struggle with everything that was going on, but after a few frantic moments, the tightness in her chest loosened and her breathing normalized. She opened her eyes and felt a little fatigued from the panic attack, but overall she was feeling better. The thudding in her ears had died down, and the creeping darkness that had been encroaching on the edges of her vision withdrew.

Finally, she heard movement from outside and scrambled to her feet. Gadjet stepped through the door, followed by a very rough-looking Ronan.

"Brin!" Ronan said as soon as he saw her. He stumbled over to her, and she intercepted his steps before he fell and hurt himself further.

"Ronan," Brin said as she lowered him to the floor. "Sit. Now. I'm healing you immediately."

He nodded. He could feel the same thing she could—the Flame was barely holding on. They didn't have much time to pull this off.

She laid him on the floor as carefully as she could and focused. Niradim's Flame flickered on the edge of her senses, and she pulled it into herself, focusing on Ronan's injuries. Steam curled up from his wounds as they began to close. It was working—Ronan was going to be okay.

And then the power abruptly cut off. Ronan's eyes went wide with surprise as they met hers.

The corruption of Niradim's Flame was complete.

13

Ronan

Ronan looked up at Brin from the floor, struggling to breathe through the pain. At least a few of his ribs were broken, and from the way his shoulder was screaming in pain, he suspected it had been dislocated. They'd slapped another pair of those magical suppression cuffs on his wrists before locking him up, so Brin was his only hope of getting healed. For a brief moment, the healing magic washed over him before dissipating all at once.

The Fallen Star had accomplished their goal to corrupt the Flame, and he'd been powerless to stop it. What did this mean for their god? What would become of Niradim, now that Celestian's magic tainted the Flame? He stared up at the roughly hewn rock of the room's ceiling, contemplating his failure, when Brin spoke.

"I'm sorry, Ronan," Brin said. "I didn't get here in time."

Ronan's eyes snapped to Brin. "Hey, don't blame yourself. There's nothing you could have done."

He groaned as she helped him into a sitting position against the wall, each tiny movement bringing a fresh wave of pain. A heavy silence permeated the room as the weight of what had just happened settled over them.

Brin broke the silence first. "Was it like this the entire time?" She gestured at his wounds.

Ronan looked down at himself. Tattered clothes hung from his broken body after several days spent in captivity, caked in blood, sweat and dirt. Most of the blood was fresh, though.

"No, this is the worst of the physical abuse. I spent most of my time between the Heart Forge and the cage they kept me in." Ronan tilted his head toward Brin. "You'll never guess who's in charge."

Brin's expression darkened. "Oh, don't tell me Kyros is here. Although it would be nice to get a little payback for what that monster did to our home."

Ronan grunted in agreement, instantly regretting it as pain flared in his chest. "Close. Turns out our least favorite novaborn has a twin brother. His name is Falrose, and he's just as bad as Kyros, maybe worse if you can believe it. Though I gather the twins aren't exactly fond of each other."

Brin huffed. "Doesn't surprise me. Being a terrible person must run in the family." She shook her head. "Gadjet told me they wanted you to create a new Mythril Soul, is that true?"

Ronan nodded. "I spent my time in the Heart Forge taking the Phoenix Trial. Completing the Trial is supposed to create a new Mythril Soul."

"The Phoenix Trial? Is that like the Shaping Trial we took?" She'd perked up at the mention of it. That's right, Brin wouldn't know about the Phoenix Trial. This was going to be a lot for Brin to take in.

He slowly pushed himself further up the wall so he wasn't slouching as much before explaining. "Sort of. As you know, the Shaping Trial is the last step for us to become Disciples. We don't have a step after that." He paused and gathered himself. "But Niradim's first people, the mythrali, did."

Ronan watched as Brin processed the last thing he said, before she shot up to her feet.

"Wait, what!? Niradim created a people *before* the dwarves?"

"I was surprised too," Ronan said. "You saw the man who threw me back in the cage?" Brin nodded. "His name is Steel, and he's one of them—the last one. And as you could probably tell, he's working with the Fallen Star."

"The mythrali…" Brin said as she collapsed back to the ground. "Ashes, this is just crazy, Ronan. Were they all that huge? I don't know if I've ever met anyone big enough to wear that much armor!"

Ronan shook his head. "That's not armor. Niradim forged his first people from mythril itself."

Brin's jaw dropped.

His time in captivity, though only a few days, had felt like ages. He'd learned so much in that time that was still completely unknown to the rest of the world. An entire race of people was forged from Niradim's legendary metal itself. It was unheard of.

Brin didn't have a response for that, and he wondered how this must have felt to her. Until now, she'd assumed that the dwarves were the only race Niradim had created. One of her core beliefs had just been turned upside down.

"I've learned quite a bit about them during the Trial," Ronan said, attempting to jar her out of her stunned state. "For example—they didn't have access to Niradim's magic like the dwarves do."

Brin's mouth snapped shut, and her focus found Ronan again. "What do you mean?"

Ronan smiled to himself. He knew she'd be curious about that. "They couldn't channel Niradim's magic at all until they reached the rank of Disciple. Even then, they had to share Niradim's magic between them. Only four people could use Niradim's magic at a time, and only if they had one of four Mythril Souls, which they would place in their chest."

"Wow," Brin said. She lifted her arm, tapping a finger to her cheek as she thought. "So if that's how the Mythril Souls used to work, why would the Fallen Star want you to create a new one for them?"

"They need it to create something called a Starsoul, but I don't know what they're planning to do with it, and I don't want to find out," Ronan said. Brin lent him a hand as he struggled to his feet, grunting in pain with each slight jolt of movement. Ashes, he was in bad shape, but he couldn't afford to rest. He didn't know what the Fallen Star had planned, but they'd already done too much for Ronan's comfort. "We need to steal back the Mythril Soul I created. Thank Niradim the other one is still in Midral. If we can manage to get them both back there, we can keep them safe."

Brin shifted uncomfortably. "Umm, about that…"

She reached for her bag, shuffling things around slowly at first, then more frantically when she didn't immediately find what she was looking for. Eventually, she dumped out the contents of her bag before raising both hands to her head.

A pit began to form in Ronan's stomach. "What's wrong, Brin?"

"It was here just a moment ago…" Brin said. "Gadjet, have you seen-"

She stopped as she looked around at the empty room. Gadjet was gone. Neither of them had noticed the small draken sneak out amid the shock of the Flame's corruption.

Brin buried her face in her hands. "Oh, no…"

The pit in Ronan's stomach grew. Brin was trembling. "What's going on, Brin?"

"Ronan…" Brin started. "The Mythril Soul isn't in Midral. Gadjet and I brought it here with us."

"You what!?" he yelled, flinching as fresh pain tore through his broken ribs.

Brin's eyes widened at Ronan's sudden outburst. "She said it was the only thing that could purify the Flame!"

Ronan forced himself to calm down. There must be a reasonable explanation for this, even if he couldn't see it immediately. He needed to give Brin a chance to tell her side of things. "Okay, back up. Explain."

Brin told Ronan about how she met Gadjet, and the events at Niradim's Cathedral. Her decision to take the Mythril Soul, and how Druden had given the order to kill Gadjet in secret to keep her from telling her story. He was trying to give her a chance to justify her actions, but the more he heard, the more frustrated he became.

"So let me get this straight." Ronan said, hands clenched in the cuffs he still wore. "After you caught a draken stealing the Mythril Soul from Niradim's Cathedral, you decided it would be a good idea to *help her* deliver it straight to the Fallen Star? What were you thinking?!"

"I was *thinking* that I wanted to save you when nobody else would!" Brin's face was red and her fists were curled into tight balls by her side.

"You can't just put my well-being before everyone else's!" Ronan said. "I was willing to die to keep you all safe. Now, this has all been for nothing!"

"You can't seriously be mad about this," Brin scoffed. "I risked everything to come save you. I can't go back to Midral, Ronan." She placed a hand on her chest. "My home. I can never go back to my *home*."

"I didn't ask you to do that!" Ronan yelled, earning him a glare that caused him to look away. Those hadn't been the right words. He'd known it as soon as they'd left his mouth.

Ronan cleared his throat, breaking the uncomfortable silence. "So now your little draken friend has the Mythril Soul and is probably delivering it right to Falrose or Agent Steel."

Brin finally looked away and started nervously tugging on her braids. "I don't know. I just… I can't believe that she would do that. She must have some other reason she needs the Mythril Soul." Brin shook her head and wiped her eyes. "She hates them, Ronan. I saw the way she looked at them when they mistreated her tribe. She wouldn't help them."

"Unless they promised her something in return," Ronan said. "Or she was just a good liar. She could have used your feelings for me to manipulate you."

This was a nightmare. Ronan still didn't know why Falrose wanted to create a new Starsoul, but now he had two Mythril Souls to work with, and one of them contained the last pure spark of Niradim's Flame. And Brin had delivered it right to them. Brin was about to speak again when they heard some commotion outside the building.

"Ashes, they must have finally realized I escaped," Ronan said. "Brin, we need to move."

He looked over at her, but she wouldn't meet his eyes. Instead, she walked past him to the entrance of their hiding space.

"Let's hurry," she said. He could tell she was still mad at him, but they couldn't stay put. "We need to go deeper into the ruins, and you can't move as fast as usual. Maybe we can find some way to get those cuffs off you as we go."

Ronan nodded and pressed up against the wall next to Brin. She peeked her head out the door to make sure it was clear, and then led them deeper into the ruins, away from the draken camp.

He still couldn't believe what she'd done. Was she really that easily manipulated? She'd put all of Midral in danger by taking the Mythril Soul away from the Earth Sector. She should know him better by now. He'd gladly trade his life to keep the people of Midral safe.

But… was he really being fair? He needed to put himself in her shoes. If she had been captured, could he have left her to the whims of the Fallen Star? Would he have made the same decision if the tables were turned? Now, thinking about it, he wasn't as sure of himself. What would Niradim have wanted him to do?

He shook his head. Well, it didn't matter now. This was the mess they were in, and they needed to get out of it. Brin paused in the middle of an intersection between two paths to decide which way they should go, and he finally took the time to look at the surrounding buildings. There was something familiar about them...

Then it struck him. Of course it looked familiar! He'd been having visions of this place for the past three days. This was Midralen, and they were only a few streets over from the original Great Anvil. The council room would be a good place for them to rest and come up with another plan, and it should be far enough away from the main draken camp that they wouldn't be discovered.

Brin made up her mind and turned down one of the paths, but Ronan caught her arm to let her know that he'd had an idea. She turned, and Ronan's words died on his lips.

Her cheeks were stained with tears.

"What," she demanded, quickly wiping the tears away.

"Um, I was just going to say that I know of a place we can go," Ronan stumbled over his words. He hated seeing her cry—even worse that he'd been the cause of it. "Brin, I-"

"I don't want to hear it," Brin snapped. "Just lead the way, if you know where to go."

Ronan's gaze lingered on her a moment longer before he led them toward the council chambers. They moved as silently as they could through the ruined streets, stepping carefully over the rubble left from a millennium of abandonment and disrepair. It was difficult to navigate based only on Clash's memories, but enough of the original structures remained for Ronan to recognize where they were going. They could hear the draken behind them growing more distant. He didn't know if they were heading in this direction or not, but hopefully they'd be able to lose them.

After a few more minutes of travelling in uncomfortable silence, Ronan saw their destination up ahead. Unlike the rest of the buildings in the area, this one had been somewhat maintained. Ronan could see repairs in a few places to keep its structure mostly intact—it barely looked different than it had in his visions.

As they crept closer, they heard a noise coming from inside the building, and they glanced at each other. Someone was there. Ronan battled over what to do next. The tribe of draken were still behind them somewhere, so whoever was out here was probably on their own. Could they handle an enemy in the state they were in? Ronan was a broken shell of his former strength, so he'd only be a liability if it came down to a fight.

Still, there was something in the back of his mind pushing him in this direction. It wasn't just that it was the only familiar place he could think of for them to hide. There was a history in that room that he needed to see for himself. He took a step forward, but Brin caught his arm before he could go any further.

"What are you doing?" Brin hissed. "There's someone in there. We need to find somewhere else to hide."

"I can't explain it," Ronan said. "But I have this feeling that I need to go in there."

"Ronan, as you're already pointed out, I've made the incredibly stupid decision to come all this way to save you," Brin pushed a finger into his chest. "I'm not going to let you walk right into a trap and get captured again, even though you seem so *insistent* on sacrificing yourself when there are people who actually care about what happens to you. I don't care if you don't like what I did. I'm not sorry about it, and I would do it again."

"Brin... I'm sorry about my initial reaction." Ronan met her eyes. "I'm still not convinced you did the right thing, but I can admit that if our roles had been reversed, I don't know what I would have done. I've tried putting myself in your shoes, and it's a really tough decision. Wouldn't Niradim want us to protect Midral over saving one person?"

"It's not one or the other, Ronan. Midral is just a place. A place full of people—*strong* people—that can protect themselves or move if they need to." Brin let her hand drop. "Niradim would save the one in trouble. I know you would do the same, even if you don't know it yourself."

Ronan sighed to himself. He wasn't so sure she was right, but now was not the time for a religious debate. They needed to do something before someone discovered them.

"We can discuss this more later," Ronan said, getting them back on topic. "Let's get closer and see if we can figure out how many people are inside the building."

"Fine," she huffed. "But don't be a hero. If there's a threat in there, we leave."

He nodded. "Deal."

They snuck across the street up to the council building. Now that they were closer, Ronan could see a flicker of torchlight coming from the building. It also sounded like there was someone... crying? That was odd.

They lined up on either side of the door and peeked in. Brin gasped, and before Ronan could react, she drew her weapon and sprinted inside.

"You!" she screamed, slamming a small red draken with one arm against the wall. They'd found Gadjet.

Brin's blade pressed tightly against the draken's throat, but Gadjet didn't fight back. Her head slumped in Brin's arms.

"It didn't work." Gadjet was sobbing. "I was so sure it would work."

She looked over at the wall, and Ronan followed the draken's gaze. There sitting against the wall with Midral's Mythril Soul embedded in its chest was a figure Ronan instantly recognized.

Clash.

Ronan stumbled backwards. What was Clash's body doing here? Had he died in this room somehow, in a vision Ronan hadn't seen?

The way he was positioned seemed more like he'd been deliberately placed there. But by who? He was the last mythrali, aside from Steel, and Steel had been imprisoned until recently. It didn't make sense.

Brin was still holding Gadjet against the wall with Ronan's old blade pressed against the small draken's neck, almost to the point of drawing blood. Gadjet was blubbering—something about a plan that had failed.

Ronan noticed Brin's flared nostrils and wide eyes as she held Gadjet in place. She'd put an enormous amount of trust in Gadjet, only to be betrayed. At least they'd found the Mythril Soul before Gadjet turned it over to the Fallen Star, if that was indeed her intent. Though Ronan was less sure about that now.

He looked around the room—it was almost exactly the way he remembered it. A large chamber opened around them, with the original Great Anvil marking its center. It looked the same as the Great Anvil in Midral, before Kyros had destroyed it, except for the four bowl-shaped recesses in the top where the mythrali council would place their Mythril Souls when they convened.

Well, and then there was the sword. The ornate sword with the folded wings on either side of the hilt had been driven deep into the center of the Great Anvil. He'd seen the moment Ashe had done it. Just before she was murdered by the same monster that had inflicted Ronan's current injuries.

The sword was covered in the ashes that marked it as inert—waiting to be picked up by its rightful owner so it could shed the ashes and roar back to life with Niradim's Flame. Only... Ronan knew its owner would never return. Would it remain in this state forever? Condemned to rust and lost to history? Ashes gently flaked off the surface of the blade, drifting down into a pile that had built up over the hundreds of years since it was last wielded. Ashe had claimed it was just a sword—but it could be so much more in the right hands.

Ronan let his eyes slide back over to Clash's body, leaning against the wall. His Anvil Hammer rested next to him. Seeing it in person was surreal. The handle was at least six feet long, and the head of the hammer was almost as large as the Great Anvil. Only a mythrali would be able to wield a weapon so large.

A thought struck Ronan as he surveyed Clash's remains—why had Gadjet placed the Mythril Soul in his chest like that? What was she trying to accomplish...?

"I'll give you one chance to explain yourself, Gadjet," Brin's words broke Ronan from his thoughts. "I thought we'd become... well, if not friends, then at least allies on our journey here."

Gadjet couldn't look Brin in the eyes. "I'm sorry, Brin. I didn't exactly lie to you, but I didn't tell you the full truth."

"Then tell us now," Ronan said from over Brin's shoulder. He tried to project strength, despite being so worn from his imprisonment here. The broken ribs he was dealing with made it tougher, but he wouldn't look weak in front of someone who might be an enemy if he could help it. "What is the Mythril Soul doing in Clash's chest?"

Gadjet's eyes widened in surprise as her attention snapped to Ronan. "You know of the Clash?"

"Yes," Ronan said. "Now, answer me. What is your goal here?"

Gadjet sniffed before continuing. "I've studied the history of this place that was once called Midralen. And what I learned led me to believe that if I could return with a Mythril Soul that still contained a Soul Flame, I could resurrect the Clash by putting it in his chest." Her head hung in defeat for a moment, before she looked back up at Brin. "But I was wrong. I'm sure I inserted it properly, but the Soul Flame has done nothing to bring him back. I wanted him to convince my tribe to take up arms and drive the Fallen Star away. I thought that if they wouldn't listen to me, surely they would listen to the one who gave us a purpose so long ago." Her eyes pleaded with Brin. "I truly thought that bringing the Mythril Soul back to Midralen would help save Ronan. But I am sorry I wasn't completely honest with you. I didn't know if you would bring it if I told you the truth."

Brin shoved herself off Gadjet, who slumped to the ground, still upset.

"I don't know if I would have trusted you or not, Gadjet," Brin said, fresh tears forming in her eyes. "But now you've betrayed my trust, and I don't know if I can believe anything you say anymore."

Gadjet just nodded, still sullen against the wall. While she sulked, Ronan walked up to Clash and gently placed his hands on the Mythril Soul embedded in his chest. He could feel the power there, wanting to be released. What if he could do something?

He concentrated for a moment on the Soul Flame within the Mythril Soul, but no matter what he did, he couldn't channel anything from Niradim with his hands still bound by the cuffs that blocked his power. He stepped back, shaking his head.

"I feel so useless with these on," Ronan said, looking down at the cuffs binding him. "Whatever this is, it completely blocks me from Niradim. I can sense his power still, even with the Flame being corrupted, but I can't get to him."

Gadjet looked up and seemed to notice Ronan's cuffs for the first time. "Oh, mister Phoenix, I'm sorry. I can help you get those off if you want."

Ronan spun toward her, wincing at the sharp pain in his side as he did. "You can get these off? How?"

"I have some tools here that should be able to pick the locks," she said as her hand went to her pack. Brin leveled her sword at Gadjet's chest before she could reach inside.

"It's okay, Brin," Ronan said. "I know you don't trust her, but I understand her motives. She's trying to save her people. Right, Gadjet?"

Gadjet slowly nodded, not moving any more than she had to with

Brin's blade at her chest. Brin stared at her in frustration, but eventually lowered her sword. "Don't make me regret this, Gadjet."

"I won't," Gadjet replied. "I promise I can get him free."

She finished reaching into her pack and removed two small metal pins that had slight curves in them. She wrapped one around her pinky claw and held the other between her thumb and index claw.

"It was pretty tough at first to learn how to pick locks with only one hand." Gadjet stepped up to Ronan and inserted the picks into a small hole in the side of the cuffs. She put pressure on one, holding it steady, as the other worked its way deftly into the lock, moving around in small motions and occasionally making little clicks. "But after so much practice, I can pick a lock faster with one hand than any thief can with two."

Less than five seconds passed before Ronan heard a satisfying click and the cuffs slid off his wrists. The dam holding back the Flame broke, and Niradim's power flooded his senses. He immediately reached out and channeled Niradim's healing magic. As it flowed through him, small white wisps of power began to rise from his body and heal his wounds. He gasped as his ribs popped back into place and the cuts on his body sizzled and closed. When it was done, he stood up and finally took a deep, painless breath.

"Oh, that feels much better," Ronan said, stretching his arms out to the sides. "Thank you, Gadjet. It seems I am in your debt."

"How did you do that?" Brin asked, running over to him and inspecting him. "I can't channel enough of Niradim's power to heal by a long shot."

"Maybe it's the difference in our ranks," Ronan guessed. That felt like the right answer, somehow. "As we learned recently, Phoenix is a rank higher than Disciple. I've seen glimpses of what that means from the Phoenix Trial, but I think that my rank as a Phoenix means I rely less on the external Flame in the Forge, and more on the Soul Flame that is inside me."

"So, you're at full strength?" Brin asked.

"It's hard to tell, but I think so," Ronan said. "And if my theory is correct, then it means anyone under the rank of Disciple will have a very hard time channeling any of Niradim's magic. They might not be able to channel at all."

Ronan's heart sank even as he said the words. It meant Midral was even more defenseless now. Only the few Disciples remaining in Midral would be able to use magic to defend the city in the event of an attack.

"And until we can purify the Flame," Brin added. "Nobody can take the Shaping Trial, so there won't be any new Disciples."

She was right—the situation kept getting worse and worse. His eyes drifted back to the large mythrali sitting next to them, and a thought popped into his head. Maybe now that he had access to Niradim's power...

"Ronan," Brin said as Ronan slowly reached his hand out and placed it on the Mythril Soul. "What are you-"

Ronan connected with the Soul Flame housed within the Mythril Soul and *pushed*. This time, the Soul Flame responded. A pulse of light burst from Ronan's palm and radiated across Clash's body as the Soul Flame filled it. Ronan heard a click as the Mythril Soul settled deeper into Clash's chest and locked into place. Gadjet gasped.

So did Clash.

The large mythrali's eyes burst alight as Niradim's power surged through him. Ronan took a step back as Clash looked around the room. Then, with a burst of speed that Ronan would have had a hard time believing the large man was capable of if he hadn't experienced it himself, Clash jumped to his feet, snatched the Anvil Hammer from the ground next to him and swung it at Ronan.

Ronan didn't flinch as the warhammer stopped inches from his face.

Brin stumbled back at the sudden attack and began to draw her sword, but Ronan held up his hand to stop her.

"Who are you?" Clash asked.

"My name is Ronan," he said. "And this is Brin, and Gadjet. We're friends, Clash. You can lower your weapon."

Ronan's muscles relaxed as Clash did lower the hammer to the floor with a solid clunk.

"How do you know my name?" Clash said. "And what are two humans doing this far north in Midralen?"

"Clash, you may want to sit back down for this," Ronan said. "You've been gone for a long time."

14

Brin

Brin studied Clash as Ronan finished his story.

"And that's why we're here," Ronan said. "The Fallen Star has corrupted the Flame, and we need to figure out a way to purify it and save Niradim."

Clash sat silently as he processed everything Ronan had told him. He'd been gone for centuries, and Niradim had created a whole new race of people. Clash had been resurrected at the worst possible time—when Niradim's Flame was already corrupted. Brin wondered what he'd think about all of this. Would he feel as if Niradim had abandoned the mythrali and moved on? She didn't know how she would feel in his shoes.

After a moment of contemplation, Clash finally broke the silence. "So, he really did it? Niradim created a new race of people to succeed the mythrali?"

Ronan nodded. "He did."

Clash put his head in his hands, and Brin's heart sank as she watched the enormous man begin to cry. Ronan shifted on his feet and looked away. It wasn't an unusual reaction for someone finding out that their god had moved on, but somehow she hadn't expected such an imposing figure to weep. She couldn't read Gadjet's expression, but her head was bowed in respect.

Clash composed himself and looked up at Ronan, wiping away the tears that streaked his face. "So then… my sacrifice wasn't in vain. Niradim created life again!"

"Wait," Brin said in surprise. "You're not upset? Or angry?"

"Of course not," Clash said, his voice still raw with emotion. "The mythrali are gone because of *me*. So before I died, I anchored Niradim's Flame in a new location south of here. I prayed he would create a new, better race of people. I never thought I would be blessed with finding out whether my sacrifice made a difference."

"*You're* the one who created the Great Anvil in Midral?" Brin asked.

"Yes," Clash replied. "It was the only way to prevent Steel from corrupting the Flame while he was imprisoned."

"Can you tell us what happened?" Brin asked.

"Of course." Clash's eyes grew distant as his voice softened.

"Let me tell you about my greatest failure—the fall of the mythrali."

* * *

Over 1000 years ago

Clash led a group of mythrali to the Heart Forge. These were the ones who hadn't turned on their god and accepted Celestian's gifts. They'd been skeptical of trusting him at first, but when he showed them Ashe's body, they saw he'd been telling the truth about Steel murdering her, and they trusted him despite Celestian's corruption pulsing in his chest.

You really don't want to do this, Agent Clash, Celestian whispered in the back of his mind. *I've already warned the others you're coming. This will only end with the death of everyone you care about.*

I don't believe you, Clash replied to the now-unwelcome presence in his mind. *They'll listen to reason.*

The low rumble of Celestian's chuckle in his mind made his metallic skin hum, and he couldn't help but shiver. *As you wish,* Celestian replied. *Don't say I didn't warn you...*

Clash held Ashe's body in his arms as he and his people marched to the forge. Her blade had refused to budge from its position in the Great Anvil for any of the other mythrali. She'd said it was a Phoenix-level weapon, so maybe only a Phoenix could pull it free. He didn't know if he'd ever reach that level now—not after his betrayal of Niradim's people.

"A sword is just a sword, Clash..."

Her last words ate at him as he walked. What did she mean? And what had she been about to say? That sword had become the symbol of the highest level of Niradim's faith ever since she emerged as Niradim's Phoenix. If he couldn't wield it, then he was nothing. Worse than nothing, since he'd helped cause all this suffering. He didn't know if he was strong enough to fix this mess without it.

As they approached the Heart Forge, it became clear that Celestian hadn't been bluffing about warning the others. A large group of corrupted mythrali assembled in front of the doors to the Heart Forge, weapons drawn and Star Crystals glowing in their chests. Beyond them, he could see two mythrali doing something to the Flame. That would be Cinder and Saber. Whatever it was, Clash needed to stop them.

Clash stopped a few feet in front of the gathered group and held Ashe's body before him.

"My fellow mythrali." He projected his voice out to them so they all could hear. "We've been betrayed!"

"Steel has murdered our first and only Phoenix!" Murmurs began to sprout up from the corrupted mythrali, but he continued. "Celestian has corrupted us with his promises of power, but it's not too late to turn back to Niradim! So long as the Flame burns, there is still time to fix this!"

Cinder stood at the back of the group and yelled to Clash.

"Where is your proof, Clash?" Cinder yelled. "You've brought us Ashe's body, but how do we know you didn't kill her yourself? I think you're the one who has betrayed us!" Voices in front of Clash began to pick up. "Yes, I think you are here to claim the power for yourself. Agent Steel isn't here to defend himself, which is pretty convenient, wouldn't you say?"

The murmurs grew, and Clash could tell he was losing them, so he placed Ashe's body to the side to keep it safe. "I'm telling the truth! You can see the blade marks from Steel's greatsword. Please, we have to stop this before it goes any further!"

"We're trying to bring the power of our Starsouls to every mythrali!" Cinder gestured to the surrounding people. "Now that you've eliminated Ashe, there are only two of us who rival you in strength. We won't let you hoard this power all to yourself, Clash—your treason against the mythrali ends here!"

The mythrali in front of him all drew their weapons, and the ones behind him did the same. Before Clash could continue, the front lines of the corrupted mythrali surged forward and began to attack. He couldn't do anything but defend himself, so he drew his Anvil Hammer from his back and did his best not to hurt anyone too badly.

The skirmish was brutal. Never, until Steel had killed Ashe, had a mythrali raised a weapon against another mythrali. They'd been a peaceful people, intent on being left alone in the greater world. Now they surged with unearned power, tainted by a foreign god who had wormed his way into their chests. The temptation had been too great for them.

The corrupted mythrali had an advantage with the powers they wielded, but Clash's side had greater numbers. Past the fighting, Clash could still see Cinder and Saber working on the Flame, so he pushed forward and through the corrupted mythrali, relying on his strength and massive warhammer to keep the enemies away from him.

He finally burst through the back ranks and into the Heart Forge itself. As he crossed the threshold, he pulled a lever, and the massive stone doors slammed shut behind him. It was just him and the two other mythrali who'd converted their Mythril Souls into Starsouls. The three of them represented the most powerful mythrali alive. Cinder picked up a large staff, reinforced with weights at either end, and Saber drew her twin scimitars from her waist. Their weapons began to glow with a pale purple hue—a corrupted version of Niradim's power.

"Please," Clash begged them. "Reconsider what you're doing here. You know this is wrong."

Saber leveled one of her swords at him. "Sorry, Clash. We will spread Celestian's power to the rest of Niradim's people. It's time we served a generous god instead of one that withholds his full power from us."

It's true, Clash, Celestian said. *You and the others here have my favor. When the power of the Flame combines with my influence, your power will only continue to grow. You can lead my armies, Clash. Agent Steel himself will bow to you—I promise it. Your power will dwarf even that of Niradim's Phoenix. All you need to do is allow Cinder and Saber to complete their work.*

Shut up! Clash thought back.

As if he'd heard Clash's thoughts directly, Cinder shook his head. "Wrong answer."

Saber leapt forward as Cinder swung his staff and sent a wave of power at Clash. He sidestepped the magical attack and blocked Saber's initial flurry with the shaft of his hammer. Saber was smaller than Clash, but more agile, and she could attack faster than Clash could defend with his large hammer. He backpedaled and found an opportunity to take a swing at her, which she easily dodged. The attack bought him some space, but he had to pivot quickly to block another wave of power from Cinder, which drove Clash back a few feet.

He hated having to fight his own people, but it was time for him to stop holding back. Dragging out the fight would only serve Celestian, and he was done with that. He wouldn't let them corrupt the Flame. No, he would do as he should have done from the start—defend his god.

Clash focused on the swirling purple-white power within him, corrupted as his opponents were. But as he focused, he realized the two opposing powers didn't completely combine into one. A spark of hope ignited within him as an idea struck.

Without knowing what would happen, he seized a thread of pure-white energy from the swirling mix in his chest and pulled with everything he had. His body vibrated with the effort, threatening to shatter him as he attempted to tear the two powers apart. Just when he felt he'd reached his limit, the head of his hammer burst aflame with a blinding white light, pure and free from the purple taint of Celestian's corruption.

Saber held up her hands at the sudden light, and Clash took that opportunity to surge forward. He slammed his hammer into the ground in a massive explosion of pale flames, crushing her body below it. As the dust settled, Clash withdrew his weapon to reveal the shattered Starsoul embedded in her chest.

NO! He heard Celestian scream in the back of his mind. *How-*

Suddenly, Celestian's voice cut out as Niradim's power flowed through Clash's body and cut off the connection.

Cinder roared at the sight of Saber's broken body. "How dare you! You've destroyed one of the most powerful artifacts ever created!"

"Yes, one down." Clash rested his mighty hammer on his shoulder as he straightened up and leveled his gaze at Cinder. "Now only two remain." He pointed to Cinder's chest, then his own.

"I'll be careful to take you apart piece by piece so we can recover your Starsoul for someone more worthy than you," Cinder growled through clenched teeth.

"Everyone is more worthy than me," Clash said, voice barely above a whisper. "I'm a traitor."

Cinder screamed as he leapt forward, swinging his weighted staff glowing with the corrupted power of the two gods over and over in a fury. Streaks of pale violet light hung in the air as the staff spun between his hands. Clash met the attacks blow for blow with his anvil hammer, ablaze with Niradim's pure Flame, despite the tainted Starsoul in his chest.

Cinder was the more experienced fighter of the two of them, so Clash was pushed back as Cinder's attacks flowed from one to another. He blocked an attack aimed at his head, but Cinder immediately brought the bottom of his staff in a circle and swept Clash's legs out from under him. Clash barely rolled out of the way as the other end of Cinder's staff smashed the ground. A violet shockwave sent Clash tumbling before he used the momentum to roll back to his feet.

He took a deep breath and focused as Cinder rushed at him again. This wasn't a simple duel—he was fighting for Niradim, for Ashe, and for his people.

Losing wasn't an option.

Cinder began his next assault, but this time Clash held. His focus narrowed to a razor's edge, and his movements grew more precise with each swing. Wisps of white energy streamed from his skin as the Flame of Niradim lent each of his blows more power than he'd ever experienced before.

Cinder's eyes flashed wildly as he suddenly felt the momentum of the battle shift. Clash planted a foot into Cinder's chest, pushing him back a few feet. Before he could regain his stance, Clash leapt high in the air. At the top of his leap, Clash's anvil hammer erupted with

Niradim's Flame, leaving a trail of white fire in an arc as he brought the full force of Niradim's fury down on his former friend. Cinder's staff shattered in an explosion of purple and white, sending the corrupted mythrali flying toward the back wall of the forge, where he crumpled into a heap.

Clash breathed heavily as he lifted his hammer off the ground. Cinder was slowly pushing himself into a sitting position against the wall, but it was clear this fight was over.

"You've killed us all, Clash," Cinder spat at him from a jaw that hung crooked on his face. "Your little army of magic-less mythrali out there murdered the ones that were loyal to Celestian. But Celestian just informed me that Agent Steel returned and slaughtered the survivors. He's waiting for you just outside these doors, Clash. After you kill me here, it'll just be you and him. The last two mythrali."

Clash's heart rate spiked. "You're lying."

Cinder let out a low chuckle that morphed into a cough. "I'm not. But you'll find out for yourself soon enough…"

Clash watched as the light left Cinder's eyes, leaving the husk of another of his fallen brothers behind. The Starsoul still pulsed in his chest like a heart continuing to beat, despite the lifeless body it inhabited. Clash walked over and took a deep breath.

"I'm sorry, my old friend," Clash said before he slammed his hammer into Cinder's chest, shattering the Starsoul.

Clash looked over his shoulder back at the entrance of the Heart Forge. If Cinder wasn't bluffing, Steel was on the other side of those doors, waiting for him. Though he'd won the battles with Cinder and Saber, the fights had left him tired and beaten. Facing Steel would be a death wish, but Clash knew there was no other choice. He had to take on Steel and hope he still had the Mythril Soul with him. That was the only hope of saving Niradim. So Clash walked over and pulled the lever to open the large doors.

As they opened, Clash's heart sank. Littered across the ground were the corpses of his brethren. Steel stood among several bodies that didn't have Star Crystals in their chests. He stalked toward Clash, reaching his arms out to the sides as they split in two. Four hands reached up to his massive greatswords and unhooked them from his back as a tempest of unbridled rage vibrated from his mythril body.

"CLASH!" Steel swept his swords around, gesturing to the bodies piled around him. "How could you betray us? This—*all of this*—is your fault!"

"I know," Clash replied, his shoulders dropping with the admission. "And I have to do this to atone for my sins. I'm sorry I let it get this far, Steel. I should have stopped you before we ever accepted the novaborns' gifts. Now, hand over the Mythril Soul."

Steel laughed. "Oh, I don't think so, Clash. Once I crush you, I'm going to finish the work Saber and Cinder were doing on the Flame and take this final Mythril Soul back to Lumenova. The novaborn think they've figured out a way to swap my Star Crystal for the Starsoul, so I can finally have the power I deserve."

Clash shook his head. "You never deserved this power, Steel. None of us did. Niradim gifted it to us—that's what made it precious."

"Easy for you to say, with all the power of the Starsoul in your chest," Steel replied. "Last chance, Clash, step aside. There's only two of us now, and I know you're not going to exterminate the only other member of your race."

Clash looked around at the fallen mythrali around him. They were his friends, loved ones, and he'd failed them, one and all. No, he didn't want to be the one who exterminated his own race, the people he knew Niradim loved. But Steel didn't truly belong to Niradim any longer. Not for a long time, even before Steel had accepted the Star Crystal.

"I will do what I have to do in order to protect Niradim," Clash said, raising his hammer. "Ready yourself, Steel. This ends now."

Steel's swords flared to life with Celestian's power, and the Star Crystal pulsed an angry violet. Steel's Star Crystal had grown to fill the recess in his chest, integrating itself further into his anatomy as he grew in power since it was installed.

Clash focused on that pure power within him, bypassing Celestian's corruption and drawing only on Niradim's Flame from within his Starsoul. Some of his wounds healed, but he was significantly weaker than when he fought the other two. It was difficult to focus on pulling power only from Niradim when the temptation to use Celestian's power was right there. But he'd made his decision. If he couldn't win using only Niradim's strength, then he was resigned to die trying.

Power flared in his Anvil Hammer as Steel rushed forward with his two blazing greatswords. They roared with violet flames as he began his attack. Similar to Cinder, Steel had been around longer than Clash, and that showed itself in the first few moments of their battle. He was a deadlier opponent than the other two were, and Clash immediately found himself on the back foot, having to focus on defense as those two huge swords did everything they could to find purchase in his mythril flesh.

He kicked Steel back to create some separation and swung his hammer in an arc. Steel leapt over him, slashing downward with both swords and cutting into Clash's back, causing him to fall to a knee. He pulled the shaft of his hammer around to stop what would have been a finishing blow from Steel, but it left him open to a kick to his chest, sending him tumbling backward into the Heart Forge.

"You're no match for me, Clash," Steel said as he strode forward into the Heart Forge. "You limit your own power by only using Niradim's magic. How foolish."

"I will never use Celestian's power again," Clash said, between deep breaths. Clash hated to admit it, but Steel was right. Clash was losing this fight. He had to figure out another way to save the Flame. "My loyalty belongs only to Niradim now."

Steel hooked one of the greatswords to his back and removed the Mythril Soul from a compartment on his body. He held it up for Clash to see. "This is all that remains of your precious Niradim. Just the Soul Flame inside this Mythril Soul." He set it down on the anvil in front of the Flame "And when I finish with you here, I will take what remains of Niradim to Lumenova and make him regret ever creating us." Steel chuckled to himself. "Not many people get to outlive their own god."

Clash glanced at the Mythril Soul, and a small fraction of the tension he was holding left his body as he realized there was indeed still some hope left. It was here. An idea formed in Clash's mind, but it would be difficult to pull off. He'd only get one shot at it, but it was the only chance he had to save Niradim.

Clash got to his feet and readied his warhammer. He hoped he could at least count on Steel to be predictable. Steel drew the greatsword from his back, and fortunately, left the Mythril Soul sitting on the anvil next to him. Clash rushed forward again, taking a mighty swing at Steel, who leapt again over Clash's head. This time, Clash rolled under Steel's aerial attack, flared Niradim's power into his hammer, and threw it as hard as he could at Steel just before he landed.

Steel had no time to dodge as Clash's Anvil Hammer streaked through the air like a comet, trailing Niradim's white Flame. The massive warhammer slammed into Steel's chest, causing him to drop his swords as the momentum from the attack cratered him into the wall on the far side of the room. Clash snatched the Mythril Soul from the anvil and plunged it into the corrupted Flame. He pushed the pure Soul Flame into the Heart Forge and drove out Celestian's corruption. Now that the orb in his hand was empty, he formed an intricate connection between the Mythril Soul and the purified Flame within the Heart Forge and pulled.

A heartbeat later, his own hammer slammed into his side, sending him sprawling back towards the doors of the Heart Forge. He clenched the Mythril Soul to his chest, now glowing again with Niradim's Flame, as he slid to a stop next to his hammer.

Steel was wounded, but not finished. Clash knew his attack wouldn't be able to finish Steel off, but he'd hoped to have a little more time. He needed to stall just a little longer…

"Clever little trick, Clash," Steel said, stepping over to where his swords lay on the ground. "I've never seen you throw the hammer before. Caught me completely off-guard. Too bad it didn't work."

Clash picked up his hammer and struggled to his feet. There was no way he could continue fighting in this state.

"I've got the Mythril Soul," he said, limping back out of the Heart Forge. "I knew I couldn't beat you one-on-one, so instead I'll have to settle for locking you away." Clash focused a ball of white fire into his hand and released it at the lever that controlled the doors to the Heart Forge from the inside, destroying it completely.

"What a ridiculous notion," Steel said as he casually bent down to pick up each of his swords. "Those doors also respond to the Flame's power. If you shut me in here, I'll simply corrupt the Flame and use the power to open the doors back up." He latched both swords onto his back. "And then I will hunt you down, Clash. Celestian has Agents everywhere. There is nowhere you can hide where I won't be able to find you and that Mythril Soul."

"No, I don't think you will," Clash said, reaching for the lever on the outside and pulling it to drop the doors. "You see, I'll be taking the Flame with me." He held up the Mythril Soul, now blazing with the full might of Niradim's Flame. "Goodbye, Steel. And for what it's worth…" Clash's voice lowered. "I'm sorry it came to this."

Steel's face contorted with fury as he glanced at the now-empty Heart Forge. Clash had indeed been able to forge a strong enough connection to siphon the rest of the Flame from the Heart Forge before

Steel had knocked him away. He'd kept Steel talking just long enough for the rest of the Flame to transfer, and now it was safely tucked away within Niradim's last Mythril Soul.

Steel couldn't corrupt the Flame if there was no Flame to corrupt.

Steel sprinted forward as the doors shut, but he and Clash both knew he wouldn't make it in time.

"I'll get out of here, Clash," Steel screamed before the door completely shut. "And when I do, Niradim will feel my wrath!"

As the door slammed shut, Clash turned and looked upon the remains of his people. He'd saved Niradim, but he hadn't won.

Because of him, the mythrali were no more.

* * *

Present day

The room was silent as Clash finished telling his story.

"So you and Steel really are the last of your people," Brin said. "I'm so sorry."

"But you saved Niradim," Ronan said. "A whole new people exist because of your actions."

Clash nodded. "Yes, but I still made the wrong choice. I was too blind to Niradim's true heart back then to realize it. It's why I was never able to obtain the rank of Phoenix."

"What was the right choice?" Brin asked.

"I should have-"

A sound outside the building cut Clash off, and they all turned to look at the entrance. Gadjet hissed off to the side and ran for the door to peek out. They'd all been so captivated by Clash's story that they'd forgotten about the clan of draken searching for them.

Gadjet was flung back through the door, and Clash got to his feet, grabbing his hammer next to him. Brin drew Ronan's sword from the shield strapped to her left arm, and Ronan backed away from the door. He was still unarmed.

"They're here," Gadjet said as she got to her feet.

Several draken poured into the room, leveling crude weapons at their small group. Upon seeing the towering mythrali, they paused and gave him a wide berth, but kept their weapons up. A larger draken with green scales walked through the door holding a curved scimitar. This was clearly their leader.

The draken's eyes looked to each of them and finally rested on Ronan. "Phoenix, my apologies, but we must escort you back to our camp."

"I'm sorry, Dak'thor," Ronan said. Brin was surprised at the level of familiarity in Ronan's voice as he addressed the draken. "I can't go with you this time."

Gadjet ran forward and gestured with her one arm to Clash. "Dak'thor, don't you see? The Clash lives again! I told you it could happen."

"You are the descendants of the dragonkin I tasked with guarding the Flame?" Clash asked.

"Yes, we are," Dak'thor said. "But we cannot trust your judgement. We have seen how your kind treats others."

"But the Clash is different," Gadjet pleaded. "He can take up the Sword of Ashes and lead us to victory."

"The Sword of Ashes?" Clash asked, clearly confused.

"Well, yes," Gadjet said, uncertain. She pointed to the sword buried deep in the anvil. "You told our ancestors to guard the Sword of Ashes along with Niradim's Flame."

"I told..." Clash said. He put his hand up to his head. "I told them to guard Ashe's sword. She was the Phoenix who gave her life rather than take up arms against her own people. Ashe's sword—not the Sword of Ashes."

"It doesn't matter what it's called. You must take it up and lead us,"

Gadjet said. "Dak'thor, you wouldn't deny the Clash if he took up the Sword of Ashes, would you?"

"No," Dak'thor said. "That part of our oath stands. If there is one worthy to wield the Sword of Ashes, we will follow them. But nobody has ever been able to pull it from the Anvil."

"The Clash can!" Gadjet cried.

Brin glanced at Ronan, whose somber face mirrored Clash's own. Gadjet looked over pleadingly. Brin knew this was the moment Gadjet had been betting on to save her people. Her final gambit to gain their independence and freedom from the slavery that had plagued them for generations.

"Please, you must take it," she begged.

Clash looked at the sword jutting from the anvil for a long beat before his shoulders slumped and he turned back to Gadjet.

"I can't," Clash said. "I'm not worthy of that blade. The dragonkin chief is correct. I should not be trusted to lead anyone after I failed my own people."

Clash set his hammer on the ground and sat back against the wall, head in his hands.

"I'm sorry, little one," Clash said. "I am not the person you believe me to be."

15

Ronan

Ronan watched as Gadjet fell to her knees in defeat, eyes glazed over in shock.

And why wouldn't she be? She'd risked everything to free her people, and it had just fallen apart in front of her. Clash was in the same state, hunched against the wall with his head buried in his hands. Dak'thor and the draken weren't much better off. They'd resigned themselves to a life in slavery rather than try to stand up for themselves.

Ronan was in a room full of people who'd given up their hope, their faith. These people deserved to know that they could be reforged, like he had. He'd once lost his faith as well—he looked over to Brin, who had tears forming in her eyes at Gadjet's suffering—and it took the acts of those he loved to bring him back from it. From being broken.

Dak'thor snorted, venting smoke from his nostrils. "You see, it is as I said. The metal ones cannot be trusted. Now stand aside, little one. The Phoenix will come with us now."

Dak'thor pointed his scimitar at Ronan, and two draken on either side of him with spears stepped forward. Brin dropped into a defensive stance, but Ronan waved her back. This wouldn't be settled with bloodshed. He had an idea, and even though he wasn't sure it would work, they had nothing else to lose. He had to try.

"No." Ronan jumped up onto the anvil behind him. "I won't be going with you this time, Dak'thor."

"Phoenix," Dak'thor said calmly. "We will bring you in, one way or ano-"

He cut off as Ronan's hand moved to hover over the blade embedded in the anvil. Clash and Gadjet noticed the sudden interruption and looked up, eyes jumping with surprise as they realized what Ronan was about to attempt.

"You said your people would follow whoever wields this blade." Ronan held Dak'thor's stare with a fiery intensity. It wasn't a question, but Dak'thor still gave a silent nod in response. "Well, Dak'thor, prepare your tribe for battle."

Ronan's hand wrapped around the hilt. Dormant power stirred deep within the blade at his touch, sending a gentle vibration through his hand. The blade longed to be resurrected by a Phoenix once more. It had remained buried in ashes for too long.

"That sword has not answered anyone's touch in a thousand years," Dak'thor said, voice barely above a whisper. Even so, they all heard his every word in the suffocating silence that filled the room. "What makes you think you are any different from the countless that have tried before you?"

Then Ronan finally spotted it. The faintest embers in their eyes that he'd been searching for since he arrived. The craving for something more—something different from the oppression they'd known for generations. Hope still flickered deep within them, buried deeper even than the sword before them in the ashes of their past. The recent events had begun to blow those ashes away to reveal the last sputters that remained within them. But those ashes could still be reignited. All they needed was a spark.

"Because I know something you've all forgotten." Ronan's eyes flared to life with Niradim's power as his grip around the hilt tightened.

"This sword has been waiting for a Phoenix."

Wings of white fire exploded behind Ronan, and his body lit up with the full might of Niradim's power. The ashes on the sword burned away as Ronan pulled it out of the anvil in one swift motion. The wings on the hilt spread to mirror Ronan's own, and the blade roared to life with Niradim's holy Flame as Ronan held the Sword of Ashes above him.

"Today, we free your people from the Fallen Star's grasp and fulfil the oaths your ancestors made," Ronan said. "Today, we will save the Flame."

Ronan stared out at the people gathered before him. All the draken behind Dak'thor immediately dropped their weapons and bowed. Dak'thor dropped to his knees, scimitar clanging to the ground next to him.

"Yes, my Phoenix," Dak'thor said, tears streaming down his face. "Today, we will save the Flame."

Brin and Gadjet were both frozen with their mouths hanging open—clearly they hadn't expected him to try to draw the sword. In fact, he hadn't even considered it until Dak'thor mentioned he'd follow its wielder. From his time in Clash's memories, he remembered Ashe saying it was a Phoenix-level weapon, so he'd hoped that would be enough to pull the blade free from the anvil. Thankfully, his hunch had paid off.

Clash was still sitting against the wall, watching the scene unfold before him in silence. "What about you, Clash?" Ronan lowered his blade and held out his hand to the silent mithrali. "Will you help me?"

Clash was unreadable as he got to his feet and walked over to Ronan, holding his mighty warhammer at his side. Even with the extra height Ronan had from standing on the Great Anvil, Clash almost met him eye-to-eye. Ronan held his breath as Clash raised the head of the hammer and placed the bottom of the shaft on the ground next to him. Then, the entire room gasped as Clash knelt before Ronan and bowed his head.

"I promised myself long ago that if another Phoenix rose up to take Ashe's sword, I would follow them without question." Clash raised his head and looked up at Ronan. "If you are even a fraction of the Phoenix that Ashe was, you are the only one worthy to carry that blade. I trust Niradim's judgement, and so I trust you. My hammer is yours to command."

Ronan's eyes softened. "I'm just a man, Clash. I can be wrong, just like anyone else." He paused to steal a quick glance at Brin. "In fact, if I didn't have people who loved me enough to challenge my choices, we wouldn't even have this chance to save the Flame. So if you're going to follow me, don't do it blindly. Do it to keep me accountable."

Clash smiled. "You sound like her already. Alright then, I swear it."

Ronan smiled back and hopped off the anvil to join the rest of them. Dak'thor was the first to rise, and the rest of the draken followed. Excited whispers filled the room as the draken rose, chatting quietly with each other about what they'd just witnessed. He could see hope beginning to grow in each of them. Since their birth, they'd only known one kind of life, but now they had a chance at something more. Something better.

Dak'thor approached with a fist over his heart and bowed to Ronan. "I'm sorry for my part in this, my Phoenix. After our battle with the Fallen Star, I will accept any punishment you see fit to deliver. I ask only that you spare my people. They were simply following my leadership."

"Nobody is getting punished, Dak'thor. I meant what I said before. You did the best you could for the survival of your tribe. Now the situation has changed, and you have the ability to make different choices." He rested a hand on Dak'thor's shoulder. "We're going to do better. Together."

Dak'thor nodded as Ronan lowered his hand. "I have one more apology to make." He turned to Gadjet and knelt before her as well. "Please accept my deepest apologies, Dragonslayer."

Dragonslayer? What was that about? Brin's jaw almost hit the floor for the second time in the last few minutes. Gadjet's lips curled up slightly as she, too, noticed Brin's reaction. He'd have to ask Brin about that later.

"It's okay, Dak'thor, I'm just glad this many of us have survived." She cleared her throat, and Dak'thor glanced up at her. She was still shorter than he was, even while he was kneeling. "But if we're going to square off against the Fallen Star, I'd like my arm back. As well as the rest of my… things."

"Yes, of course." Dak'thor stood and snapped his fingers, and two of the draken nearest to him stepped forward. "Ri'jahd, Pareem—take the Dragonslayer to where we have stored her… trophies. And gather the rest of the tribe. Tell them the Sword of Ashes has been reclaimed."

Gadjet turned to Ronan. "I'll be much more useful in the coming fight if you let me get the rest of my stuff, but I'll only go if you allow it. Like the others, I will follow your command, Phoenix."

"Please, enough of the formalities. You can call me Ronan. That goes for you too, Dak'thor." Ronan gave the taller draken a look before turning back to Gadjet and taking her hand. "Thank you for leading Brin here and helping her save me from my poor judgement. What you've done is incredibly brave, and you're the reason we even have a shot at this. I'm in your debt, Gadjet."

Gadjet beamed at his words and shook his hand. "Oh, don't worry, Brin and I have already talked about a way you can repay me," Gadjet shot a quick wink in Brin's direction. "Now we just have to make sure we all survive this so I can collect on my bet!"

Ronan looked over at Brin, who was tugging on her braids. "Oh, you have, have you?" Brin mouthed the word 'sorry,' and Ronan chuckled before turning back to Gadjet. "Well, I'm happy to help with whatever Brin promised you. Go collect your things. I'll send someone after you to discuss the plan once we've got one."

She nodded and ran over to Brin to give her a big hug before running off with the two draken. They didn't have much time to spare. It hadn't been long since the Fallen Star finished corrupting the Flame, but Falrose could leave at any moment with the Starsoul. They needed to make sure that didn't happen.

Ronan held up his hand for attention, and the room quieted. "Thank you all for your help. I want you all to know that I will do my best to protect you, but the fight in front of us won't be an easy one." Ronan hesitated. He didn't want to admit the next part, but he wouldn't lead these people into battle without being completely honest with them. "That being said, we still have one big problem. I don't know how to purify the Flame."

Murmurs broke out among the tribe members, and they began to shift uncomfortably where they stood. Fortunately, Clash spoke up before things got out of hand.

"I can assist with that." Clash gestured to his chest. "This Mythril Soul still contains a Soul Flame. If we can drive the Fallen Star out of the Heart Forge, I can use this to purify Niradim's Flame."

One of the draken spoke up. "But even if we do that, what's stopping them from corrupting it again?"

"We'll destroy the door's mechanism from the outside," Ronan said. "Clash destroyed the lever inside the Heart Forge, which is why Steel wasn't able to escape until now. After we purify the Flame, we'll destroy the mechanism on the outside as well so it can't be reopened so easily."

"That could work..." Clash thought for a moment. "It wouldn't be a permanent solution—the door responds to Niradim's magic, so anyone who can channel the Flame could still open the door.

And theoretically, someone wielding a large amount of Celestian's power could eventually destroy the door, but that would take years of concentrated effort."

"Either option buys us time," Ronan said. "If we purify the Flame and seal the door or drive off the cultists, we'll use the time that buys us to bring in forces from Midral and any willing allies to secure this city against any further Fallen Star incursions."

The draken were nodding in agreement, and Clash also inclined his head in approval. Brin stood off to the side, but he caught hints of a smile on her face as she watched him.

"Dak'thor, how long will it take to gather your tribe and get them ready to fight?" Ronan asked.

"We can be ready quickly, but I have to warn you," Dak'thor said. "We have not been in many battles. We will need someone to lead us."

Ronan brushed a hand through his hair as he thought about the best course of action. He'd studied some battle strategy in the Niradim Protectors under Ginmar, but he'd never actually led troops himself. It wasn't ideal, but he'd have to take what little he'd learned and put it into practice.

A straight-on attack wasn't likely to work against the Fallen Star camp. They were outnumbered and lacked experience, it was too risky to try. However, the ruins surrounding the camp could give the tribe the upper hand. If they split into two groups and hid among the ruins, they could take the cultists by surprise. That could tip the scales in their favor.

With 2 small groups instead of one large one, he'd need to make sure each group had someone in charge with real battle experience to guide them—so that meant Clash, Brin, or Gadjet. Taking Steel and Falrose away from the main fighting would also give them a better chance of success, so he'd need to find a way to distract them. If they could pull all of that off, it should be enough to win this fight.

"Okay," Ronan said. "Here's what we're going to do. Dak'thor, I want you and Gadjet to take half of your tribe along the left side of the Fallen Star camp. Clash, you'll take the other half and sneak along the right side. Use the ruins as cover to get as close as you can without being seen. Brin and I will approach from the center and try to get Steel and Falrose to fight us directly. You'll wait for my signal and then swoop in from the sides to take out as many as you can before they realize what's happening."

"You intend to fight Steel?" Clash asked.

"Yes," Ronan replied. "Hopefully, Falrose as well."

Clash shook his head. "It won't work. Steel may not serve Niradim any longer, but Ashe's sword can't be used against a mythrali. Your blade won't be able to harm him. Plus, as soon as he sees me, he will abandon his fight with you, I'm sure of it."

Slag and ashes, Clash was right. In Clash's memories, Ashe was adamant that her sword could never be used against Niradim's people, and a magical artifact would obey that kind of intent from its creator. That kind of restriction would stay with the blade, regardless of its owner. And Steel would absolutely go after Clash as soon as he sensed him. He'd have to go with Ronan as a part of the distraction, which meant… He looked over at Brin.

"I'll do it." She'd already made the connection. "Clash is right, plus he's fought Steel before. If anyone's going to help create a big enough distraction for us to pull this off and guarantee Steel takes the bait, it's the person Steel hates the most. I'll lead the draken forces on the right side of the camp."

Ronan held Brin's eyes, exchanging a subtle nod with her before turning back to the group. "It's decided then. I will give you all time to get in place, and then Clash and I will march on the camp. Remember to wait for my signal before you attack. I want them to be completely focused on our battle before you engage. Dak'thor, I'll leave you to choose who goes with each group."

"It will be done, my Phoenix," Dak'thor said. Ronan left him to divide the tribe how he saw fit and walked over to Brin.

"I don't like how we've left things between us the last two times we've been together," Ronan said.

"I don't either." She crossed her arms and looked away.

"So let me just say this." Ronan took a deep breath. "I'm sorry."

She smiled and met his eyes before rushing forward and embracing him, burying her head in his chest. "I'm just glad you're okay."

"Thanks to you," he said. "I have to admit, I wish I could have you fighting next to me in the coming battle."

"I know, me too." She pulled away. "But this is the best chance of success, and I can handle myself."

"Oh, trust me, I have no reservations about that," Ronan said, chuckling. "Just give those cultists the glare you give me when we're arguing and they'll run for their lives."

She gave him that glare.

"Yes, that one!" Ronan laughed.

She grabbed him by his collar and pulled him down into a kiss. After a moment, they pulled apart, and he brushed a strand of hair out of her face.

"So." She held up Ronan's sword and shield. "I guess I'm going to need to borrow your weapons for a little longer. Hope you don't mind."

"Actually, I had a thought," Ronan said. "I have the Sword of Ashes now…"

"It's not called the Sword of Ashes, it's Ashe's sword…" Clash grumbled from where he was sitting against the wall.

Brin giggled. "I think you might have to let that one go, buddy."

"Regardless," Ronan continued. "I think I'll be using this sword for the foreseeable future. You gave me a wonderful gift from your Trial, and I think it's only fitting I give you a gift from mine. They're yours now."

Brin's eyes went wide. "Ronan... are you sure?"

He'd used those weapons for years after his Trial. The signature design of his sword storing directly into the shield was something he'd come to be known by. It had become a symbol of the one human who'd gained Niradim's favor—the only Disciple to have created more than one artifact in his Trial. But it was only a sword, and it didn't matter which one he was holding when he served Niradim.

He nodded and gave her a wink. "Besides, they suit you."

She gave him another hug, but then pulled back. "Speaking of my gift to you, where exactly *is* the Phoenix Armor? That's not something you should make a habit of losing."

"Yeah, about that..." Ronan said. "There's this whole thing that happened, where I was kidnapped. Maybe you remember it?"

She punched him in the shoulder.

Dak'thor cleared his throat from behind Ronan. "I can help with that."

He disappeared into a side room and came out with a bundle. "We took this from you before delivering you to the Fallen Star. We may have been serving them, but we weren't eager to help them with their mission any more than they demanded." He held up his arms to reveal Ronan's Phoenix Armor.

"Oh, that's a sight for sore eyes." Ronan took the breastplate and began to put on his armor. "Thank you, Dak'thor."

As he finished getting his armor into place, he realized he could attach his new sword to his back and it would stay in place—the magic locking it in when he let go and it went inert. As he felt the armor synchronize with Niradim's magic, he took a deep breath and smiled at the familiar warmth that flooded him. He paused for a moment to inspect the gathered forces in the room. They might be a small and random bunch, but they risked their lives to fight by his side. He would do his best to protect them.

"Dak'thor, have you divided your tribe?" Ronan asked.

"Yes, my Phoenix," he replied. "We are ready."

"Then take your team, meet up with Gadjet, and make your approach," Ronan said. "As for the rest of you, Brin will be leading your group. Be quick, but silent. This only works if we have the element of surprise."

Both groups looked at him, bodies shifting uncomfortably, avoiding chatter and eye contact with one another. Their nerves were getting to them as they realized they were about to go into battle, many of them for the first time in their lives. He remembered being in their shoes, but he'd had Ginmar to help him shake off the nerves and focus on what he was fighting for. He didn't remember what Ginmar had said, but he did remember how it made him feel. These people needed that kind of leader. He jumped back up onto the anvil, and all eyes focused on him.

"Today, we fight to reclaim your freedom." Ronan's voice dominated the air as the room stilled. "For centuries, you've endured—surviving what would have broken lesser souls. But your ancestors made an oath of protection, and today you fulfill that oath. The blood of dragons courses through your veins—ancient, unstoppable, *powerful*. Feel that power rising and burning within you. Use it to show your enemy that you will not be quelled any longer."

He paused and watched the sparks in their eyes ignite and grow brighter. Hands gripped their weapons tighter, shoulders straightened, and black smoke curled through bared teeth.

"We are children of ashes and flames—shaped by our past and reforged into something better. Today, the Fallen Star will learn what happens when they try to stand against the combined might of a Dragon and Phoenix!"

The entire mood of the room shifted as he finished. Where

once stood a group of scared draken, he now saw confidence and determination. The reminder of what they'd survived gave them faith that they had the power to change their own destiny.

Ronan lowered his sword and nodded to Dak'thor and Brin. Brin came over and gave him one last kiss.

"Nice speech," Brin said. "Now, don't die on me, okay?"

"Been there, done that," Ronan said with a grim smile. "I don't recommend it. Stay safe, and light them up."

He gave her hand one last squeeze before she turned and led her forces out the doors. He knew she'd be fine, but he really wished they could fight side by side in this battle. There was no one he'd rather fight beside. But this was the best course of action. It would provide them with the best chance of surviving the fight and saving Niradim. He sighed as he turned back to the room.

"So now we wait?" Clash asked.

"Yes." Ronan took a seat across from the mythrali. "Now we wait."

Ronan always found this to be one of the hardest parts before a battle. The waiting. It gave your mind too much time to think about everything that could go wrong. He preferred to be doing something, but they really did need to give the others plenty of time to get into position.

"Can I ask you a question?" Clash asked.

"Of course." Ronan was happy for any distraction that would take his mind off their monumental task.

"You seem to know more about my time than you should," Clash said. "How is that possible?"

Ronan's brow furrowed. What a strange situation he found himself in. He'd been having visions through Clash's eyes for weeks. Having lived through snippets of Clash's life made Ronan feel like he knew Clash intimately, but Clash didn't know anything about him. It was a strange dynamic.

"Niradim has been giving me visions of events that happened in the past," Ronan said. "And each one of these visions happened through your eyes."

Clash took a moment to process Ronan's words. "So, you've seen my transgressions then," he said solemnly. "You saw how I succumbed to Celestian's temptations and doomed my people."

"What I saw," Ronan said, carefully. "Was someone who was slowly and meticulously betrayed by a person he trusted. Someone who took advantage of his position to put you in tough situations without all the information needed to make a good decision."

Clash grunted, rolling his eyes. "That's kind of you to say, but my actions can't be excused so easily."

"I'm not excusing them." Clash glanced back up, and Ronan locked eyes with him. "You're fully accountable for your actions, and you absolutely made some terrible choices. But it's important to realize the circumstances of those choices."

Clash nodded, but Ronan could tell he was still beating himself up for everything that had happened. If he didn't get out of his own head before they fought Steel, Ronan was afraid Clash wouldn't be able to handle that fight. Maybe another tactic would work.

"You didn't choose to take a Star Crystal right away when others like Steel did. Why was that?"

Clash sighed. "I didn't know if it was a power we could trust. It felt like a betrayal of Niradim. But there were selfish reasons too—I believed I was on the cusp of completing the Phoenix Trial and wouldn't need the Star Crystal."

"But still, you were cautious," Ronan said. "Rightfully so, as we now know."

"I still ended up taking the power eventually, in a worse way," Clash said.

Ronan shook his head. "Clash, hear me. I'm not saying that you should be absolved of everything that happened. But you need to give yourself some grace and look forward. In the end, you saved Niradim and rejected Celestian. I don't see a Starsoul in your chest, so at some point, I know you made the right choice. Even if you made a dozen wrong ones along the way, there's a whole race of people alive now because of you. That is also a fact. If you're going to count all the bad, you also have to count the good."

Clash nodded, and a gentle smile broke across his face. "You're wise, like she was." He gestured to the sword Ronan had placed across his lap. "She would have loved to see another Phoenix like you join her ranks."

"She seemed like a great person, from what I saw of her in your memories," Ronan agreed.

"It is odd though, to see a human reach the rank of Phoenix," Clash went on. "Humans were around in my time, but only the mythrali had access to Niradim's power. Has Niradim shared his gifts with everyone then?"

"I'm a bit of an anomaly, you might say," Ronan admitted. "I am the only non-dwarf who has ever been able to channel his power. Well, aside from the mythrali, I guess. I grew up with the dwarves and consider them my people. I don't know exactly why I'm able to wield the Flame, but until my resurrection, I was among the weakest of the Disciples."

"Your resurrection?" Clash asked. "You died?"

Ronan nodded. "That's how I attained the rank of Phoenix. Is that not how Ashe did it?"

"I don't think so," Clash said. "Though I can't truly be sure, as I didn't ever complete the Phoenix Trial."

"It seems Niradim changed some things when he created the dwarves," Ronan said. "For example, Disciples don't have to share power like you did with the Mythril Souls. Each dwarf is born with a piece of Niradim's soul inside them, so dwarves that haven't even achieved the rank of Disciple are able to channel some of Niradim's magic if they practice."

"Interesting…" Clash said.

It was interesting. It seemed even gods could learn from their past. Ronan stood and brushed some of the dirt off his armor. "We should get going. The teams will be getting into place soon."

Clash nodded and picked up his Anvil Hammer.

"Let's finish this," Clash said.

They rose and made their way out of the council chambers and through the ruins. As they approached, Ronan could hear that the Fallen Star camp was busier than usual. There weren't any of the familiar sounds of battle from what he could tell, so the plan was still in motion, but the cultists had probably discovered his escape by now. When they closed in on the border of the Fallen Star camp, Ronan put his hand up to stop Clash.

"Let me go out and talk to them first," Ronan whispered. "We'll keep you in reserve in case I can't lure Steel and Falrose out myself."

Clash gave a quick nod and crouched down behind one of the ruined buildings. Ronan took a deep breath and walked out into the open. He didn't see the two Agents anywhere in the vicinity, so he walked forward until a group of cultists saw him and ran off to tell their superiors.

He only had to wait a moment before someone approached him, but it wasn't who he expected.

"Well, well," Treyla stepped out from the group in front of him. "I'm surprised you aren't halfway back to Midral by now, little Phoenix. It seems I have lost a bet with some of my peers!" A few cultists around her chuckled. It seemed the new nickname Steel gave him had caught on. "To what do we owe the pleasure?"

"I'm not here for you, Treyla," Ronan said. "Why don't you go fetch your boss for me so I can talk to someone with real authority around here."

Her nostrils flared before she sneered back at him. "Oh, I don't need an Agent to deal with you, Ronan. I will handle you myself."

She walked forward, and magical armor spread out around her body. Translucent with a slight purple hue. It looked like an inferior version of Kyros' when he'd fought the novaborn back in Midral. She also withdrew a long, hooked blade from her waist, which ignited with purple energy. Waves of heat radiated from its length as she leveled it at Ronan.

"Prepare yourself, little Phoenix," Treyla said. "Our restrictions against harming you have been lifted. Let's see if you'll be able to resurrect this time without your god!"

She rushed forward and swung her blade. Just before it connected, Ronan sidestepped, drew his sword, and slashed all in one fluid motion.

Treyla took two more steps past Ronan before she crumbled into ashes and her sword fell to the ground.

The entire group of cultists in front of Ronan collectively took a few steps back in shock.

Ronan calmly returned the blade to his back. "I'm only going to ask this one more time. Someone go get Steel and Falrose."

It turned out he didn't need to ask again. Falrose hovered up out of the crowd, and he saw Steel shoving his way through the cultist ranks.

"Oh dear." Falrose drifted over to hover above the front ranks of cultists. "I knew you were dull, but I didn't expect you to be quite this stupid, Ronan. Seriously, how did my brother ever have trouble dealing with you?"

Ronan smirked. "Why don't you come down here and find out?"

"Now why would I ever do that, when I have a small army here at my disposal?" Falrose gestured to the ranks of cultists below him.

"Let me finish him," Steel said. "I'd love to wipe that smile off his face for the last time."

Falrose rolled his eyes. "There's no need. We don't use a hammer to swat a fly. Let the soldiers handle him." He gave a signal with his hand to a few of the people waiting below.

Five cultists rushed forward with weapons drawn. He could probably handle them easily, but his draken forces should be in place by now. The longer they waited would risk their being discovered before they could spring their trap. He looked to where Clash was hiding and nodded.

A pulse of white light spread through Clash's body, originating from the Mythril Soul in his chest. Ronan watched him close his eyes and take a deep breath as Niradim's power washed over him, a warm smile on his face, before his eyes snapped open and he came shooting out of the ruins. His Anvil Hammer swept through all five of them, sending them careening through a nearby wall in an explosion of rock and dust.

Falrose's eyes went wide with shock. So, he wasn't as completely unflappable as he pretended to be. Clash set the head of his hammer on the ground next to him and straightened up to his full height.

"Hello, Steel," Clash said. "It's unfortunate to see you again."

"CLASH!" Steel roared. His arms split into four and ripped the two massive greatswords off his back in a frenzy. Before Falrose could restrain him, he rushed forward to engage Clash.

Ronan drew the Sword of Ashes. The blade roared to life in his hands, and his wings flared out behind him.

The battle to save Niradim had begun.

16

Brin

Brin moved forward, leading her small group of draken around the right side of the Fallen Star camp. They kept to the shadows as they crept through the dilapidated ruins, but Brin was the only one making any noise as they approached. After spending so much time with Gadjet the last few days, their ability to move so silently didn't surprise her.

It helped that there was a flurry of movement in the camp, so her small missteps went unnoticed by the enemy. Clash and Ronan had made their appearance, and it was causing quite a stir. Their plan was working—most of the cultists had filtered toward the disturbance to watch things unfold.

She didn't know how much time they had left to get in position, but Ronan could give the signal at any moment. Steel's head poked up above the rest of the crowd, and he was shoving his way toward the front of the camp. She hoped Falrose was with him. From the little Ronan had explained, they were dealing with Kyros' twin brother, and Falrose had already proved he shared the same disregard for others' lives as his sibling.

She started directing the draken into positions around her, still hidden in the surrounding rubble. She had about thirty draken with her hiding among the ruins, and Dak'thor and Gadjet would have similar numbers on their side. Their combined forces still weren't enough to overcome the numbers of the Fallen Star—they had to have close to a hundred people in their camp.

With the vast majority of the Fallen Star focused on Ronan, they just might cut down enough of them to level the playing field before they could rally. They would have a lot of soldiers in the camp to keep the draken in check and hold this area, and their priests could also prove to be dangerous. At least some of them could wield Celestian's magic.

But despite their lack of experience, the draken wouldn't be an easy fight for the cultists. Brin didn't know much about draken physiology, but they should all have access to at least some draconic magic. Plus, they had Ronan and Clash on their side. Brin wasn't a pushover herself, though she was weaker than usual from the Flame's corruption.

And Gadjet... Well, perhaps Gadjet hadn't been embellishing her accomplishments after all. If the Dragonslayer could help them survive this mess, she'd gladly hold up her side of their little bet.

Just as the draken settled in place, Brin heard the cultists at the front of the camp cry out in surprise and back away. Ronan must have done something impressive. She chuckled to herself. He'd never admit it, but he did tend to have a flair for the dramatic sometimes.

Once the crowd had settled down, she could hear distant voices talking. That had to be Falrose and Steel. A few moments later, there was a loud crash.

Then she heard Steel scream in fury and saw him rush forward. Any second now... She looked to the draken around her and nodded.

"Be ready to move," she whispered to them.

Just as she finished speaking, she saw Ronan's wings flare out behind him. That was it! She held up her hand and brought it forward to signal the draken behind her to move, and then she was off. Hurdling over her cover, she sprinted toward the camp, adrenaline filling her veins and propelling her forward.

The tents on the perimeter were separated from the rest of the tents gathered in the center of camp. This meant they'd have to rush past that first line of tents and across some open ground without being spotted before they'd get to the heart of the camp and actually start their attack.

Something about the isolated line of tents nagged at her as she ran. Why would they leave them exposed, away from the main camp?

As she got closer, she could see they lacked the tidy order of the rest of the camp. None of them faced the same direction, and there were even gaping holes which revealed crates and barrels inside some of them. Who—or what—would they be keeping in these tents? They didn't look fit to sleep in. It was almost as if...

"Wait!" she yelled as she grabbed a draken that had sped ahead of her. She threw the draken behind her just before an explosion detonated in front of her and sent her sprawling backward.

She slammed into something hard, and her world went dark.

***

5 years ago

Brin walked alongside her parents as they traveled on the main road out of Midral. She'd always wanted to go with them on one of their adventures, and so they'd chosen this one as a way to give Brin what she wanted without risking her safety too much.

This road was one of the safer ones, with a heavy presence of Protectors who would regularly patrol and keep the peace. In fact, that's why her parents were on this mission. They were assigned to guard a trade caravan on its way to Spine's Crossing. She'd gone on a few personal trips with her parents before, but this was the farthest she'd ever gone. She was so excited she barely slept the night before they left.

But there was another reason she was excited about this trip. She'd finally get to see what her parents did as part of the Protectors, which was good, because she'd be joining their ranks in just a couple of years. Sure, this trip had been boring so far, but at least they got to explore interesting places! And surely some of their assignments would be more interesting.

They'd only had one minor disturbance in a small town they'd stopped at the night before, but fortunately they'd resolved things without any fighting. A small group of thieves had been harassing the area around the town, but they'd run off when they saw the Protectors guarding this larger caravan. Still, Brin had to stay back with the rest of the merchants and their families while her parents scouted ahead with a few other Protectors to make sure things were clear. She couldn't wait to sign up for service as soon as she was old enough so she could be the one exploring and keeping people safe.

Brin shifted in her seat as her parents returned. "Mom, how much longer until we arrive?"

Her mother smiled and swept her hand along one of Brin's twin braids. "We'll be there soon, my little sweet bun."

Her father squirmed, tugging at his clothes as he kicked one of his legs out to the side. "The sooner, the better. This armor is beginning to chafe!"

"Oh, Daddy," Brin said, giggling at how silly he looked. "You always say that!"

"And I mean it every time!" he said with a smile.

Her mother tugged on her hand and pointed ahead of them in the distance. "See there, Brillenia? You can see the tops of some of the buildings if you look hard enough."

"Yes!" Brin said. "Can we see what kind of meat pies they have when we get there? I'm starving!"

Her father chuckled. "As long as you let me get out of this armor first, I'll buy you as many meat pies as you can eat!"

"No, Delvin!" Her mother gave him a playful push. "I don't know if we can afford *that* many meat pies!"

"Hey!" Brin exclaimed, putting her fists on her hips in feigned offense.

Her father brushed a hand through his thinning hair. "Whoops, you're right, Bellina. Ok, how about three meat pies?"

"It's too late. You already promised!" She punctuated her statement by sticking her tongue out at them.

They all laughed as they continued down the road. Daddy better be ready to pay up. She was *really* hungry today!

* * *

Brin's father groaned as he buried his face in his hands. "Seriously, Brillenia, *five whole meat pies*? Where does it all go?"

Brin shrugged with a grin as she settled back in her chair, patting her belly. She was stuffed! These meat pies were almost as good as the ones from Heart of the Forge back in Midral. Though to be fair, nothing was better than the meat pies back home, she was sure of it.

"Hey, you're the one that said I could have as many as I wanted!" Gods, there was nothing better than a belly full of fresh meat pies.

"Well, I certainly learned my lesson!" her father said as he stuffed the last bite of his second meat pie into his mouth.

"I should hope so, dear." Her mother poked a finger into his chest. "Otherwise you're going to have to pull extra shifts just to afford our daughter's food!"

"Oh, don't even joke about that," he said. "If I had to spend any more time in that uniform, I don't know what I'd do."

Brin frowned. "You don't like being a Protector?"

"Oh, that's not it. I love what I do," he said. "But the uniform and armor—they're just so outdated and uncomfortable. Plus, it barely offers any real protection compared to what comes out of the mountain every day. Ashes, I'm probably the third generation of dwarves wearing this very armor!"

"It's traditional, honey," her mother corrected.

"Oh, that's just a fancy word for outdated," he joked. "Your mother hates it too. Don't let her fool you!"

"Really, Mom?" Brin asked. "You don't like the uniform either?"

"Let's just say I wouldn't put up a fight if they decided to make a few modern changes. For the safety of the Protectors, of course." She slipped a quick wink in Brin's direction.

"Leave it to your mother to be nice about it," he said with a chuckle.

"Well, I kind of like it," Brin said. "It's what the Protectors have always worn. I don't know if I would like it as much if it changed all the time."

"Oh, just wait until you're wearing it yourself in a couple of years." Her father tipped back his mug and finished his drink. "You'll change your tune quickly enough."

"Oh, that's enough, Delvin," her mother said. "She'll look great in the traditional uniform. I can't wait to see her in it."

Her father laughed and gave her a kiss on the cheek. "Me too, dear. Me too."

Her mother stood up and brushed off her clothes. "Well, dinner is finished, and we've a long day of travel ahead of us. Best we get some rest."

Her father got up and took their plates back to the tavern keeper.

"I wish we could stay longer," Brin said, sinking a little further in her chair.

"Me too, sweet bun," her mother said. "Maybe we can come back sometime, just the three of us. How does that sound?"

"Yes, I would love that!" Brin said. "There are still so many meat pies I didn't get to try this time."

Her mother laughed. "Good, it's settled then! For now, it's time for bed. Good night, Brin."

Brin got up from the table and made her way to her room. "Good night!"

* * *

Clouds marred the sky as their caravan gathered in front of Spine's Crossing. A couple of wagons were joining them for the trip back to Midral to benefit from the presence of the Protectors. After arranging themselves at the back of the caravan, they were off.

A cold front had blown in overnight, so Brin wrapped her cloak tightly around her as they rode. Her parents were stationed at the front of the caravan today, so she had a wonderful view of the long road ahead.

Brin's father looked up at the sky and frowned. "Figures the nice weather wouldn't hold up for the whole trip. Are you sure you don't want to ride in the back of the wagon, Brin? It would be much warmer."

"No, this is fine, Daddy," Brin replied. It was cold, but she knew that this would be a normal experience when she joined the Protectors. She wanted to prove she could handle a little cold weather.

The morning passed quickly, but the sun just couldn't seem to find its way through the clouds. A little after midday, they approached a narrow pass just south of the little town they'd stopped at on their way to Spine's Crossing. Brin's father slowed the caravan and prepared to hop down and lead on foot so he could scout for any potential danger. Passes like this would be prime areas for bandits to ambush unsuspecting caravans.

Brin's mother put a hand on his shoulder to stop him. "Actually, why don't you let me scout ahead, dear? I'm tired of riding. I want to stretch my legs."

"Are you sure?" he asked.

"Yes, please," she said, stepping down from the front of the wagon and stretching her limbs.

"Oh, can I go too, Mom?" Brin asked. "I want to see how it's done!"

Brin's mother and father exchanged a look before her father gave a shrug.

"Sure, I could use the company, my little sweet bun," she said.

"Okay, but be careful," her father warned. "Remember that there's been bandit activity recently."

Brin's mother waved her hand in the air. "Oh, they ran off when we approached a few days ago. Besides, it was a pretty small group. A caravan this large would be too dangerous a target for them—especially with this many Protectors guarding it."

"Still," her father said.

Her mother smiled. "We will, honey, I promise." She turned to help Brin down from the wagon.

The caravan waited as Brin and her mother scouted the narrow pass.

"Ok dear." Her mother drew her sword as they proceeded slowly along the road. "There isn't likely to be any danger here, but as your father said, you always have to be careful and alert. Draw your sword and follow me closely. I'll show you what to look for."

Brin drew her sword and felt a nervous excitement as they made their way slowly through the length of the pass. It wasn't very long, but there were high walls on either side, which would be a good place for bandits to hide and wait.

Her mother pointed out several areas where she noted that there had been bandits recently, confirming what they already knew. They'd even caught glimpses of some crates and barrels among the boulders at the top of the pass, likely discarded after the bandits had to make a quick getaway. Fortunately, the tracks they found were a couple of days old. There were no fresh signs of bandits in the immediate vicinity, so it didn't look like they'd come back after they fled a few days before.

Once Brin's mother was satisfied they weren't in any danger of bandits jumping out from behind the surrounding rocks, she waved the caravan through. Brin sheathed her sword and gave her mother a hug. It was really great to see her work. She hoped that one day she'd make both her parents proud as a Protector. She wasn't sure if she'd ever take the Shaping Trial—neither of her parents had completed it—but being the first member of the Dawnstar family to reach the rank of Disciple would bring a lot of honor to their humble little family. But those were silly dreams. She didn't think she'd actually ever do it. She was happy following in her parents' footsteps and living the simple life they had. It had been good enough for them, so it would be good enough for her.

Most of the caravan had made its way into the pass, but the last two wagons that had joined their group in Spine's Crossing were having some trouble. They'd stopped at the entrance, and she could see the drivers checking the wheels. The Protector assigned to the back of the caravan was walking back to help, but they waved him off.

"I wonder what's happening back there," Brin asked, noticing the small commotion.

Her mother squinted and held her hand up to shield her eyes as she tracked the disturbance. "I don't know, but look, your father is handling it."

Her mother was right. Her father handed the reins to a merchant to continue on as he walked back to investigate.

The next part happened too fast for Brin to process, but it would be seared in her memory for the rest of her life.

The Protector who had been helping the unmoving wagons, seized and took two steps back before falling to the ground. Immediately, a dozen people poured out the back of the two wagons, weapons drawn. Her father shouted and drew his sword, sprinting toward the group, but one of the ambushers readied a bow and fired a single arrow. It pierced her father's chest, straight through his armor, and he fell to the ground, unmoving.

"Daddy!" Brin screamed and ran towards her father.

Her mother chased after her, whipping her sword out as she ran. "Brin, no!"

The same archer who'd shot her father readied another arrow, but this one looked different. The tip ignited as he drew his bow, and he fired a flaming arrow toward the crates and barrels Brin and her mother had spotted moments before at the top of the pass. As the arrow struck, Brin heard an explosion, and the force of the blast tripped her to the ground. She rolled over to see boulders falling from the wall in her direction. In seconds, she'd be crushed.

A strong hand grabbed her by the front of her shirt and threw her backward through the air, out of the way of the avalanche of rocks. She landed hard, and felt something in her leg snap, causing her to scream. She watched through tears of pain as the rocks slammed into the caravan. Then time slowed down. Her mother, who had just saved her life, was hit in the chest and pinned against the wall by one of the falling boulders that had been meant for Brin.

Brin's mind raced. She heard shouts and fighting happening behind the new pile of rocks, and finally she realized she needed to move. The pain in her leg made it hard to focus, but she channeled Niradim's power the best she could. Only a handful of dwarves her age could manage any healing magic, and even though she was still learning, she should be able to help. If she hurried, she could save her parents. She was sure of it.

Her hands hovered over her leg, and she pushed Niradim's magic into the area she felt the most pain. It was clumsy, but she screamed as she felt her leg snap back into place. She didn't realize healing could hurt so much. Fortunately, it quickly faded to a more manageable ache. She didn't have time to heal it completely—fixing the break would have to do for now.

She got to her feet and limped as fast as she could. Her mother was still moving! Brin focused more of Niradim's power into her limbs and pulled at the boulder that had her mother pinned. She could do this. She just needed to get rid of the boulder and give her mother a little healing. Then, they could heal her dad and save the rest of the caravan. She could do this. She *would* do this!

"Brin," she heard her mother wheeze. "Go… run…"

"It's okay, Mommy, be still. I'm going to help," she said. Her mother obeyed and stayed quiet as Brin lifted and pushed with all her strength, powered by Niradim's magic flowing through her. Finally, the boulder gave and rolled away. Brin quickly knelt and ripped open the front of her mother's uniform. She needed to get the breastplate off to heal-

The breastplate had crumpled like parchment under the boulder's weight.

She looked up at her mother's face and saw why she'd gone quiet. It wasn't because Brin had asked her to. Her mother's lifeless eyes stared blankly back at her.

Brin's heart raced and her chest tightened as a wave of dizziness hit her. She stumbled back from her mother's body and vomited into the dirt. Her breathing quickened, but she felt like her lungs wouldn't fill. She couldn't get air. Where had all the air gone? Why couldn't she breathe?

Frantic shouting and clanging metal hovered around the haze of her senses, and she fought to focus through the panic. It was growing closer. Faces she didn't recognize climbed over the pile of rocks, even as she heard more fighting beyond. Some people in her caravan were still alive, despite the ambush. Fear gripped her as the bandits descended and their eyes found her.

She wanted to run, but her legs wouldn't move. She wanted to scream for help, but her voice wouldn't work. What was she going to do? What could she do? What would her mother-

The storm in her mind was snuffed out, and the world around her froze as her brain completed the thought.

What would her mother do?

Bellina would get up, draw her sword, and save whoever she could. That's who her mother was, and so that's who Brin would be. People were still in danger, and if her mother couldn't help them, then she would.

So, Brin fought through the pain in her leg. She fought through the fear gripping her chest. And she fought through the air that wouldn't enter her lungs. And she stood.

Three men with swords approached her. She wiped the tears from her face and took a breath that filled her lungs. She drew her sword and focused once again on Niradim's power.

The men thought they had found some easy prey, but they didn't know. They didn't know that they stood against a Dawnstar. She was her mother's daughter, and these bandits were about to find out what that meant.

* * *

In the end, Brin saved two full wagonloads of people, and the bandits had been killed to the last. None of the Protectors had survived, so Brin led the caravan back to Spine's Crossing herself to report that the road ahead was blocked.

She learned later that the bandits her parents had driven off on their initial voyage had retreated to Spine's Crossing to join with a larger group. They posed as merchants so they could assault the larger caravan on the way back.

A month later, she was back in Midral, and she'd requested an urgent meeting with Elder Druden, the Elder in charge of outfitting the Protectors. It had taken him weeks to agree to meet with her.

"What brings you here today, young Brillenia?" Elder Druden asked her from across his desk. He hadn't looked up when she entered, instead continuing to read some correspondence he was holding.

Brin slammed two breastplates down on his desk, causing the Elder to jump and finally acknowledge her presence. One breastplate had a single hole through the chest. The other had almost been turned inside out from the damage it had sustained.

"What is this?" Druden asked.

"This is my parents' armor." She pointed to her father's breastplate. "My father was killed because this breastplate couldn't deflect a simple arrow away from his vital organs." She pointed to her mother's armor. "My mother was killed because her breastplate crumpled under the force of a boulder I was able to move by myself."

"Yes, I was sorry to hear of your parents' passing." Brin didn't miss that Druden's voice lacked the sincerity one would expect from someone who was actually sorry. "Normally, parents pass down their armor to their children when they join the Protectors. Is that what this is about? Surely you have been forging long enough to repair either of these breastplates for yourself."

Brin fumed, but held her temper. She wouldn't yell at someone so far above her own station.

"No, Elder Druden." Brin's knuckles went white at her sides as she clenched her fists. "I am requesting that we upgrade the standard armor for the Niradim Protectors to mythril. We have the resources to have the best-equipped forces in the world, yet we ask the Protectors to put themselves in danger without even giving them the protections they deserve. If my parents had been wearing mythril, they'd both still be here today."

Druden crossed his hands in front of him and sighed. "The uniform of Niradim's Protectors is a symbol, Brillenia. Our enemies know us by our armor. Who knows how many people have been saved because the uniform deters people from attacking us? We can't simply change it every time someone dies."

Brin clenched her jaw in frustration. "I'm not asking we change it every time someone dies, I'm just saying we upgrade-"

"Perhaps you should speak with Captain Landren," Druden cut in. "Had they been trained better, perhaps your parents would have been wise enough not to let some simple bandits get the better of them."

"Training had nothing to do with it!" Brin yelled, her anger finally breaking through. "My parents were among the best-"

Druden quickly rose from his chair, knocking it over behind the desk with a loud thud. "That's enough, child!" Her mouth snapped shut. "You would do well to know your place. Without Niradim's own blessing, the armor of the Niradim Protectors will not be changing. Now, I have some matters that are *actually* important to attend to, so please see yourself out. And take these scraps with you to be melted into something useful." He gestured to her parents' breastplates.

Brin snatched the armor from Druden's desk and stormed out without another word. So, he wouldn't upgrade the armor without Niradim's blessing, would he? Well, then she'd just have to go get Niradim's blessing. And she knew exactly how to do it.

She needed to get to work. It looked like she'd be taking the Shaping Trial after all.

17

Ronan

Ronan's wings flared behind him as Clash and Steel began their fight. He prepared to launch himself at Falrose when two enormous blasts erupted from either side of the camp, right where he'd told the two flanking forces to position themselves.

Brin! Ronan thought in a panic.

"What," Falrose said with a chuckle. "You didn't think I'd be stupid enough to leave our camp exposed to a flanking attack, did you?"

Anger burned in Ronan, but he pushed it down and settled his mind. Falrose was just trying to rile him up to get him off-balance. He trusted Brin could take care of herself—he just hoped that Gadjet and Dak'thor were okay on their side.

Falrose held his arm out to the side, and an amethyst crystal rapier blinked into existence and settled into his hand. It had a long, thin blade, with an ornate handguard that protected his knuckles. He gave a mock salute with the sword, a wry smile plastered on his face, and then beckoned Ronan forward to engage.

Fine, Ronan would take the fight to him. He crouched and burst into the air, rocketing towards Falrose. He couldn't spare more than a quick glance, but he noticed the enemy forces had parted toward each side of the camp to counter the failed surprise attack.

As he closed in on Falrose, he swung his blade, but his sword slashed through open air. Falrose disappeared right as Ronan's attack was about to land, throwing Ronan off-balance. Surprised by the unexpected move, he didn't see Falrose appear above him, but he felt the magical blow that hit him in the back, hurling him like a meteor into the ground.

Fortunately, his Phoenix Armor absorbed most of the blow, but Ronan coughed up a little blood as he got to his feet. He channeled some of Niradim's power to heal his wounds as he straightened up. Falrose was floating in the air above him, stifling a fake yawn.

"Again, I ask—how did my brother have so much trouble with you? If Kyros hadn't played around for so long in your city, maybe Celestian wouldn't have had to tag me in to clean up his mess."

So, Kyros had fallen out of Celestian's favor. Good, it served him right for what he did to Ronan's home. Still, his brother seemed at least an equal threat, if not worse. Ronan was beginning to suspect that destroying Midral hadn't been Kyros' or Celestian's main goal. They wanted the Flame. Setting giants loose in Midral must have been a cover for Kyros as he attempted to steal the Flame back in Midral. Ronan and a few other heroes had thwarted that plan. Now his brother was making a play to corrupt the Flame here. Whatever Celestian's plans were, the Flame of Niradim was a key component. Ronan couldn't let them have it.

He readied himself as Falrose beckoned again. Sounds of battle raged around him, though none of the cultists moved to engage him directly—the memory of what he'd done to Treyla still fresh in their minds. Clash may insist that this sword wasn't called the Sword of Ashes, but Ronan thought the name fit pretty well considering what it could do.

He rose in the air to match Falrose's height, and Falrose faked another yawn. "Well, little Phoenix, shall we continue? Or have you had enough already? I do need to be off soon."

Ronan smirked as he gathered Niradim's power into his sword and slashed forward, sending a wave of power from the blade streaking towards Falrose. Falrose casually raised his hand in front of him, and Ronan's blast exploded against a shield Falrose had summoned.

Ronan was pleased to see the momentary shock on Falrose's face as he burst through the smoke of the blast. Falrose hadn't expected him to follow up on that attack so quickly. Ronan slashed again, and the shield shattered. This time, the force of Ronan's attack sent Falrose careening down into the middle of the Fallen Star's camp, destroying some of the tents.

When the dust cleared, Falrose was stumbling to his feet among the rubble, his clothing dirty and torn. He wiped some blood from the corner of his mouth and sneered at Ronan. The noble air of indifference was gone. Ronan finally had his full attention.

"You know, it's funny," Ronan said. "Seeing you careening through the air brought back such pleasant memories of the last time I saw your brother."

"Okay, little Phoenix." Falrose spat blood to the side before raising his blade and settling into an actual swordsman stance. "Now we begin in earnest."

He disappeared again, but this time Ronan was ready. He spun and met Falrose's blade with his own behind him as Falrose coalesced in midair. Ronan tried a counterattack, but Falrose was too quick. He parried Ronan's attempt and pushed forward with a flurry of attacks, driving Ronan backward. Ronan had been hoping Falrose was all show, but those hopes were quickly dashed as Falrose expertly shifted from one attack to the next.

"Are you surprised, little Phoenix?" Falrose asked as he transitioned perfectly into another series of attacks that Ronan had trouble defending. "My brother shirked his studies as a child, favoring politics over real power." He found an opening in Ronan's defense and pressed his palm against Ronan's breastplate. A ball of fire erupted against his armor and sent Ronan flying into the ground again.

He rolled to his feet and blocked another attack as Falrose didn't give him any time to rest. "As you can tell, I didn't inherit the same pathetic work ethic that he did."

Falrose kicked Ronan backwards several feet, then held up his free hand, and Ronan felt invisible forces grab his body. Falrose pulled his hand back, and Ronan came flying towards Falrose against his will. He was barely able to twist his body away from Falrose's blade to avoid getting impaled.

They were on the ground now, amidst the chaos of the rest of the battle. Ronan heard the clanging of steel against steel, and flashes of amethyst light were met with spouts of flames as the Fallen Star and draken used their magics against one another. His eyes caught Clash fending off an onslaught of attacks from Steel, who still seemed to be in a rage. This fight wasn't going their way at all.

Suddenly, Steel smashed one of his greatswords down through Clash's arm, shearing off his hand and forcing him to drop his Anvil Hammer. He followed up the attack with a kick to Clash's chest, who stumbled back and fell off the side of the camp, down toward the river of lava.

Falrose paused to laugh as he saw Clash disappear off the edge. "Looks like my metal man is better than yours."

Steel caught their eyes across the battlefield and stalked towards them, casually cutting down a draken without missing a step until he'd reached Ronan and Falrose. "Little Phoenix! I believe I have a score to settle with you, now that my former student has been dealt with."

Ronan was worried about Clash, but he couldn't afford to let his guard down for a second against this madman. He readied himself, raising his blade and beginning to channel Niradim's magic.

Steel squinted as he noticed the sword Ronan was holding. "Is that Ashe's old sword? Hah! How did you get that rusty old blade out of the anvil?"

"Oh, it came right out for me." Ronan smirked. "What, you weren't strong enough to lift it?"

Steel's eyes darkened again. "Falrose, you may take your leave. This little Phoenix needs a lesson in how he should speak to his betters."

"You sure you're up for it, old man?" Ronan said, dropping into a crouch.

Steel leveled his two huge swords at Ronan. "You can ask Clash in a moment when you join him."

Falrose dismissed his blade, which shattered into tiny crystals and evaporated into the air. "Very well. Just don't toy with him for too long. Let's clean up this mess so we can deliver the Starsoul to Lumenova."

With that, he flew off, leaving Ronan facing this metal beast before him. Steel didn't give him any more time to prepare, leaping toward him with both blades. Ronan rolled out of the way of the initial attack and blocked the follow-up. Each attack that smashed against Ronan's blade felt like he was deflecting a boulder. Only Niradim's strength kept him on his feet.

Steel was faster than Ronan expected, and he wasn't holding back. Plus, Celestian's magic bolstered his already heavy attacks. He wove Celestian's magic directly into each strike, instead of utilizing spells like Falrose had. Though Ronan suspected Falrose wasn't only using Celestian's magic when he fought, but some of his own as well. Each of Steel's attacks fell heavier than the last. Ronan's defenses would break quickly if he kept this up. He had to go on the offensive.

Ronan jumped over one of Steel's greatswords and twisted his body in the air. He channeled Niradim's magic into his blade as he swung down toward Steel's exposed shoulder, but the Sword of Ashes extinguished as it met Steel's metal flesh, completely devoid of any power. As Ronan landed on the ground in front of Steel, the sword burst back to life, but he was so stunned by the sudden loss of power that Steel backhanded him and sent him tumbling across the ground.

In the heat of battle, he'd forgotten. The Sword of Ashes was useless against Steel. Worse, Steel had just realized it as well.

"Oh, poor little Phoenix!" He laughed as he towered over Ronan, enormous blades filling with pulsing violet energy. "It looks like you put your faith in the wrong place. Say hello to the sword's previous owner for me, and tell Niradim to stop sending his little birds my way, or I'll just keep sending them back to him."

Steel raised both of his massive swords above his head, and Ronan watched as death descended on him.

18

Brin

Brin heaved a boulder off her chest with a grunt. Her mythril-reinforced breastplate hadn't even dented at its weight. She looked around and assessed the damage. Thankfully, because of her warning, only a few of her forces had been killed or injured by the explosive traps. Unfortunately, the enemy was alerted to their presence and rallying to their position.

As she got to her feet, she drew Ronan's sword—no, *her* sword—from the shield on her arm. The draken she'd thrown backward just before the blast went off was also shakily getting to his feet. She was relieved he didn't seem too injured.

Slag, this wasn't good though. Their entire strategy had relied on being able to catch the enemy off-guard, and instead they'd announced themselves to the whole group.

The time for stealth was over—the fight was coming to them fast. "Everyone, get ready! They're on their way!"

Her short sword flared to life in her hands as she channeled Niradim's power into it. She might not be at full power, but she had more than enough to deal with these cultists. The draken were slower to respond, but got their feet under them and their weapons out before the first wave of cultists slammed into them.

She weaved her way into the fray, cutting down most cultists she encountered with relative ease. She was better equipped, and, to her relief, most of them didn't have any magical ability. But what they lacked in power, they made up for in numbers. For every cultist she cut down, it felt like two took their place.

The draken were holding their own pretty well. Most of them could breathe fire, and a few of them could enhance their strength as well. Between those two abilities, they held the cultists at bay—for the moment.

She wished she had access to her healing. With the Flame's corruption, only Ronan could use Niradim's healing magic, so she wasn't able to patch up any draken that were wounded in the fighting. When she was able, she'd come to the aid of any draken she saw struggling, but that number began to pile up as more cultists joined the fight.

Little by little, her draken forces were dwindling. Brin ducked under an attack and plunged her blade into its owner's torso before turning to assess their situation. They were engaging the enemy in their own camp. That would have been fine if their initial plan had worked, but now that they'd lost the element of surprise, they needed to find another advantage. Then an idea struck.

She jumped onto some nearby rubble so her forces could see her and raised her sword in the air. "Draken! Fall back and prepare the wall!"

The call passed between the members of the tribe, and the draken arranged themselves into a line as they fought. Brin danced from skirmish to skirmish to pull as much of the attention away from the tribe as they got into position. Finally, the last draken was in place, so she pulled back and slid behind the line.

Brin took a deep breath and screamed at the top of her lungs.

"FIRE!"

A wall of flame erupted from the line of draken as each of them added their breath to the raging inferno. The draconic fire consumed the cultists within thirty feet of the draken line, setting them ablaze and leaving many dead or incapacitated. The rest had stopped their pursuit and backed away from the heat, waiting for the flames to abate before pushing forward again.

The draken maneuver was a good delay tactic, but it wouldn't be enough to even the odds against them. The cultists still had the greater numbers. Maybe there was a way she could help fan the flames a little... Brin sheathed her sword and put her hands on of the two draken in the center of the line. Channeling as much as she could, she pushed Niradim's power into them with all her might.

A wave of power pulsed outward from the center of the line until every draken had been infused with Niradim's magic. The white Flame of Niradim combined with their draconic fire before blossoming and exploding forward. Swirling flames of red and white billowed from the wall of draken, reaching deep into the cultist camp.

Piles of ash and bones were all that remained of the cultists standing within a hundred feet. Several more beyond that range had caught fire and dropped their weapons, screaming in agony and terror.

Brin sagged from the effort, and the flames died down. The remaining cultists fled, and now Brin's forces were the ones with the advantage. She knew that had taken a lot out of them, but they needed to press while they could. The cultists didn't know how much of a drain that had been—they were too frightened to think of anything but retreat.

Brin took a second to catch her breath, and then drew her blade once again and held it in the air. "Charge!" As she yelled, the tribe sprinted forward with her.

While they pursued the enemy, Brin tried to catch what was

happening with the rest of the surrounding battle. Ronan and Falrose had been battling in the air, but she wasn't sure who was winning that fight. They weren't flying around anymore. Was that good or bad?

She needed more information. Her draken forces had reengaged the cultists up ahead and were holding their own, so she could take a moment to scan the battlefield. She just needed some height.

Channeling Niradim's magic to enhance her strength, she pushed off the ground next to one of the taller buildings in the area. Her hands barely grasped the roof's ledge, and she hauled herself up. Once she did, she sheathed her sword and surveyed the battle.

Ronan was parrying a string of impressive attacks from Falrose, putting Ronan on the back foot and losing ground. Falrose was a lot more skilled than she expected, but she knew Ronan would be okay—he was the strongest person she knew.

She shifted to the battle between Clash and Steel. That wasn't going well either. Steel was in a full rage, and Clash didn't look like he was used to fighting with limited strength. He'd be feeling the same weakness in his power as Brin did in hers. They were both of the Disciple rank, so they'd be equally hampered with the Flame's current corruption.

Finally, she turned her focus to the battle happening across the camp. Now that they'd burned away most of the cultists on their side, Gadjet's group had more enemies to contend with than Brin's group. She'd need to direct her forces to help flank the enemy across the camp to help Gadjet's squad soon so they didn't get wiped out. She chided herself again for not recognizing the trap sooner. But as she did, her attention shifted back to Ronan, and she noticed something odd.

Steel had joined Falrose over by Ronan. What happened to Clash? She'd missed something.

Falrose flew off toward the Heart Forge and left Steel with Ronan, who immediately started fighting. Steel was relentless in his attacks, but Ronan held his own—as she knew he would—so she let her eyes track back over to Falrose. He landed in front of the Heart Forge and proceeded inward, so she decided that's where she would be needed most. If Ronan had to fight Steel, she needed to go take on Falrose before he got away.

Before she descended from the building, she took one last look at Ronan's fight. He dodged an attack from Steel, and Brin saw a clear opening. Ronan had too. His sword flared with power as he swung, but sputtered out at the moment of impact. The blade clanked harmlessly off of Steel, and he sent Ronan sprawling across the ground before Ronan could recover.

Brin watched in horror as Steel stalked over to Ronan. He lifted both his massive blades in the air and brought them down in a powerful blow. Brin's heart stopped in her chest.

A small blur of red and white with a glint of metal shot out from the ruins across from her with incredible speed, coming to a halt between Steel's blades and Ronan.

Brin heard a massive boom as Steel's magic-enhanced greatswords crashed against a gleaming mythril arm attached to a small red draken.

Gadjet had joined the fight.

19

Ronan

Ronan opened his eyes to one of the most incredible sights he'd ever seen.

Standing over him was Gadjet's small, red draken form, wearing glistening white dragon-scale armor from the neck down. On her head, she wore a bone-white helmet, carved into an intricately detailed dragon's head. She held a long spear, carved from the same bone, tucked under her right arm behind her. Her left arm, made completely of mythril and crackling with draconic magic, crossed above her—upon which rested the two largest greatswords Ronan had ever seen. They were still vibrating with shock from the impact.

Gadjet had blocked both of them with one arm.

Steel's eyes went wide with shock, unable to process what had just happened. While he was still stunned, Gadjet's spear lit up with pale-blue energy, and she thrust the point into Steel's chest. A burst of draconic power blasted from the tip and sent Steel flying away, buying them a moment to recover.

Gadjet straightened up and shook her mythril arm.

"Dragon's above, that *hurt!*" she said. "Wow, I am seriously going to feel that one tomorrow."

Ronan just sat there, mouth agape.

Gadjet raised her helmet, revealing a faint smirk playing across the little draken's face. "What, you're surprised? I killed a *dragon*, Ronan. You think I can't take a hit from this lunatic?"

She extended her mythril hand to him, hauling Ronan to his feet.

Ronan composed himself as he dusted the dirt off his clothes. "Well, you have incredible timing, Gadjet. Looks like I owe you even more."

Gadjet's smile widened. "Oh, don't worry. What your girlfriend promised me should be more than enough to pay me back!"

Ronan shook his head. "At some point one of you is going to need to explain to me just what I've been volunteered for." He picked up his sword and latched it onto his back. "Hopefully, it's enough to cover one more request. I'm afraid I'm going to have to ask you for a little more assistance. This sword is useless against Steel. Clash was right. It can't be used against a mythrali."

"I gathered as much," Gadjet said. "It's okay, I'll keep Steel busy until Clash gets back."

Ronan sighed. He'd rather give her this news in a different setting, but she needed to know that she wouldn't get any more help from Clash. "Gadjet, I'm sorry, but Clash is dead. Steel pushed him off the edge during their fight."

Gadjet raised a single eyebrow. "Oh really? So the huge metal guy climbing out of the lava is some *other* mythrali I don't know about?"

"What?" Ronan asked. "He's alive?"

"There's a reason that the Heart Forge is guarded by a flowing wall of lava," Gadjet said. "Only a mythrali can walk through it." She turned and regarded Ronan. "And maybe a Phoenix, but that would be a pretty dangerous thing to test," she added with a wink.

Ronan felt a weight lift from his shoulders. That was a relief. He wasn't sure how Clash was going to swing around that massive hammer with just one arm, but he'd take all the help he could get at the moment.

"You're sure you're up for keeping Steel occupied?" Ronan asked as he watched Steel climb out of some rubble. "He's not going to be happy about what you just did to him."

Gadjet waved her hand in the air. "I'll be fine. You need to go stop Falrose. I'll send Clash your way when he gets back up here. You'll need his Mythril Soul to save the Flame."

That's right, Clash still had the Mythril Soul! Thank Niradim for the mythrali ability to survive molten rock.

"Take care of yourself, Gadjet," Ronan said. Gadjet nodded and slammed her helmet back down into place. Steel had retrieved his swords and seethed at the small draken. The crystal lattice running through his chest began to pulse and glow with mounting violet energy, and purple sparks of lightning crackled across his body and blades.

"You're going to regret that, you little wyrmling!" Steel raged.

Gadjet leveled her dragon-bone spear at the monstrosity facing her. Her eyes flared blue-white with draconic power, and her armor frosted over. Cold steam vented from the scales she wore, pooling around her feet. She snorted smoke from her nostrils.

"We'll see."

And she leapt into battle.

Ronan only spared a moment to watch Gadjet dancing between Steel's blades, before he turned and sprinted towards the Heart Forge. He needed to focus on his task. Falrose had retreated to the Heart Forge, which meant that's where Ronan needed to be.

He'd expended a lot of power in his initial bout with Falrose, so even though flying would be faster, he opted to run instead so he could conserve whatever energy he could. As he ran, he spared a quick glance over at Brin's forces, which seemed to have the upper hand. In fact, some of them were flanking the cultists attacking Gadjet's group. They were still outnumbered, but they were doing well considering their initial plan had failed. He didn't see Brin, but he still trusted she was okay. She wouldn't go down that easy.

He couldn't help but worry about how they were going to win this fight. Sure, the draken were doing well against the rank-and-file cultists for now, but Falrose and Steel were a bigger threat than they'd calculated. Ronan had hoped that since the corruption hadn't affected his power like it had the others, he'd be able to stop Falrose without too much trouble. Especially after obtaining the Sword of Ashes.

He'd beaten Kyros despite the two artifacts in Kyros' possession, but Falrose was a different kind of ruthless in battle. Kyros had wielded his power like a club, but Falrose directed his with practiced precision, honed from a lifetime of training. Clash was wounded, Brin was weaker than normal because of the corruption, and Ronan could only fight Falrose because his sword wouldn't harm Steel.

On top of that, every moment that passed was a boon to the cultists, who had more battle experience than the draken. The more they could rally and organize, the less effective the draken forces would be. Their advantage could change in a heartbeat. But if they could finish off Falrose and Steel, that would ensure their victory. They had to hurry.

Ronan broke through the far edge of the camp about the same time as a small dwarven woman with twin braids through her hair skidded to a stop in front of him. A huge smile broke across her dirt-stained face as soon as she saw him, and his heart skipped a beat.

"Brin! I'm glad you're okay."

They shared a quick embrace before she took a step back and gestured back at the Fallen Star camp. "Yeah, no thanks to them. I should have known they'd have defenses set up around the perimeter of their camp. I'm sorry, Ronan."

Ronan shook his head. "Like you could have predicted that? Besides, it was my plan. But what are you doing here? I thought you were with your draken."

"I saw your fight with Steel and watched Falrose retreat to the Heart

Forge," she said. "I didn't want to let him get away, so I thought I'd keep him busy for a bit. Though I have to say, I'm glad you're here already. I wasn't looking forward to facing him alone."

Ronan nodded in agreement. "Yeah, he's stronger than I thought he'd be. I was hoping he'd be all bark, no bite. That doesn't seem to be the case."

"Well, let's go together then." She pulled him down and gave him a quick kiss before unsheathing her sword from the shield on her arm.

"Well, isn't that cute?"

Falrose emerged from the Heart Forge holding the Starsoul Ronan had helped create, but instead of being empty, it was pulsing with pale-violet magic. A corrupted version of the Flame of Niradim. "The love birds have come here to die together."

Ronan sneered as he removed his sword from his back, and it flared to life. "We're not letting you leave here with that Starsoul, Falrose. Drop it, take your people, and leave."

Falrose laughed. "Oh, I think you misunderstand your position, little Phoenix. We already have reinforcements on the way from Lumenova. Even if you were to somehow defeat me here and restore the Flame, you wouldn't be able to hold this location. No, I think it is you who should flee before I've wiped out you and your new friends."

"We'll gather forces from Midral." Ronan countered. "We'll be able to defend the Heart Forge just fine."

Falrose laughed. "No, I don't think you will. You see, I happen to know from a very reliable source that your little girlfriend is no longer welcome in Midral. And word is already spreading that you worked with her and the draken that attacked them to steal the Mythril Soul. Your people have as good as abandoned you already."

"How could you possibly know that?" Brin asked.

A wicked smile snaked its way across his face. "Like I said, I have a very reliable source."

Ronan didn't like the sound of that. He hated to think there was anyone in Midral that would be working with the enemy, but for Falrose to have information like that... Only someone involved in the events surrounding Brin and Gadjet could have fed him that information. It was possible that Falrose was bluffing, but how else would he know about the Mythril Soul being stolen?

It didn't matter right now. They needed to stop Falrose here, and then they could figure out the rest. "I have faith in my people." He leveled his sword at Falrose, and Brin readied herself as well. "Last chance."

"Very well," Falrose said. "Besides, I wasn't really going to let you go anyway. Killing you both will be too much fun."

His crystal blade manifested itself in his hand as the Starsoul folded out of existence. He must have some kind of pocket dimension he was storing it in. Ronan didn't know much about magic outside of what he used with Niradim, but he did know that creating a personal pocket dimension was not some low-level spell. Falrose had not been joking when he said he was gifted. They needed to be careful—he may still have some tricks up his sleeve.

Falrose raised his blade toward them as his translucent crystalline armor sparked into place around him.

Ronan looked over at Brin. "Are you ready?"

She winked at him. "I was born ready. Let's do this."

They sprinted forward, and Falrose leapt back into the Heart Forge, where there was more space to maneuver. As they crossed the threshold, two explosions rocked them from either side, knocking them both to the ground.

"I can't believe you fell for the same trick twice!" Falrose's laugh bounced off the walls of the Heart Forge, taunting them. "Like I said, killing you both will be so much fun."

Ronan rolled to his feet and closed the distance, with Brin trailing right behind. Falrose was just as sharp in his movements as before, though the combined efforts of Ronan and Brin kept him from gaining the upper hand. The issue was that Brin wasn't at full strength, so anytime Falrose went to make an attack on her, Ronan had to overextend to protect her from anything too dangerous, and Falrose knew it.

"I wonder which of you I should kill first." Falrose parried an attack from Ronan while dodging a strike from Brin. "Shall I kill the little Phoenix first and destroy Niradim's last symbol of hope?"

He kicked Ronan in the chest, sending him tumbling, and then tripped Brin after sidestepping her follow-up strike. He tapped a thoughtful finger on his chin. "Or perhaps it would be more entertaining to kill his little plaything and see if he still has the will to fight."

Ronan and Brin climbed to their feet, breathing hard from the skirmish. Ronan hated to admit it, but they were losing. Falrose was tiring as well—Ronan could see it in his movements, and he hadn't taken to the air like in their first fight—but not as fast as the two of them were.

The corrupted Flame flickered unnaturally beside them, the pale-violet glow casting twisted shadows around the room that seemed to mock them as they stood their ground. He glanced at Brin, who was struggling to catch her breath and dripping with sweat as she stood next to him. At this rate, she was going to become more of a liability than an asset in this fight. They needed to change things up.

Just then, Gadjet soared through the air and slammed against the wall next to them, crumpling into a heap. Clash came next, skidding across the ground and grinding to a stop a few feet from where they stood.

"Ah, so it seems my esteemed colleague has finished taking out some of the trash," Falrose said as Steel stepped up to the entrance of the

Heart Forge and then paused. "Though this may be as far as he makes it." He laughed at Steel's hesitation to cross the threshold.

Steel looked at Falrose, sneered, and then took a purposeful step into the Heart Forge. It looked like Steel's hatred for Clash outweighed his fear of entering his old prison. Or maybe he simply didn't want to continue looking weak in Falrose's eyes. Either way, it wasn't good news for Ronan's group.

Brin ran over to Gadjet to check on her as Clash struggled to his feet. He was still holding his Anvil Hammer in his remaining hand, but he leaned on it as he stood.

"Sorry," Gadjet said, wincing in pain. It looked like she had some broken bones. "I may have underestimated just how strong he was."

"It's okay, Gadjet," Brin said. "We'll take it from here."

Gadjet nodded as she propped herself up to sit against the wall. So they were down to Ronan and Brin. They already had trouble dealing with Falrose between the two of them, and now Steel had joined the fight. Clash could barely stand, much less swing that hammer with any real force. Gadjet couldn't move at all, Brin was exhausted, and Ronan was pushing the limits of his power even as a Phoenix.

There was only one play left, and that was to hold them off long enough for Clash to purify the Flame. Once that happened, Brin would get access to her full powers again, and hopefully that would be enough to turn the tide in their favor. With the Flame back, perhaps Brin could even heal Clash and Gadjet back into fighting shape.

Clash stood as if to help them make a final stand, but Ronan shook his head. "No, Clash, you're too wounded, and we need that Mythril Soul in your chest to cleanse the Flame. Brin and I will handle the two of them while you work on the Flame."

Brin nodded in agreement. "I'll take Steel. Your sword won't work against him. Besides…" She turned and placed a hand on Gadjet's shoulder. "I have to pay him back for hurting my friend."

"Thanks, Brin." Gadjet tried to smile, but gritted her teeth in pain instead. "Go get him."

Brin stepped over until she was across from Steel and then drew her sword. Niradim's power flickered around her and then steadied as it filled her shield and blade.

"Oh, I finally get to try my hand at one of Niradim's new breed!" Steel's arms split into four and he unhooked both of his greatswords from his back. "Let's see how you tiny things match up against the original!"

Ronan and Brin channeled as much of Niradim's power as they could manage. Wisps of white smoke rose from their bodies, and their blades gleamed with the holy power of Niradim. Ronan looked over at Brin, and their eyes met. They each gave a slight nod, and then they leapt back into battle.

Ronan saw Brin dodge Steel's initial attack out of the corner of his eye before his blade crashed into Falrose's, and then all of his focus shifted to keeping the powerful novaborn busy. Ronan pushed his advantage with the surge of strength he received from Niradim's power, but Falrose met him blade for blade. Not content to keep the fighting on solid ground, Falrose again took to the sky, and Ronan's wings flared out behind him as he pursued.

He heard the sounds of Brin and Steel's battle below, but couldn't spare a moment to see what was happening. Falrose dodged in the air around the Heart Forge as Ronan continued his relentless attack. He wasn't making any good headway in the fight, but he just needed to keep Falrose busy while Clash worked on purifying the Flame.

As he fought, he heard Clash's voice rise above the sounds of battle. "Ronan, we have a problem!"

Slag and ashes, this was not a good time to be running into complications. Clash continued.

"I can't push the Soul Flame into the Forge. It needs to be done by someone who can channel!"

That meant either him or Brin. He was the only one capable of keeping Falrose's attention at the moment, which meant Brin was their only option. She must have come to the same conclusion, because he heard her shout back. "Clash, switch with me! Now!"

Ronan pushed Falrose back and spared a glance as Clash left the Mythril Soul on the ground next to the Flame and picked up his hammer, limping towards Steel, who was getting back up off the ground from one of Brin's attacks. She sprinted past him toward the Flame. Ronan didn't know how long the transfer would take, but he did know there was no way Clash could last very long against Steel with his current injuries. Still, it was the only option they had. It would have to be enough.

Indeed, Steel easily turned away Clash's initial attack and immediately put him on the defensive, but Ronan saw a flash of pale-blue light streak out from the wall, and a blast of draconic magic splashed against Steel's back, causing him to stumble.

Gadjet!

Clash took advantage of the momentary distraction and hit Steel square in the chest with his hammer. It wasn't as strong as normal considering Clash's current state, but Steel went skidding across the ground. Brin had reached the Flame, so Ronan redoubled his efforts against Falrose. They could do this! Just a little longer…

Ronan flew forward to reengage Falrose, pouring Niradim's power into his blade for a powerful attack. He slashed forward, but Falrose smirked and winked out of existence. Energy surged out of the Sword of Ashes, cutting a deep gash along the ceiling of the Heart Forge, but missing its target. Ronan heard Gadjet shriek, and he spun.

Falrose looked up at Ronan from the ground with a cruel grin, crystal blade slick with bright crimson as fresh blood pooled next to the body lying at his feet.

The Mythril Soul rolled out of Brin's lifeless hand.

20

Brin

Brin floated above the Heart Forge, which was odd, because the last thing she remembered was reaching toward Niradim's Flame. She was about to push the Soul Flame from the Mythril Soul into the Heart Forge to cleanse it of Celestian's corruption. Everything around her was coated in shades of grey, except for a few of the magical items in the room.

Ronan's armor and sword glowed a vibrant white, illuminating everything around him. Various pieces of Steel and Falrose's armor and weapons glowed purple, a sign of Celestian's power. Parts of Gadjet's armor and weapon had a blue tint to them, which matched the draconic magic she'd seen from the powerful draken. Strangely, Gadjet's mythril arm glowed both blue and white, which seemed to imply there was some of Niradim's own power mixed with Gadjet's draconic magic within it.

The Flame itself still blazed with the swirl of violet tinged with white—Celestian's corruption completely intertwined with Niradim's Flame. The Mythril Soul glowed with a pure white light on the ground next to it. But why was it there, and why was she here? Things also seemed to be frozen, or perhaps moving very slowly? It was difficult to tell. Everything was hazy.

She tried to remember. She'd just used the last remnants of her fading power to deliver a blow on Steel to give her enough time to switch places with Clash. He wasn't able to complete the transfer of the Soul Flame from the Mythril Soul. Only someone who could channel Niradim's power could do it, which meant either Ronan or Brin would have to do it. They both knew she'd stand no chance against both Falrose and Steel, so she'd immediately made the move to purify the Flame.

She remembered a flash of orange-red in front of her and excruciating pain.

Then nothing.

Then this.

Slag and ashes... That was her body on the ground, wasn't it...

She was dead.

That slagging novaborn had killed her. She clenched her fists in frustration. Of all the people... Why'd it have to be that guy? And he still wore a smug smile aimed at Ronan while he stood over her body. She expected her heart rate to increase and her breathing to become erratic like it did so often when everything around her seemed too much for her to handle, but—nothing. The familiar panic didn't settle in. *One of the benefits of being dead,* she guessed.

She knocked her knuckles against her forehead. *Not the time for jokes, Brin.* This was all so strange. She needed to get her bearings, so she rubbed her hands over her face before deciding to look around.

Her eyes immediately gravitated to her beloved. Poor Ronan. He was hovering in the air, looking down in horror at the scene on the ground. She teared up at the sight of him. He didn't deserve to feel this pain.

She floated over to him and put a hand on his cheek, caressing his grief-stricken face. He was the strongest person she knew. If there were anyone who could get through this, it was Ronan. She planted a gentle kiss on his forehead before leaning her head against his with her eyes closed.

"I'm so sorry, Ronan," she whispered. "I really thought we could do this. Please, survive. Take care of yourself, and our people."

It took her a moment to let go. She still didn't know if there was something she needed to do before she moved on or if it would happen slowly. If it did happen gradually, this was where she wanted to be when it happened, by Ronan's side. Still, she couldn't help but wonder why she was stuck here in this limbo. Maybe there was still a way for her to help the others?

She reluctantly pulled away from Ronan and lowered herself over to Clash, who was in a heap on the floor. His fight with Steel wasn't going well, even with the help Gadjet was trying to lend to the fight in her injured state.

Gadjet... Brin approached her new friend and embraced her. They'd only known each other for a short time, but she felt such a strong bond with the little draken. She wished they'd had more time together. Gadjet was such a fierce warrior, but even her face was painted in grief at Brin's fate.

Brin walked over to Falrose and frowned at the stuck-up novaborn. Kyros had been pretty bad, but she was starting to care even less for his twin standing before her. She couldn't help herself and tried to give him a swift kick to see if she could elicit any kind of response, but nothing happened. Too bad. At least Ronan was about to make him regret every decision in his life that had led him to this moment. He didn't know what was coming for him.

Finally, she inspected the Mythril Soul that had rolled out of her lifeless hand. Strangely, it was glowing brighter than any of the other magical objects in the room, including the Flame itself. She had been so close, she thought as she reached toward it. Just a moment longer and she'd have been able to-

Her fingers brushed the orb, and holy fire roared out of the Mythril Soul, causing her to stumble and fall back. She shielded her eyes as the Flame gathered in the air. Light blanketed everything in the room until it was all she could see, even through her closed eyelids. Once it had dimmed, she slowly opened her eyes. A glorious phoenix made of the white Flame itself hovered above her.

Her breath caught in her throat. Could it really be? "...Niradim?"

YES, MY CHILD.

She laughed. It was really him! Her god was really here, talking to her! She had so many questions she wanted to ask him. Where should she start?

And then the realization of what that meant hit her. So, it was true. This wasn't a dream. She really had died.

So instead of asking him one of the thousand questions she'd had growing up, she focused on what was before her. "Niradim, what's going on? Why am I here like this?"

I WANT YOU TO SEE.

As he spoke the words, the world began to move around them. Ronan yelled at Falrose and sped toward the ground. She could see what was happening, but all the sound was muffled. Falrose dodged out of the way and back over to Steel, who kicked Clash across the ground toward Ronan. Ronan summoned a wall of flames to keep Celestian's Agents at bay and then knelt to pick up Brin.

Ronan cradled her body in his arms, and she could tell that Falrose and Steel were arguing about something. Falrose must have won, because Steel fell silent. Gadjet crawled over to where Ronan was holding Brin and wept.

She looked to Niradim. "What's happening?"

MY PHOENIX IS ABOUT TO REALIZE THIS IS THE DECISION I HAVE BEEN PREPARING HIM FOR. THE HARDEST DECISION

HE WILL EVER HAVE TO MAKE. HE WILL HAVE TO SACRIFICE SOMEONE HE LOVES FOR THE GOOD OF MY PEOPLE.

A chill ran through her. "What do you mean?"

THE MYTHRIL SOUL BESIDE HIM HOLDS A SOUL FLAME. THAT FLAME CAN BE USED TO PURIFY MY FLAME AND SAVE ME. Niradim's head turned to her. OR IT CAN BE USED TO BRING YOU BACK.

"To bring me back…" Brin said. "Like what you did with Ronan?"

YES.

Ronan still held her body in his arms. What would he choose? At that moment, one of the mysteries she and Ronan had never figured out popped into her head, and she finally had the opportunity to ask the one person who had the answer.

"Niradim," Brin said. "Why did you allow Ronan to die?"

The large phoenix before her continued to watch Ronan for long enough that Brin wasn't sure if she would get her answer. But then Niradim sighed.

IT WAS THE ONLY WAY FOR HIM TO BECOME WHAT HE WAS MEANT TO BE.

"What do you mean?" Brin asked.

HUMANS ARE NOT BORN WITH A SOUL FLAME AS THE DWARVES ARE. FOR RONAN TO BECOME A PHOENIX, HE HAD TO DIE SO I COULD GIVE HIM A PIECE OF MY SOUL.

"And then his rebirth made him a Phoenix?" she said.

NO, THAT WAS ONLY THE FIRST STEP. RONAN PASSED HIS PHOENIX TRIAL WHEN HE PUT HIS FAITH IN ME AGAIN.

"Why couldn't you have told him why he had to die?" Brin asked. "He might have understood and trusted you again sooner!"

THAT IS NOT HOW FAITH WORKS, MY CHILD. FAITH IS BELIEVING WITHOUT KNOWING.

Ronan picked up the Mythril Soul and stared at it. He looked at the

Flame, and then down at Brin.

Niradim let out a breath and smiled.

HE HAS JUST MADE THE CONNECTION HIMSELF.

Some tension she hadn't noticed Niradim was holding melted away before her eyes. Keeping the secret of Ronan's death to himself was not something Niradim had enjoyed.

Brin looked back over at Ronan. "And now he has to decide between saving me or saving you."

YES.

Ronan was talking to Clash, tears streaming down his face. The moment of choice was coming. She could feel it in the air. It was close.

"What if he makes the wrong choice?"

HE WON'T.

"How can you be so sure?" she whispered, finally turning to look at Niradim.

Niradim's eyes met hers, and a gentle smile spread across his face.

I HAVE FAITH.

21

Ronan

Ronan screamed.

Brin was dead. No, this couldn't be happening. Brin could not be dead.

He dove through the air, slashing at Falrose in a wild frenzy to get him away from Brin. Falrose easily dodged the attack and retreated over to Steel, who'd just kicked Clash across the room.

Niradim's power flared within Ronan and he swung the Sword of Ashes in a powerful arc. Fire burst like a geyser from the ground, cutting Falrose and Steel off from the rest of them. It wouldn't last long, but he needed them to stay away.

She couldn't be dead. This was just a nightmare. He was about to wake up, and Brin would be lying next to him, gently snoring like she did after a hard day of work. It always sounded like she was purring in her sleep. Yes, this was just a bad dream.

Then why did it hurt so bad?

Falrose laughed from across the Heart Forge as Steel pulled his blades out and prepared to attack, but Falrose held Steel back with his hand.

"What are you doing?" Steel shrugged out of Falrose's grip. "Let's kill him now and be done with this!"

"Wait for the flames to die down," Falrose said. "Besides, I'm enjoying the show! Look at how broken he is. Niradim's little phoenix, reduced to tears. It's delicious!"

Ronan could barely hear them as he held Brin's body in his arms. She was dead. Not dying. If she were dying, he could heal her and save her life. No, she was truly dead. Falrose had been precise with his strike. He'd pierced her heart.

And in doing so, pierced Ronan's as well.

Sobs crashed over him in waves as he held her. Gadjet crawled over to join him in his pain. Clash pulled himself to his knees and rested a gentle hand on Ronan's shoulder. "I'm sorry, Ronan."

"What do we do now, Clash?" Ronan asked through the tears.

His time with her had been too short, and too riddled with chaos. She'd been the one that helped him through his darkest moments—when his faith was dead. They'd spent countless hours together in his forge as he taught her the techniques that would help her pass her Shaping Trial.

Unlike everyone else around him, she didn't try to force him back into the faith. She accepted him as he was, and respected his decision. He didn't know if she always knew he'd put his faith back in Niradim eventually, but it meant the world to him that she let him work through his issues without feeling pressured.

And now she was gone. He'd never get to work in the forge with her again. See that spark in her eye when a new idea popped into her head. Or watch her demolish a plate full of meat pies while she sketched new armor designs late into the night in the light of a flickering candle.

She was dead.

He had to focus on something else right now. He picked up the Mythril Soul. It was warm, almost hot to the touch. That was different. He'd never felt this kind of warmth from the palm-sized orb before. A gentle pulse, almost like a heartbeat, vibrated from its core in his hand.

The Soul Flame within resonated with him, and the greatest mystery in his life finally clicked into place.

The Soul Flame—that was why Niradim had let him die. As a human, he didn't have one, but now he did. Niradim had given him a Soul Flame from the Soul Forge when the flames washed over him and brought him back to life.

And in that moment, he knew. He could save Brin. But it would use the Soul Flame in the Mythril Soul, which meant they would lose their only chance at saving Niradim. Saving Brin would mean sacrificing his own god. And *he* had to choose. This was the moment Niradim had warned him about. Only, it hurt so much worse than anything Ronan could ever have expected.

"Clash." Ronan stared at the Mythril Soul in his hand as he spoke. "You said that you had made the wrong choice back then. What was the right one?"

Clash looked at him and whispered. "I should have saved my people."

Niradim would save the one in trouble. I know you would do the same, even if you don't know it yourself. Brin's words echoed in his mind.

She was right.

He looked up and met Clash's eyes. "Yes." Ronan nodded. "That would have been the right choice."

He placed the Mythril Soul against Brin's chest and pushed the Soul Flame out of the orb and into her body. Holy fire surged out from the Mythril Soul and engulfed Brin. As the fire consumed her, Falrose stopped laughing. Ash crusted over her from head to toe before falling away. All of her wounds had been healed.

A tense silence filled the Heart Forge for the length of a heartbeat before one beautiful ragged cough shattered it. Brin wiped the ash from her face and looked up into Ronan's teary eyes.

"Niradim wanted me to tell you," Brin said as she placed her hand on his cheek and wiped away his tears.

"He knew you'd make the right choice."

22

Brin

Brin felt the power of Niradim flow through her like it never had before. Flakes of ash fell from her body as she got to her feet, dissolving in the air around her. Gadjet almost knocked her back over with an embrace, but then gave a small yelp of pain.

"Oh, Gadjet," Brin said with concern. "Here, let me help you with that."

She placed her hand on Gadjet's shoulder and let Niradim's power pour into Gadjet. Gadjet shuddered as bones popped back into place. The wounds covering her body sizzled as if being cauterized, and then sealed shut. Gadjet gasped as the healing finished.

"Oh, that feels *much* better," Gadjet said. She embraced her again, much stronger this time. "Thank you, Brin."

She then looked over at Clash, who was still kneeling on the floor, his mythril body broken and chipped in so many places. He looked like he was in great pain, but he was beaming with pride at the choice Ronan had made. He truly had learned Niradim's heart from the tragic events of his past.

His eyes and smile turned to her. "Welcome back, Lady Brin."

"Thank you, Clash," Brin said. "Now hold still."

She placed her hand, so tiny compared to his large mythrali body, on his forehead and again focused on pushing Niradim's power into him. In much the same way, his body vibrated as Niradim's healing power flowed through him. The chips, bends, and breaks along his frame heated to white-hot as if in the fire of a forge and then molded back into place before cooling back to his normal metallic dark grey, though with a bit more shine than when they'd first found him. He was as good as new, minus the hand he'd lost in battle. He got to his feet and took up his hammer in his one good arm, resting it on his shoulder.

That healing had been so easy! It was like up until now, she'd been running with a full set of heavy plate armor, but now all the weight had been removed. She was astonished at how well she resonated with Niradim's power.

She could still feel the corruption, the *wrongness*, of what was happening with the Flame. But it didn't hinder her abilities now as it had moments ago.

The Flame... they'd lost their only way of cleansing it of Celestian's corruption to bring her back. She didn't feel worth that cost, but Niradim had told her to have peace with his decision. As Ronan had correctly assessed, Niradim would gladly sacrifice himself for his people. And he'd left her with one last parting gift.

She lit up like a roaring fire with Niradim's power as she turned to regard her killer. Falrose's eyes widened, and he took an involuntary step back as her gaze locked on him. He quickly regained his composure, and a look of understanding replaced the momentary shock.

"Wait... Am I to understand that you used the Mythril Soul to resurrect your girlfriend instead of saving your god?" He doubled over in laughter. "Congratulations, that is the most profoundly stupid thing I have ever witnessed!"

She couldn't wait to wipe that smile off his face.

Steel looked over at Falrose. "So that's it? Niradim is gone?"

"Niradim will never be gone, so long as his Flame lives within his people," Ronan said. "The people he loves so much, he would rather sacrifice himself than lose one."

"How ridiculous!" Steel said.

"I'm sure it seems like it to you," Ronan said, then a sly smile spread across his face. "But then again, you did fail your Phoenix Trial what—three times? So I wouldn't expect you to understand."

Steel growled at the insult and drew his blades again. "Why don't you come over here and I'll show you again what I traded that measly Phoenix power for."

Ronan leveled his sword at Steel. "Maybe when I'm done with Falrose, you and I can-"

"Actually," Brin said, cutting him off. "Why don't you go ahead and give Steel what he wants? I'd like to give Falrose a chance to *deeply* regret his actions in the last few minutes."

Ronan lifted an eyebrow. "You sure?"

"Oh yes." Brin's eyes didn't leave her target as a smile spread across her face. "I'm sure."

"Are you two seriously deciding which of you gets the pleasure of dying by my blade?" Falrose's rapier manifested in his hand as he spoke, and he pointed the tip at Brin. "I'm happy to kill you a second time if once wasn't enough, child. But don't worry, I'll make it quick so the grownups can continue to play."

Ronan smiled. "Oh boy, he doesn't know he's getting the short end of the stick, does he?"

Brin's smile deepened. "Nope!"

Gadjet and Clash stepped up next to Ronan and Brin.

"This time, we can help." Gadjet slammed her helmet back into place and raised her spear, which had a spiderweb of cracks through the length of the shaft. Clash nodded in agreement as he shifted his stance and gripped his hammer closer to the head with his one good hand.

"No, you two have a more important mission." Brin pointed to the ruins beyond the Heart Forge's entrance, where the rest of the tribe was still engaged with the remaining cultists. "You need to get everyone else out of here to safety. Go help them defeat the last of the cultists and lead them out of the mountain. The Fallen Star will reinforce this position, and we no longer have the means or the need to protect the Heart Forge now that the Flame can't be saved. We need to shift our focus to saving your people."

Gadjet hesitated, but then nodded. "Thank you, Brin." She spared one last glare at Steel and Falrose before she ran out the doors of the Heart Forge to join her tribe in battle.

"Now if we're finished with our meaningless little heart-to-hearts, can we be on with this?" Falrose said. "Once we've killed you all, I have a long trip back to Lumenova that I'd like to get started on."

Brin drew her blade. "Gladly."

Brin lunged forward at incredible speed to engage Falrose, but he flew into the air to dodge her attack.

Hovering just outside of her reach, he laughed down at her. "Oh, I'm sorry, are you having trouble reaching this high with your little arms?"

Brin smirked as wings of white flame exploded from her back and she launched herself into the air. Falrose's laughter cut off as the smug look on his face was replaced by her fist, sending him shooting through the air and bouncing off the ceiling.

Gods, that felt good.

23

Ronan & Brin

Ronan watched with pride as Brin smashed into Falrose in mid-air. The power behind her fist sent the cocky novaborn smashing into the ceiling with a loud crash. Rocks came tumbling down with the force of the blow.

Steel chuckled. "It looks like the little phoenix has a tiny phoenix to keep him company now. Enjoy it for the few moments you're still alive. I don't know how you think you'll stand a chance against me with that useless blade. This won't even be fun."

Clash growled beside Ronan. "I hate to admit it, but he has a point. How do you plan on fighting him if you can't use Ashe's sword against him?"

Ronan took the Blade of Ashes off his back and slammed it point-down into the Great Anvil of the Heart Forge. It sank almost down to the hilt and then crusted over with ash as Ronan released it. It was in the same position Ashe had left it so many years ago. Fitting, to give Clash a chance at redemption. A chance to believe in himself again.

Ronan turned to Clash. "Actually, I'd like to borrow your hammer, if you don't mind. In the meantime, I won't have you be defenseless. You can borrow my new sword." Ronan gestured to the blade buried in the anvil.

Clash's eyes widened, and he took a step back. "No, Ronan, I can't. You know as well as I do that I've tried wielding that sword before. I'm not worthy enough."

Ronan placed a hand up on Clash's shoulder. "I believe in you, Clash. You are not the same mythrali you once were. It's just a sword."

Clash placed his hammer on the ground and tentatively reached toward Ashe's former sword. Ronan took a step back as Clash's hand hovered next to the hilt for a moment. He looked up.

"Just a sword..." he whispered. "She said the same thing before she died. But there was more... And I think I finally understand."

Ronan nodded. "I think you do."

"A sword is just a sword..." Clash wrapped his hand around the hilt of the blade and met Ronan's eyes. "Until someone with the heart of a Phoenix wields the blade."

He ripped the Sword of Ashes free from the anvil, and the blade roared to life in his hand. The inferno blazed around the blade as he held it high, casting bright light to every corner of the Heart Forge. Tears streamed down his face as he pulled it down to eye-level.

"You have the heart of a Phoenix, Clash," Ronan said. "Even if you don't have the powers yet."

"Thank you, Ronan," Clash whispered. "I will protect this with my life and return it to you when our task is done here."

"Protect the people, Clash," Ronan said. "Niradim and I believe in you."

Clash nodded as he placed the sword on his back. He reached down and picked up the empty Mythril Soul and slotted it back into his chest before turning and running after Gadjet to assist with their escape. The Anvil Hammer rested on its head next to Ronan, with its handle rising straight up beside him.

"Now, it's long past time I dealt with you." Ronan squared off against

Steel as he cracked his knuckles and placed one hand on the shaft of the massive hammer.

Steel scoffed. "And what do you plan on doing with that, little phoenix, you can't even lift-"

Ronan exploded with power as the mantle of a burning white phoenix settled over him like a cloak. Wings of fire trailed behind him, and the visage of a phoenix folded over his own like a knight's helmet. The eyes glowed pure white with Niradim's Flame.

He lifted the Anvil Hammer off the ground with one hand as if it weighed no more than his blacksmith tools, and casually rested it on his shoulder.

"I'm sorry, what were you saying?"

He didn't give Steel a chance to respond before he dashed forward and slammed the hammer into Steel's chest.

* * *

Brin zipped through the air around Falrose, relentless in her attack. He tried teleporting, but she'd seen that trick before. He tried firing bolts of magic at her, but they bounced harmlessly off her shield. Every hit she landed against him sent cracks through Falrose's magic crystalline armor.

He was at his weakest since they'd begun, and she was the strongest she'd ever been. Plus, he'd used her to hurt Ronan. He didn't stand a chance. This battle was over—he just didn't know it yet.

* * *

Ronan pursued as Steel rebounded off the mythril wall of the Heart Forge. Before he could fall to the ground, Ronan slammed the Anvil Hammer into his side and sent him flying again. As Ronan went for a third hit, Steel finally recovered and got his swords up in time to block the follow-up attack, but Ronan didn't let up.

He spun under Steel's counterattack and swept the shaft of the hammer across the ground, taking Steel's legs out from under him and knocking him to his back. Ronan flipped in the air above him and brought the hammer down, barely missing Steel as he rolled out of the way. The Anvil Hammer hit the ground like a meteor, cratering the ground where it struck.

Ronan lifted the hammer and rested it on his shoulder again as Steel got to his feet. The Star Crystal in his chest pulsed with a deep violet glow as he pulled more of Celestian's power into him. Crystal veins that weaved their way through his mythrali frame seemed to spread further into his body and pulsed in time with the Star Crystal in his chest, almost as if it was a heart pumping Celestian's power through his veins.

The Mantle of the Phoenix had given Ronan an enormous boost of power, but it wasn't endless, and it was running out fast. He'd have to finish this quickly if they had any hope of escaping. Steel roared with fury and sped forward. Ronan rushed to meet him.

***

Brin landed hit after hit, and Falrose's composure was breaking with each one. He grew angry, and that anger made him sloppy. She dodged under a swing and brought her shield up to slam him in the face. He tumbled end over end in the air before righting himself.

His broken nose bled from where she'd hit him. So, she'd finally broken through his magical armor. He gingerly wiped his face and sneered when he saw the blood staining his sleeve.

Falrose spat blood mixed with saliva to the side. "You're going to pay for that, child."

"It's the least of what I owe you," Brin replied.

She shot forward, pouring Niradim's power into her blade for an attack she knew would end this fight. As she got close, she saw Falrose's eyes flick down to the battle between Ronan and Steel and back to her. A smirk crossed his face, and he vanished before she reached him.

There was no time to think, so she reacted purely on instinct. She pivoted in the air and sent the wave of power from her blade toward the ground.

Directly at Ronan.

* * *

Ronan jumped back as Falrose appeared in front of him, stabbing forward with his crystal blade.

Just before it pierced his chest, a wave of Niradim's power blasted Falrose from above. The explosion tore through him, and he went flying out the doors of the Heart Forge, back into the Fallen Star camp.

Without missing a beat, Steel appeared from the smoke in front of Ronan and slashed down with both of his blades. Ronan spun out of the way of the attack and swung his hammer in a large arc. He poured Niradim's power into the head of the hammer as he swung, and fire burst from the back of the hammer, propelling it around at a speed far faster than Ronan would have been able to manage with his strength alone.

The attack landed with a force worthy of the Anvil Hammer's name.

A commanding boom shook the air, and Steel went flying out the same doors as his ally. Just as Falrose was getting to unsteady feet, the massive mythrali slammed into him and they tumbled backwards in a heap.

Brin landed on the ground next to Ronan, sheathing her sword back into her shield as she stepped over to him.

"Nice shot," he said. "I thought I was done for."

"Falrose pretends to have plenty of tricks, but I realized he tends to rely on the same ones over and over. By the way, I like the new look. It's hot." She winked at him.

Somehow, despite the insane circumstances they found themselves in, Ronan blushed.

"Yeah, likewise," he replied. She beamed.

Just then, the Mantle of the Phoenix snuffed out around him, and Ronan sagged from the sudden loss of power. Brin caught him before he hit the ground. Wow, that had really taken a lot out of him.

"Sorry," Ronan said between heavy breaths. "That's about... all I've got, I'm afraid."

"That's okay," Brin said. "I've got you."

* * *

Brin watched as Falrose and Steel slowly got back to their feet, but neither one of them looked like they were eager to continue the fight. Both were furious, but mostly because they knew they were beaten. Ronan was also done, but she knew that her power alone would be enough to handle the two of them now.

Unfortunately, it didn't seem like it would come to that.

"Enjoy your meaningless little victory while you can," Falrose spat at them. He was gripping his sides and wincing in severe pain. "This is the last you'll see of the outside world. Do it, Steel."

"With pleasure." Steel reached over and yanked on a lever on the ground. He then charged his blade with Celestian's power and sliced through the mechanism so it couldn't be used again. The doors of the Heart Forge creaked, but didn't shut as Steel had clearly intended.

Unfortunately, the other defense mechanism of the Heart Forge activated, and a curtain of lava began to close in from either side of the entrance. A wall of molten fire was about to block their only way out.

She pulled Ronan's arm around her neck and pulled them towards the exit. The curtain was closing fast, but they could make it if they hurried. Beyond the bridge, she watched Falrose take a crystal out of his robes and smash it on the ground. A circular portal ripped open in the air, and Brin saw a city in ruins on the other side.

Falrose stepped through in a hurry, and Steel followed closely behind, watching Brin and Ronan as they attempted to escape. They were almost to the entrance—just a few more steps, and they'd make it through before the river of fire blocked their path.

Before the portal closed, she saw a flash of purple light, and a large beam of violet energy blasted out from the Star Crystal in Steel's chest. She dropped Ronan to the ground and got her shield up just in time. A barrier of protection surrounded them and absorbed the hit, flickering with the force of the blast.

As the smoke cleared, she heard Steel laughing in the distance. "Enjoy my old home!"

The last thing she saw was Steel's crazed grin, and then the curtain of lava sealed them inside.

24

Ronan & Brin

Ronan settled up against the wall of the Heart Forge, the pale-violet Flame flickering to his right, illuminating their new prison. It was more spacious than his previous one, but also more ominous. The uneven light seemed to highlight the evidence of the Heart Forge's previous occupant. The deep scars that cut across the walls from Steel's massive blades gave the impression of a trapped animal trying to claw its way to freedom. He thought Steel must have felt that way much of his time in here.

How long before he felt the same way?

He rested his head against the wall as Brin finished searching for anything that would help them escape. He knew her efforts would be fruitless, but it made sense to at least check. And he was in no shape to help at the moment. The Mantle of the Phoenix had one very large drawback to its massive power boost. His body felt like it had torn itself to shreds holding so much power at once. It probably didn't help that he'd been swinging around a weapon that weighed several times his own body weight.

Brin walked over to him and sat down, leaning her head against his. She didn't have to say anything. For now, it was nice just to have a break from all the fighting and turmoil that had plagued them over the last week. Right now, it was just him and Brin. And that was all he needed at the moment.

"So..." Brin said, breaking the comfortable silence between them. "I wanted to say sorry for our fight earlier-"

"Brin, are you kidding me?" Ronan asked in disbelief. "I'm the one who owes *you* an apology!"

"Well, I mean, I wasn't going to say anything, but..." she joked, nudging him in the side.

He laughed. "Well, I *am* sorry. And you can write this down since I'll probably never say these words in this order to you again, but... you were right."

She feigned a shocked look and put a hand up to her ear. "I'm sorry, what did you just say? I'm sure I didn't hear that right..."

"I said I wouldn't say it again!" He returned her smile and gave her a nudge of his own. "But seriously, Brin, thank you for everything."

"I believe in you, Ronan," Brin said. "Just like Niradim does."

"Or at least, did," Ronan corrected with a frown.

"No. *Does.* Like you said, as long as his Soul Flame is within his people, Niradim still lives. We'll figure out another way to cleanse the Flame." She glanced around the room. "You know, assuming we can get out of here."

Ronan nodded. Yes, that was the first thing they needed to focus on. Saving Niradim would come after, and he shared her belief that Niradim wasn't lost to them forever. They would find a way to save him.

She laid her head back against his shoulder, and they sat there for a few more moments, taking the break they had thoroughly earned, before the sound of clanking footsteps on the stone ground broke the silence. Someone was walking *through* the wall of fire toward them, and Ronan's heart raced as the looming form of a mythrali slowly stalked towards them.

"Steel." Ronan grunted as he rose to his feet. Brin hopped up and drew her blade. He wasn't sure how the mythrali had healed enough to return so quickly, but Brin was still at considerable strength and he could defend himself if absolutely necessary. Steel wouldn't find them easy prey to kill.

After two more booming steps, their hands tightened on their weapons and Ronan prepared to don the Mantle of the Phoenix again, when the mythrali emerged from the flames.

It was Clash.

Ronan and Brin immediately sighed in relief and dropped their weapons. Ronan plopped back down on the ground against the wall.

"Apologies," Clash said. "Am I interrupting?"

Ronan couldn't help it—he burst out laughing in relief. Brin joined, and they shared an extended fit of laughter while Clash stood there and cocked his head in confusion. Once Ronan was able to gather himself, he finally answered. "No, Clash, you are not interrupting. We were just getting comfortable with our new accommodations. Not the most comfortable place to spend the rest of our days, but it seems we don't have many options, unless you're able to shut off that wall of magma, or find some way to shelter us through?"

"I'm afraid not..." Clash said. "But I must admit, I am relieved to find you both alive. I feared the worst when I saw Falrose and Steel escape and you two were nowhere to be found."

"We're still here, I'm afraid." Brin let out a long sigh. "It's too bad we're not mythrali though, since you can walk right through the fire."

Not mythrali... Ronan thought. What had Gadjet said before about the wall of lava?

Only a mythrali can walk through it.

And maybe a Phoenix.

"Actually, Brin," Ronan stood and held out his hand. "I have a crazy idea if you're willing to try it."

"Of course, my love," Brin said, taking his hand in hers. "I have faith in you."

***

Brin stepped out of the flames still holding Ronan's hand, safely out of the Heart Forge. She looked up to see Gadjet at the front of what remained of her tribe, a look of worry on her face until she saw them emerge. A cheer rose from the gathered draken, and several of them even breathed fire into the air in celebration.

She squeezed Ronan's hand and met his eyes for a second before running to Gadjet, who was already halfway to her. They embraced and cried into each other's shoulders for a moment while Ronan went and clasped hands with Dak'thor, who she was glad to see had also survived the battle.

"How are you holding up?" She asked Gadjet after they finally released each other.

"They fought fiercely. Truly, I'm proud of how they handled such a tough situation. Our ancestors would be proud." Gadjet looked back at her tribe, and sadness replaced the pride in her eyes. "But we lost a little over a third of our people in that fight. There are only about sixty of us left."

Brin placed a comforting hand on Gadjet's shoulder. "I'm so sorry, Gadjet."

"But for the first time in over a thousand years," Gadjet said, turning to look Brin in the eyes with a gentle smile. "My tribe is free."

"And we're going to help it stay that way," Brin said. "I promise."

"That's right," Ronan said, joining them. "Do you know where you will go, now that Midralen is compromised?"

"Oh yes," Gadjet said with a sly smile. "I know the perfect place for us to settle."

* * *

Every head turned as Ronan strode through the still-damaged Crucible Gate. By the time he reached the Forgehold, he'd attracted quite a crowd that waited to see what news the Phoenix brought about Niradim's Flame. Good, he wanted what he was about to say to be public knowledge. The people deserved to know the events of the last week and the danger they were in.

"Ronan!" a very familiar voice yelled, as Ginmar broke through the gathered dwarves. Ronan enveloped his adopted father in a huge embrace. "You have got to stop doing stuff like this, son. I'm going to have to keep a closer eye on you around here!"

Ronan smiled and placed a hand on Ginmar's shoulder and gave it a soft squeeze. "I wish that were possible, Ginmar. I really do."

Ginmar searched Ronan's eyes with a frown. "What do you mean?"

"Let's wait for the Elders," Ronan said. "It's a long story, and I'm afraid I'll only get the chance to tell it once."

Ginmar lowered his voice. "Ronan, what's happened to Brin? By the time I got back, I heard she'd stolen the Mythril Soul and joined the enemy. Vorkin's in jail for aiding them, but nobody is allowed to question him. I know what they say about her has to be a lie—Brin would never betray Niradim!"

"It's a truth mixed with a lie," Ronan said solemnly. "Brin is well. She did steal the Mythril Soul, but she is no traitor. I promise I'll explain once the Elders arrive."

Ginmar nodded, but Ronan could tell the news troubled him. Well, he would find out soon enough about everything.

Fortunately, they didn't have to wait long. Druden marched through the doors first, followed by each of the Elders, with Oren bringing up the rear. They arranged themselves in a semicircle in front of the Forgehold. Then, Thalga and the rest of the Disciples, many that Ronan hadn't seen in years, filtered out of the building as well. They surrounded Ronan with hands on their weapons. He hadn't expected a warm welcome, but receiving this much hostility was disappointing. Maybe Falrose had already warned his informant about what had happened back in Midralen.

Oren held up his hands for silence. "Phoenix Ronan," he said once the noise of the crowd died down. "We are glad to see you are well and free from the enemy's clutches. Please join us inside so we may debrief you in private."

Ronan folded his arms in front of him. "I'd rather have this conversation outside, thanks."

"It wasn't a request, Phoenix," Druden spat from the side. "It was an order."

Ronan turned his head to look at him. "I will be telling my story out here, Druden. Feel free to leave if you think what I have to say is going to be uncomfortable for you to hear. But I think you are all going to want to hear what has happened to the Flame."

Whispers spread through the crowd. Yes, they wouldn't be able to force him inside now. Everyone wanted to know what was happening. If they tried to force the issue, it would look as if they were trying to hide something from the people.

Druden's face contorted in anger, but Oren cut him off before he could say anything more. "We will be glad for any news you have, Phoenix Ronan. Especially concerning the status of the Flame. Have you a way to bring it back to the Soul Forge?"

"The Flame has been corrupted by the Fallen Star," Ronan said. The whispers of the crowd grew to murmurs, and several people began shifting on their feet. "Brin and I attempted to save it, but we were rebuffed by two Agents of Celestian. One was the twin brother of the novaborn who attacked Midral a few months ago. The other..." Ronan's eyes locked on Oren. "...was a mythrali."

At the mention of the mythrali, all the Elders tensed, and Oren's facial expression shifted. So, they all knew of Niradim's first people, which meant knowledge of the mythrali had been kept from the rest of the dwarves on purpose. He suspected that one of the Elders was the traitor feeding information to Falrose, but even if only one of them was actively working with the Fallen Star, it was clear that none of them could be trusted.

"Ronan," Oren said. "I must insist we take the rest of this conversation inside."

Ginmar turned to Ronan. "What is a mythrali?"

Niradim bless that man for a perfect response. Some tension Ronan didn't know he had released from him. He realized there was a small part of him that was worried Ginmar also knew the truth but had never told him. It seemed that the secret of Niradim's original people was only for the Elders to know.

"The mythrali-"

"Ronan, please-" Oren said, trying to cut him off.

"Were Niradim's first people," Ronan said over him. "The people he created before the dwarves."

At that revelation, the crowd burst into a cacophony of conversations that Ronan only caught fragments of.

"Is this true-"

"That's ridiculous-"

"Niradim is *our* god-"

Ronan and Oren locked eyes across the courtyard in front of the Forgehold as Thalga and the rest of the Protectors switched from threatening Ronan to holding back the frenzied crowd. For the first time in his life, Ronan saw anger flash across the Flame Elder's face. Electricity seemed to spark between the intensity of their stares as the dwarves shouted around them. Oren subtly shook his head in disappointment, and the other Elders took a step back in panic. All except Druden, who was also staring daggers at Ronan.

Eventually, the Protectors got the crowd under control, and Oren raised his hand again for silence. The command wasn't obeyed as quickly this time. He'd regained his composure during the commotion, but Ronan still sensed the wrath simmering below the surface of the serenity Oren projected.

"It is clear," Oren raised his voice to silence the crowd. "That you and Brin have been working together against Niradim, perhaps from the start. Spreading these lies is only another way to sow division within Niradim's *only* people and is part of the reason we were so hesitant to allow a human into our ranks to begin with. Druden, you can take it from here."

Druden stepped forward with a smug smile plastered across his face. He was lucky Brin wasn't here. Ronan was sure she would have had a hard time holding herself back from lashing out at him.

"Ronan Flamestriker," Druden yelled above the crowd. "You are hereby under arrest for treason and heresy against Niradim. You will be stripped of your rank and escorted to prison to await your sentencing. Please put down your weapon, and things will proceed peacefully. If you don't, we will have no choice but to resort to using force."

Ronan ignored him and shook his head at the Flame Elder. "I'm disappointed in you, Oren."

He turned his back on the Elders and addressed the crowd, raising his voice so that as many people as possible could hear him. "You all deserve to know that the Fallen Star has control of the Flame, further north in the Midral Mountains at a location once known as Midralen."

"That's enough, Ronan-" Druden tried to yell over him.

"The Flame rests in its original home, the Heart Forge." Ronan continued, louder. "But Brin and I have joined forces with-"

"I said that's ENOUGH!" Druden screamed and released a large ball of fire at Ronan.

Wings of flame burst from Ronan's back as the Mantle of the Phoenix settled over his face, morphing it into the visage of Niradim himself. He spun and caught Druden's fireball in his palms, squeezing until the flames snuffed out harmlessly between them. Druden's eyes went wide with shock at the show of power, but Ronan wasn't finished yet.

He reached back and drew his blade.

The crowd backed away as the legendary sword burst alight, blazing with the holy Flame of Niradim. Fire roared in a tempest around him, silencing the crowd and drawing all attention to Ronan.

"This is the Sword of Ashes," Ronan yelled above the roaring of the flames. He turned in a circle, holding the ancient blade up for all to see. "Pulled from the Great Anvil in Midralen, placed there by Niradim's first Phoenix, and reclaimed when a new Phoenix emerged to protect Niradim's people. With this sword, I give you all my word-"

He stopped turning and leveled the Blade of Ashes at the group of Elders.

"I *WILL* RESTORE THE FLAME."

* * *

Brin walked through the little village that Gadjet had led them to. It was still in shambles, but Gadjet's tribe, with the help of Brin and Clash, had already repaired a few of the homes. They didn't know the official name of the town—it had been destroyed years ago by the very dragon that had enslaved the tribe for centuries.

The same dragon whose corpse lay just outside the village's borders, slain by Gadjet and a group of adventurers just five years ago.

But, a village needed a name, and so it only felt right to give their village a name that honored its recent history—Dragonfall.

Dragonfall was far enough away from Midralen that they weren't in any danger of the Fallen Star accidentally stumbling across them. Before the dragon Nivalthyr wiped out its inhabitants, the village had belonged to another tribe of draken, so this location was unknown to any but Gadjet's tribe and the few people who had assisted Gadjet in Nivalthyr's defeat. She assured them that the group was trustworthy.

Scanning the sky as she walked, she finally spotted what she'd been waiting for—a small dot of light in the sky that was coming closer. She ran to the front of the village, passing Gadjet and Clash on the way.

"He's back!"

Ronan barely had time to touch both feet to the ground before she jumped into his arms and gave him a huge kiss.

"What, did you miss me?" Ronan said with a grin.

"Well, I didn't know how that trip was going to go after what happened when I left," Brin said.

Not being able to return home was going to hurt for a long time, but she was determined to help Gadjet's tribe start their new home here. The tribe had already inducted Ronan, Brin, and Clash into its ranks, so they were as welcome here as any of the draken were. They were now part of the tribe.

"Yeah, they weren't exactly thrilled about the news I brought them," Ronan admitted. "And they gave me the same treatment they gave you. I'm no longer welcome home either."

"I'm so sorry, Ronan," Brin said. She knew exactly how he must be feeling. He'd lived there practically his whole life.

Ronan sighed. "It's alright." It wasn't, but she knew what Ronan meant. There was nothing they could do about it right now. Maybe someday things would change. Ronan shrugged and began to dig around in his pack for something. "Anyway, I brought you a surprise..."

He pulled out a bag that was stuffed to the top with something. Brin snatched the bag out of his hands as a familiar smell wafted up to her nose.

"Wait…" Her eyes lit up. "Is this-"

She ripped open the bag and yanked out what at this moment seemed like the most beautiful thing she'd ever laid eyes on.

"Meat pies!" she yelled before stuffing one in her mouth.

"Brin, they're not even warm!" Ronan said.

"I don't care," she said through her stuffed cheeks. Tears began to fall down her cheeks. "Oh, I'm going to miss these! I guess I should ration them since these are the last ones I'll ever have."

"Actually…" Ronan said, and he pulled out a small roll of parchment and handed it to Brin. It was a letter from Dorna, the sweet old dwarven woman who owned Brin's favorite bakery, Heart of the Forge.

Dearest Brin,

I was so sad to hear that you will no longer be able to visit our little store. I will miss seeing the joy on your face every time you walked in. Know that you will be missed greatly by many here in Midral.

Your boyfriend, who is very cute, I might add, stopped by and made a request that I was all too happy to grant. On the back of this letter, you will find the recipe for your favorite meat pie, but with a new name that I think you'll like. Now you can have a little piece of Midral with you, no matter where you go.

Take care of yourself, little one. Niradim's Blessings be with you.

With all my love and support,

Dorna

She flipped the page over, and there it was—the recipe to her favorite food in the world. But when her eyes climbed to the top of the page to read the name of her favorite treat, her breath caught in her throat and her eyes blurred with fresh tears.

The Dawnstar.

"Oh, Niradim bless you, you amazing man!" Brin jumped back into his arms and sobbed on his shoulder. This was the best present she'd ever been given. He laughed and squeezed her in a powerful embrace, then wiped the tears of joy from her eyes.

Gadjet and Clash emerged from one of the homes being worked on and greeted Ronan. After they updated him on Dragonfall's progress, he caught them up on how his recent trip to Midral went.

"So, we're on our own, then?" Clash reached up and rubbed his metallic head. "Perhaps I should have gone with you, to give them proof-"

Ronan held up his hand to stop him. "It's okay, Clash. The truth will come out in time—when they're ready to hear it. For now, we need to organize, and I had a long flight to think of a few ways to do that. Why don't we head inside and get out of the cold to discuss?"

As they trudged through the snow, Brin turned to her new little draken friend. "Gadjet, I've been meaning to ask—have you talked to the tribe about your little project?"

Gadjet smirked. "I've already had a few people volunteer. But I think some of them just like the name."

Brin laughed. "Well, it *is* a pretty cool name!"

"We'll leave it to you to make the final decisions, but I think you should settle on a few specialized fighters, rather than a larger number," Ronan said. "The Dragoons will function as an elite group to take on uniquely difficult missions. Make sure you only take the best of the best."

The humor faded from Gadjet's face, and she nodded. "I agree. I'll think about it some more. In the meantime, we're almost finished building the forge. We'll need to use the Sword of Ashes-"

"Ashe's sword." Clash cut in.

"To provide Niradim's Flame so we can forge mythril." Gadjet continued. "But once that's done, I have some ideas on how to repair Clash's hand. And *then*, I think it will be time to pay up..." Gadjet raised an eyebrow in Brin's direction.

Brin laughed. "Yes, yes, I will upgrade your armor."

"And I will strengthen and upgrade your spear," Ronan said.

"I too wish to contribute," Clash said. "I will help with upgrading your arm."

"Oh, I can't *wait* to get this thing finished!" Gadjet hopped from foot to foot, giddy with excitement. "Best bet I've ever made!"

They all laughed as they approached the center of the village. Members of the tribe waved to them as they passed, carrying wood they'd chopped from a nearby forest to assist with ongoing repairs.

"Dak'thor," Ronan called out as they passed a group of draken. The large draken set down his tools and jogged over. "Do you have a moment?"

"Of course, my Phoenix." Dak'thor placed a fist over his heart and bowed.

"Come with us," Ronan said.

They all followed him into one of the larger buildings in the center of the village. A grand table carved of stone sat in the middle of the room, which Clash, Gadjet, and Brin had created and brought in while Ronan was away.

They all gathered around it, and Ronan removed his blade from his back and laid it on the stone, the blade coating in ash as he removed his hand. Clash removed the Mythril Soul from his chest and placed it in the center of the table, where a small recess had been carved out of the rock. Brin followed suit and placed her sword and shield on the table. Finally, Gadjet set her helmet and cracked spear on the table in front of her as well. They all turned to Dak'thor.

Dak'thor shifted uncomfortably on his feet and cleared his throat. "Are you sure I should be here for this? I am the one who cast out the Dragonslayer from our tribe and served the Fallen Star by imprisoning Niradim's Phoenix. I do not deserve the honor of being here."

"You are also the one who led these people during some of the toughest times this tribe has ever seen," Ronan said. "Sure, you made some mistakes along the way, but being a good leader is about learning from those mistakes and changing course when necessary instead of holding on to your pride. You are the leader your tribe needs, and I will not have them simply trade one master for another. Any decision we make that affects the tribe will involve you."

Dak'thor nodded. "Thank you, my Phoenix." He unclipped the mace he wore on his belt and placed it on the table with the rest of the items.

Ronan clapped his hands together. "Well then, it's settled. Let's begin the first official meeting of…"

He leaned forward, placing his hands on the table.

"The Knights of Ash."

25

Epilogue

Kyros was lounging in a chair, halfway through a book when the portal opened across the observatory deck from him. His brother and a massive mythrali stepped through. That must be Steel. He fired a very large blast of energy from his chest through the portal, laughing as it closed. As soon as it shut, he sagged to the ground in exhaustion. Falrose dropped next to him. Oh, it looked like things had not gone well for Falrose and Steel.

How delicious.

"What's wrong, brother?" Kyros mocked from the comfort of his chair. "Your clothes look a little singed. Haven't you been bragging about how easy defeating Ronan would be?"

"His battles were with a different Phoenix," Steel said.

"Shut up, you overgrown piece of metal," Falrose spat as he waved his hands in the air and his clothing repaired itself until not even a thread was out of place. Though the spell did nothing for his wounds.

Well, *that* was an interesting development. Kyros slapped his book shut. "What do you mean—a *different* Phoenix?"

Falrose sent a nasty glance Steel's way before focusing back on Kyros. "There are now two of them."

"Who is the other?" Kyros asked. Falrose had avoided saying who it was. Oh, it must be someone embarrassing! "Come on, you know I'm going to find out anyway."

"...it was Brin," Falrose said.

"Brin?" Why did that name sound familiar? "Brin... Brin... Wait... You mean the *little dwarven girl* did this to you!"

Kyros doubled over in laughter, actually falling out of his chair in the process. Oh, this was just the *best* day!

"Shut up, you voiding little-" Falrose's hands glowed, and he attempted to send a blast of magic at Kyros, which fizzled into nothing as it left his hand. Falrose growled with rage.

Kyros pulled himself together and waggled his finger at his twin brother. "Tsk tsk, brother. You're so quick to forget that my deal with Celestian protects me from being harmed by his priests and agents. You can't touch me."

It was one of the better parts of his contract with Celestian. If one of his agents or priests harmed Kyros deliberately, then the contract would be void, and Kyros would keep any power Celestian had bestowed upon him—permanently.

"That goes for you too, big guy." He pointed at Steel, who looked just as bad as Falrose did. "By the way, what's your excuse? Did Brin do that to you as well?"

Steel ignored him and examined the chambers. "It doesn't matter. We accomplished our mission."

Kyros' eyebrows furrowed, and his smile faded. "Really?"

Now it was Falrose's turn to crack a smile. "Yes, Niradim's Flame belongs to us now." He pulled out the Starsoul, glowing with a pale-violet light. So they actually *had* done it. Voids—that really brought his mood back down.

"And what of Ronan and Brin?" Kyros asked.

Falrose's smile grew. "Trapped in the Heart Forge behind a wall of fire, left to die next to the corpse of their god."

Kyros suspected Falrose was underestimating Ronan's uncanny ability to be a thorn in their side, but he let that go for now. If they had accomplished their mission, it didn't matter how soundly Ronan and Brin had beaten Falrose and Steel—they would both gain favor in Celestian's eyes. That wasn't good for him. He would need to put plans in motion to turn the tables. He was not about to start taking orders from his brother again if he could help it—he'd come too far for that. But for now, he had to play nice.

"Well, congratulations, brother," Kyros said. "So what happens next?"

"Tonight, we meet with Celestian. Then tomorrow…" Falrose held up the glowing Starsoul.

"We begin work on the Star Forge."

About the Author

Danny Colmenares is a Project Manager by day and fantasy author whenever time allows. Long time reader, Danny loves fantasy and sci-fi in all forms of media - from books, to TV, to games. Born and raised in Texas, he currently lives in a small town north of Dallas with his wife, two daughters, and schnauzer.

You can connect with me on:
- https://flamestrikerbooks.com
- https://www.facebook.com/FlamestrikerBooks
- https://www.instagram.com/flamestrikerbooks
- https://www.tiktok.com/@dannycolmenares_author

Also by Danny Colmenares

The Flame of Niradim
Death was only the beginning of Ronan's story.

When Ronan Flamestriker is struck down in battle, his journey should have ended. Instead, he awakens in the Soul Forge of Niradim—the very heart of dwarven power—resurrected but abandoned by the god he once served. As Midral's legendary "Phoenix" struggles with his broken faith, a shadow descends upon the once-impenetrable mountain city.

A cunning novaborn named Kyros has obtained ancient artifacts of terrifying power, bringing giants, monsters, and chaos to Midral's gates. His ultimate prize: the Flame of Niradim itself. When he succeeds in stealing it, the city's defenses crumble, and its people face annihilation.

Now Ronan must reclaim more than just the Flame—he must rediscover his purpose. Alongside unlikely allies—a revenge-obsessed elven warrior, a monk struggling with newfound power, and a florian whose loyalty runs deeper than anyone knows—Ronan stands as Midral's last hope.

But even if they survive this assault, a greater darkness lurks in the stars...

In a world where gods grant power to the faithful and artifacts corrupt the ambitious, who will rise from the ashes to defend the Flame?

www.ingramcontent.com/pod-product-compliance
Lightning Source LLC
LaVergne TN
LVHW041907070526
838199LV00051BA/2535